The Wedding Dress Quilt

A WAXAHACHIE, TEXAS, QUILT MYSTERY

Jeffree Wyn Itrich

C&T PUBLISHING
Another Maker Inspired!

DEDICATION

*I dedicate this novel to
my husband, Earl, and
my sister, Jordana,
who've never stopped
believing in me.*

ACKNOWLEDGMENTS

Thank you to my editor, Roxane Cerda,
who worked tirelessly to help me
refine it into the book you hold in your hands.
And to the many friends and family
who read the first draft and encouraged me
to bring the story to life.

Prologue

Lisbeth James was dressed in a delicate lace wedding dress that skimmed the floor. The tall, willowy redhead paced back and forth in the anteroom next to the church's sanctuary, stopping every few minutes to crack open the door to the sanctuary and scan the crowd. She closed the door and repeatedly walked back and forth, rubbing her hands together. She absentmindedly tapped her front teeth with her forefinger. Finally, she sat down in a chair and dropped her head into her hands.

"Sweetie, don't worry, he'll be here," her best friend, Maggie, reassured her, bending down on one knee and placing a hand on her shoulder.

Lisbeth looked up, worry etched in her eyes. "I don't know, Mags. The ceremony was supposed to start an hour ago. This isn't like Scott. He wouldn't be late for our wedding. He just wouldn't."

"I agree," Maggie responded calmly, hiding her own concern. "There's probably a lot of traffic."

"Maggie, there's no traffic out here, you know that. We're miles from any large city."

"That's true, and I'm sure there's a good reason why he's late."

Lisbeth rolled her lips inward, biting down on them, her bright emerald eyes searching Maggie's face. "You don't think that he's a runaway groom, do you?"

"You stop that right now, Lisbeth James! You know as well as I do that you are the center of Scott's world. There's some other reason he's late. Have a little faith in him. Was Dennis driving him?"

Lisbeth shook her head, nearly dislodging her veil. "No, Scott was going to drive."

"Well, I guess I can't blame Dennis for Scott being late. Seems to me that it's the best man's job to make sure the groom gets to his wedding on time."

"Yeah, you'd ..."

A loud knock sounded on the door. Maggie got up, walked over, and opened it. A sheriff's deputy and Dennis Dragna, the best man, stood there and stepped inside. Dennis's tuxedo was a disheveled mess, spots of blood stains on his shirt. They looked at Lisbeth, who went nearly as milky white as her dress. Her naturally blushed cheeks paled as she stood up quickly. Dennis ran to Lisbeth.

"Miss James?" the deputy asked.

Lisbeth nodded, her eyes widening.

"I regret to inform you that there's been an accident on the highway," the deputy began.

Maggie stepped to Lisbeth's side and placed a hand on one of her shoulders.

"Is your fiancé Scott Miller?" the deputy asked.

Lisbeth studied the deputy, never taking her gaze off the man. She slowly nodded.

The deputy cleared his throat, looked down, and looked back up at Lisbeth. "I'm sorry to tell you that Mr. Miller did not survive the crash."

Lisbeth fainted, falling into Dennis's arms. When she came to, she was lying on a couch in the anteroom. She looked up at Dennis.

"How ... how ... how," she stuttered, her voice cracking. "What happened?"

Dennis laid a hand over one of hers. "I don't really know. One moment we were cruising along, and the next, Scott lost control of his car. He said everything was locked up and he couldn't control the speed or the brakes. It was speeding really fast. It was as if the car had a mind of its own, and I thought we both were going to die. Then the car veered toward a big oak tree, and we hit it head on."

Tears poured down Lisbeth's face. "How did you survive and he didn't?"

"When we hit the tree, Scott's seat belt broke away and he went through the windshield. For some reason mine stayed intact, so when we crashed, the seat belt held. Otherwise, I would've been killed, too. The authorities at the crash site said that Scott died instantly."

Lisbeth broke out in a fresh deluge of tears, choking her into a coughing fit. Dennis looked at Maggie and shrugged as though asking what to do. Maggie got behind Lisbeth and began rubbing her back until the coughing ceased. Lisbeth fell back on the couch, closed her eyes, and descended into a tortured sleep.

An hour later, Lisbeth woke up, exhausted, her face swollen from the tears. "Sweetie," Maggie began. "Come on, I'll take you home."

"May I go with you?" Dennis asked. "Scott was my ride here, and after the accident, the deputy drove me. I don't have a way home."

Maggie nodded. "Help me get her to my car, will you?" Dennis barely waited to be asked. He tenderly placed his arm around her, and guided her to the exit door.

When they arrived at Lisbeth's home, Dennis carefully removed her from her seat, as though she were a fragile porcelain doll. Once inside, Maggie turned to Dennis. "I'll take it from here."

"I can stay," Dennis said.

"Not necessary, I need to get her undressed and sit with her. I may stay the night. Is there anyone you can call to pick you up?"

"Yeah, my cousin lives near here. I'll call him," he said, taking out his cell phone and leaving the house as he dialed his cousin's number.

After Dennis left, Lisbeth turned to Maggie. "He didn't have to do any of that. He's really being nice."

Maggie nodded. "Yeah, I agree. I've never seen him be so, um, pleasant."

The next day, still feeling the devastation of the day before, Lisbeth showered and dressed. She called her boss, explained what happened, and told her she would need a couple of days off to recuperate.

"Lisbeth, you already put in for a week off to go on your honeymoon. I'm sorry that now you'll need that time to deal with this tragedy. Take all the time you need."

The response from her normally demanding, difficult boss was surprisingly supportive. She thanked her, turned to all the wedding gifts piled up on top of her dining table, sucked in a big breath of air, and headed to the table to catalog the gifts and arrange to ship them back to the senders.

Early in the afternoon, her cell phone rang. It was Dennis.

"Have you had anything to eat today?" he asked.

"No, I'm not hungry."

"Lisbeth, you have to eat something. After all the trauma, if you don't eat something, you're going to get sick."

"I don't think I could eat anything even if I tried."

"I'll bet you could get down some soup. My mother makes the world's best minestrone soup. Her great-grandmother brought the recipe from Italy. In our family, it's known as 'Italian penicillin.' Mom makes a big batch every Sunday, so I know she has some on hand. I'll bring you some, along with her homemade Italian bread."

Lisbeth realized that he was dead set on getting her to eat and the soup did sound good. On second thought she decided that maybe it would make her feel better. "Okay," she finally said.

"I'll be over in an hour or so, after I swing by Mom's."

Chapter One

Over the course of the following weeks, months, and ultimately, years, Dennis slowly moved into every aspect of Lisbeth's life. He nurtured her and took care of her. Prior to the accident, she hadn't known Dennis that well and never thought of him as the type of man capable of such thoughtfulness. She learned that, with his drop-dead good looks, smooth demeanor, and devilish charm, he knew how to get what he wanted. She also came to realize that no one had ever said "no" to him.

Maggie was getting weary of Lisbeth never having time for her anymore, due to her spending every free moment with Dennis. She picked up the phone and called her.

"Hi, Maggie! What's up?"

"You know that singer you like, Sheila Felway? Get this, she's playing at the Cicada tonight. Go with me?"

"Really? Sheila Felway? Oh, I wish I could, but I'm going to a party with Dennis."

"Another one?" Maggie whined. "You're always going somewhere fancy with him. We never get together anymore."

"I know, Mags, and I do miss you."

"Then skip it, and go with me to hear Sheila Felway." Maggie pleaded as best she could.

"I don't know, Maggie. That would be kinda rude to cancel on him at the last second."

"Come on, Lis, you're with him all the time!"

"Yeah, I know. He's kinda running my life."

"Ya think?" Maggie quipped. "Why are you doing this? Are you getting serious about him?"

"Actually, Dennis wants a romantic relationship. It's getting a bit dicey."

"How?"

"Maggie, I can't give him that. I won't give him that. You know as well anyone that Scott was the love of my life."

"So, why do you keep caving into his every whim?"

Lisbeth let out a long sigh. "Guilt, I guess. I appreciate everything that Dennis did and has kept doing since Scott's death, but I also know that I can't give him the kind of relationship he wants. He takes me out to the best restaurants, to every major show that comes to town, and constantly showers me with expensive jewelry.

"I've never seen you wear anything like that."

"That's because even though I decline all the bling, he insists I keep everything. So, I put all of it in the back of a drawer."

"Seriously?"

"Very seriously! And what's worse, he often asks why I never wear any of it. So, I blow him off by saying that nothing matches what I'm wearing. And you know what he does then?"

"Uh, goes out and buys you more jewelry to match your clothes?"

"Exactly!"

"Girlfriend, I didn't know it had gotten this bad. He's trying to buy you off to guilt you into something you don't want."

"Yeah, I know. Still, I feel bad. Deep down, a voice keeps telling me that I should appreciate him for all that he's done for me and go along with whatever he wants. Because, honestly, if it weren't for his kindness, I might never have recovered from the trauma of losing Scott."

"I don't believe that, Lis. We've known each other since we were little. You're stronger than you give yourself credit for."

"To be perfectly honest, that voice is really starting to annoy me."

"How?"

"Are you sitting down? This may take a while to explain."

"Yep, I'm sitting and I've got all day to listen."

"So, you know that, early on, Dennis started taking me to opulent parties hosted by his circle of wealthy friends. What I never bothered to tell you is that they're all highly educated sons and daughters of some of the wealthiest families in Los Angeles. They all run together in a close-knit group. It's like they're all glued at the hip."

"That doesn't sound like fun."

"It's not. He insists on taking me to all their fancy parties, going on cruises around the bay in their million-dollar yachts and hanging out with them at the Del Mar racetrack. You know me. I come from a middle-class upbringing and education, and I'm proud of it. I get asked a lot of annoying questions about my background. It's become a chore to deflect the inquiries and it makes me really uncomfortable."

"Have you talked to Dennis about it?"

"I've tried a few times, but he's clueless. He doesn't see it, or he doesn't care. He seems more interested in showing me off like arm candy. It's become obvious, at least to me, that he has no sincere interest in my wants or needs, especially my uneasiness around his friends."

"Let me ask you, is he falling in love with you, or pretending to?"

Lisbeth let out another sigh. "Does it matter? Either way, I'm not falling in love with him."

"Lis, I'm worried about you. This seems really possessive. Don't you see that?"

"Yeah, I do. He wants to know how I spend my time when I'm not with him. He's always telling me how I should conduct every aspect of my life. I'm at a point where, even though I'm grateful that he pulled me out of my slump after Scott's death, he's making me increasingly uneasy."

"Well, we're going to correct that right now! Text Dennis that you can't see him tonight. Tell him it's an emergency or something. You and I are going to see Sheila Felway. And I'm not taking 'no' for an answer!"

Lisbeth felt her spirits lift and broke out in a grin. "Okay."

"Get ready, 'cause I'm picking you up in half an hour."

Not long after, Lisbeth woke one morning to sunlight streaming through the lemon-colored curtains of her bedroom. She raised her arms above her head, twisting and stretching. She started to get up when a soft paw extended across her shoulder, anchoring her to the bed. She reached over and scratched behind the long-haired cat's ears. The white, blue-eyed feline purred and blinked slowly, showing her pleasure, still not releasing her grip. Lisbeth lay there, massaging her cat and thinking about how her life had changed.

She realized that it had been three years since the accident. She imagined how different her life would be now, had Scott not died. They would probably have bought a house and perhaps had a child, maybe with another one on the way. It made her smile until Sophie pushed down harder, rhythmically kneading her shoulder like she was a batch of soft dough.

"Sophie, come on baby, let go. I gotta get up."

The cat pushed down harder, forcing Lisbeth to stay in bed, a common occurrence. Some days, like today, she felt as though she were stuck in a murky fog, paralyzed by the past and unable to move forward. Finally, Lisbeth removed Sophie from her shoulder, which was smarting from the needle-like pinpricks of the cat's nails.

"I can't stay in bed with you all day. If I don't get up, I'll lose my job and won't be able to buy you any cat food." She pointed toward the window. "You'll have to find your own food, out there. Now, you wouldn't like that would you?" Sophie pressed her nose against Lisbeth's, gave it a tiny lick, turned, and jumped off the bed.

Lisbeth slowly got out of bed, stood up, and stretched her tall, slender frame. She slipped into her favorite robe, old and frayed around the edges, soft from years of wear. Lisbeth meandered to the kitchen, yawning as she went. First, she fed an impatient Sophie, then pushed the button for a single cup of joe on her fancy coffee maker and waited for her first cup of the day to finish dripping into her favorite red mug. Just as the last drop splashed into the cup, the doorbell chimed. Lisbeth looked at the kitchen clock; it was just past seven o'clock. Wrapping her robe tightly around her, she walked across the living room and opened the front door to a delivery man holding out an envelope.

"A letter for Lisbeth James," the man stated.

"That's me," she craned her neck to read the name of the sender.

"Sign here, please," he thrust his tablet into her hands, pointing to where she should sign.

As soon as he left, she walked to the kitchen, pulled out the coffee cup from the coffee maker, and examined the return address on the envelope, which didn't sound the slightest bit familiar. She opened the envelope to find a letter from an attorney at a law firm in Dallas, Texas, with locations in Austin, Houston, and San Antonio. No ordinary letterhead, it was gold-embossed with a litany of attorneys' names running down the entire left side of the stationery. She stared at the letterhead, shaking her head slightly. She couldn't imagine why she was being contacted by a law firm in Texas. She reached for her coffee cup and took a big gulp, then sat on a kitchen stool to read the letter.

Dear Ms. James,

My name is Howard Sheridan, and I am the estate attorney for Fannie Lee Clayburne, your late grandmother. We've represented the Clayburne family and your grandmother for decades. Through our firm's research and investigation, we were able to locate you. This letter is to inform you that your grandmother has left the family home in Waxahachie, Texas, and all of its contents, to you. In addition, you have inherited a substantial sum of money.

Please contact me at your earliest convenience so I may expedite your receipt of the home and funds.

Sincerely,

Howard M. Sheridan
Managing Partner

Lisbeth dropped the letter and ran her hands through her tousled red hair, a nervous habit. The letter didn't make any sense. She didn't have a grandmother. Her parents had not been able to have children and, in their forties, they adopted her as an infant. When she got older, they told her that they were both only children who had both lost their own parents when they were teens. Cancer had wiped out every relative, including her adoptive parents by the time she'd reached her early twenties. Besides that, she was born and raised in Southern California. She didn't have any relatives in Texas that she knew about, much less know anyone in the state. She shook her head, grabbed the cup of coffee and swallowed two large gulps. She set the cup down, picked up her cell phone, dialed the phone number, and asked for the attorney. As she waited, she ran her tongue over her lips, first the top, then the bottom. A man came onto the line identifying himself as Mr. Sheridan.

"Mr. Sheridan? My name is Lisbeth James. I'm calling about a letter you sent me."

"Yes, yes, thank you for calling," he said in a deep, soothing voice laced with a slow Texas drawl.

"I think there's been some mistake," Lisbeth suggested.

"No, no mistake," the attorney assured her. "It took quite an effort to find you, and we are confident that we have the right Lisbeth James."

"You don't understand. I don't have a grandmother, or at least I didn't," Lisbeth responded.

"You were born September 15, 1995, and adopted as a baby, correct?"

"Uh, yes," Lisbeth answered hesitantly.

"Ms. James, you have quite an extended birth family in Texas."

"What?" she squealed into the phone, a little louder than she intended. "Sorry," she added in a quieter tone. "No disrespect, but I don't think you have the right person."

"Did your parents tell you about your birth family?" he asked in a gentle voice, sensing this news had come as a shock.

"Not much. They said it was a closed adoption and that the birth mother didn't want to be contacted after the paperwork was finalized." Several moments passed in silence.

"A-A-Are you still there?" Lisbeth asked.

"Yes, yes, I'm still here," the attorney proceeded slowly, choosing his words carefully. "I'm afraid that isn't quite the whole story, Ms. James. When can you come out here? I need to turn over your inheritance, and you should learn the entire story of your birth and adoption. You see, I'm not just the attorney who handled your grandmother's will and estate; I also handled your adoption."

Lisbeth paused, trying to sort out what he said, what was happening. Suddenly, she felt short of breath, as though all the air had been sucked out of her lungs. She opened her robe and unbuttoned the top of her nightgown, pulling on the collar until she could breathe more easily. "You're in Texas, right?"

"Yes, I'm in our home office in Dallas, about an hour from Waxahachie, the town where you were born and your grandmother lived."

"Uh, I don't know, Mr. Sheridan. Honestly, funds are a little tight right now, and I don't think I can afford to come out there."

"Actually, you have quite a bit of money now, Ms. James. In fact, I'd say you are a wealthy woman," he smiled into the phone, hoping that she would pick up on his sincerity. "I'll have my assistant arrange a flight, hotel, and ground transportation for you. The expenses will come out of the estate."

"I don't know ... this is all so sudden." She hesitated for a moment, then added, "How do I know you're legit?"

"Oh, I'm legitimate alright," the attorney asserted. "Look, I'm sure this has come as quite a shock to you. On the letter, you'll find my website, email address, and office address. I'll also give you my cell number and my assistant's contact information. You can check me out all you like. Please call my assistant when you're ready to proceed."

"Okay, I'll be in touch." Lisbeth hung up, feeling more than a little dazed. She slumped on the stool. It felt like the temperature of the room had gone up 20 degrees. Sweat beaded on her forehead and chest. She picked up a nearby shopping catalog and fanned herself. "This can't be real," she said out loud. She grabbed her coffee cup and gulped down the rest, not caring that it was cold. As soon as she drained the last of it, she dialed Maggie, who no sooner answered the phone than Lisbeth blurted out the whole story, barely stopping to take a breath.

"Whoa, girl, slow down," Maggie quipped. "Are you sure about this?"

"Mags, is that all you can say?" Lisbeth asked. "This is huge!"

"I'm just kinda shocked," Maggie responded. "This could be a scam."

"That was my first thought, too, but my gut tells me it's real. Maggie, all my life there's been a strange mystery around my birth and adoption. Remember how I told you that whenever I would ask about it, Mom and Dad would shut down? You knew them. I had the greatest parents in the world. It seemed like my questions really hurt them, so after a while, I stopped asking."

"Did you check out the lawyer's website? Did you Google him?"

"No, no, not yet. I called you first."

"Okay, I'm coming over after work. We're going to research this guy together, 'kay?"

Lisbeth smiled. "Yeah, that would be great. I'll open a bottle of zinfandel. I think it's going to be a long evening."

Maggie arrived late in the day, dressed in her usual dark clothing, her short blond hair spiked like a young boy's, her eyes smudged in black liner and her lips painted cherry red. She was the exact opposite of Lisbeth, whose red hair fell in curls past her shoulders. Unlike Maggie's Southern California–tanned face, Lisbeth was pale as the seagulls that soared overhead, her sweet-heart-shaped lips blushed pink. A natural beauty with clear green eyes that sparkled when she smiled, Lisbeth often turned heads because she didn't look like other women. She possessed more than outer beauty. The two women could not have been more dissimilar in the looks department, but their long friendship since early child-hood made them sisters of the heart.

When Maggie arrived, the two women picked up their glasses of wine and headed over to Lisbeth's desk, where she had set a plate of sliced cheese and crackers. Maggie opened her own laptop and went to the lawyer's website. She scrolled through the pages and then launched several programs she used at work to investigate potential employees and clients. As a security specialist in her company's human relations department, she knew how to find out everything about almost anyone. If someone was hiding even a minor infraction, she could find it.

Maggie leaned back in her chair, picked up the glass of wine, and took a long sip. "Lisbeth, the lawyer and his firm look like the real deal. You should go to Texas."

"Really?" Lisbeth asked hesitantly, arching an eyebrow.

"Yeah. I ran all the same programs that I use at work in the most sensitive searches. He passed them all."

Lisbeth sat staring at the computer screen. "This could be my chance," she whispered.

"Your chance?" Maggie asked, raising her eyebrows.

"You know how I've been in a funk lately, and work has been so overbearing? I hate what I'm doing. And you know I feel like I never have time to devote to my quilting and I'll never get really good unless I can devote more time to it?"

"Lisbeth, face it, you've been depressed. Not that I blame you. I'd be depressed, too, if I had your paper-pushing job. You are the most creative person I know, and you're not using any of it in your job."

"Mags, I feel stifled every moment I'm in the office. My job is a dead end. It will never go anywhere. Maybe this is all my life is supposed to be. Maybe I'm not that talented. Maybe I don't deserve anything better. Maybe my quilting dream is nothing but a pipe dream."

Maggie grabbed Lisbeth's hands into her own. "Lisbeth James, you stop that right now! You're just in the dumps. You do deserve better. You deserve every good thing that comes your way. And if my gut is right, this," she said, pointing to the letter from Howard Sheridan, "is that good thing."

"You really think so?"

"Absolutely!"

Lisbeth rolled her bottom lip inward, looking hesitantly at Maggie. "I know that this is a lot to ask ... could you take a few days off of work?"

"Maybe. For what?" Maggie cocked her head sideways.

"Come with me to Dallas? Moral support? I'm a little nervous about all this." Lisbeth's eyes widened, imploring, expectant.

Maggie grinned, her eyes crinkling at the corners. "Sure, I'm game. This could be really interesting," she chuckled. "Besides, I have a bit of vacation time coming to me that I might as well use. When are you thinking of going?

"How's next week?"

Maggie squeezed Lisbeth's hands. "Ok, bestie. Let's start packing."

Chapter Two

The following week, Lisbeth and Maggie settled into their seats on their flight to the Dallas Fort Worth airport.

"Hey, did you tell Dennis what's going on?" Maggie asked.

"As a matter of fact, I did," Lisbeth answered, looking sideways with a smirk.

"What's that look mean?"

"Well, let's just say that the conversation didn't go particularly well," Lisbeth grimaced.

"Come on, spill it. What happened?" Maggie pressed as she sipped on the double espresso she'd bought in the terminal. She offered Lisbeth a bite of her sprinkle-covered donut; Lisbeth shook her head.

"Nothing really. He didn't think I should go to Texas, and if I insisted on going, he thought he should be the person to accompany me."

Maggie threw back her head. "Did you just say he didn't think you should go to Texas?"

Lisbeth nodded. "Yep. He wasn't the least bit happy for me. It almost sounded like he was jealous."

"Ugh!" Maggie groaned. "Look, maybe a little time away from each other will do some good. You can decide for yourself if you want to relocate, and maybe he will appreciate you more and realize that if he doesn't stop trying to run every aspect of your life, he'll lose you. This could be a real opportunity, on a lot of levels."

"Do you really think so?" Lisbeth let out a slight moan. "This is my own fault. I've let this thing go on too long. I should have stopped it sooner. And now I'm caught in his web."

"Lis, don't say, much less think, that. You didn't do anything. Dennis took advantage of you when you were at your most vulnerable."

Lisbeth let out another sigh, low and ragged. "I know. And it has only gotten worse. Lately, he's been saying we should get married. Says it's his responsibility to take care of me since Scott isn't here."

Maggie's mouth dropped open, and her eyes bulged. Her face turned a deep shade of red. "That's ridiculous! You wouldn't, would you? Please tell me you wouldn't."

Lisbeth shook her head. "I know it probably doesn't seem like it, but I've been trying to break up with him, really I have. But he just won't accept it." She turned to Maggie. "You know how much I loved Scott. And honestly, I don't love Dennis at all. It's like Dennis wants to be Scott's replacement. Because they were best friends, he says he should step into Scott's shoes and marry me. Mags, he can never be even a tenth of what Scott was."

"No, he can't," Maggie agreed. She wondered how long she could keep her disdain for Dennis from Lisbeth. She'd never liked him, and when he moved in on her like a coyote after Scott's death, her contempt grew even more. And now Dennis was pressuring Lisbeth to marry him? Maggie got a sick feeling in her stomach.

"Maggie, this thing with Dennis, whatever it is, has gone on too long. He won't listen when I try to talk to him about it. If this inheritance is all that it seems to be, I swear, I will break up with him for good when we get home. Texas may be my chance for a new life and a new future. Without him."

Chapter Three

Three hours later the plane touched down in Dallas. They got off and walked down the corridor toward the exit. Suddenly, Maggie stopped and stared straight ahead.

"What's up?" Lisbeth paused and looked back at her friend.

"OMG, Lisbeth, look at that cowboy over there holding a sign with your name on it. Have you ever seen anything like that?"

"Like what?" she asked, looking over to where Maggie was staring.

"Jeez Louise, Lis. I wonder if all the men in Dallas look like him."

"Are you serious?" Lisbeth laughed and walked toward the tall man with dark brown hair and long, lean legs wearing tight-fitting jeans, well-worn cowboy boots, and a low-brimmed felt hat.

"Hello, I'm Lisbeth James," she smiled, stopping in front of the man. "And this is Maggie Bowen," she swept her hand toward her friend.

"Well, hello, yourself! I'm Travis," he said slowly, his voice a prolonged, smooth drawl. He took her hand and shook it, staring at her through silver-gray eyes surrounded by thick black lashes; his eyes twinkled as he smiled. "Let me be the first to welcome y'all to the beautiful Lone Star State."

"It's beautiful, alright," Maggie responded dreamily, not taking her eyes off Travis.

Travis grinned at Maggie's attempt to flirt with him. "Here, let me get your luggage," he said, taking both their cases.

"No, that's too much for you to carry," Lisbeth protested, reaching for her case. "I can carry my own."

"I'm sure you can, miss, but here in Texas, it's bad manners for a man to allow a woman to carry her luggage. You wouldn't want to make me look bad, would you?"

"Oh, oh, no, of course not. It's just that in California—"

Travis flashed a grin, dimples running down each side of his mouth. "Now then, you're not in California, are you? We do things a little differently here." Seeing the look of embarrassment on Lisbeth's face, he added, "Don't you worry, you'll get used to it. Manners and courtesy are a big deal here."

Lisbeth and Maggie traded looks of surprise as he headed toward the exit. They scurried to keep up with his long strides. At the curbside, Travis handed his parking ticket to the valet. As Lisbeth and Maggie waited with Travis, they took in the fragrant scents of spring in Texas. The valet returned with a shiny vintage pickup truck painted apple red and fully restored. Travis placed their luggage in the back and opened the passenger door for Lisbeth and Maggie. They slid onto the red-and-white houndstooth leather bench seat. The dash was as restored as the outside of the truck.

Lisbeth looked around. "This is one cool truck! What year is it?"

"A 1950 F-1 Ford. I've got a thing for old trucks." Travis strapped on his seat belt and checked to see that the women had as well. "Ready, ladies?" They nodded and he took off toward the Dallas skyline.

As they headed downtown, Travis pointed out various landmarks.

"What is that?" Lisbeth asked, looking at a tall structure with a geodesic dome at the top.

"Reunion Tower," he said. "It's 561 feet tall." Lisbeth and Maggie leaned forward and peered at the tower. "It was part of a revitalization project back in the late '70s," Travis added. "It houses an observation deck, a restaurant, and a space people can rent for events. If you have time, y'all really should pay it a visit. There's no other view like it in the whole state," he said proudly, as though it were his own.

Upon arriving at one of the skyscrapers downtown, Travis opened the door and helped the women out, transferred the luggage to the front seat, and tossed his keys to the valet who nodded at Travis. Lisbeth and Maggie followed him into the building, craning their necks to look up at the cavernous lobby, festooned in exquisite glasswork.

"Is that a Chihuly?" Maggie whispered to Lisbeth, pointing upward.

"It looks like it," Lisbeth whispered back.

"It is," Travis interrupted, pointing up. "Dale Chihuly was commissioned to create this glass sculpture when the building was designed. He was given free rein, with the only stipulation that it be unmistakably Texan. Kinda a big request considering he lives in Seattle. What do you think? Does it look Texan?"

Lisbeth stared at the massive blue glass sculpture hanging from the ceiling. "I'm not sure what a Texan sculpture is supposed to look like, but to me, it resembles a layered expanse of blue sky and clouds."

"You're quick out of the chute!" Travis barked out.

"Huh?" Lisbeth and Maggie said simultaneously.

Travis chuckled. "I do believe that you're the first person to look up there and figure it out right away. It bewilders most people."

"That's because she's a quilt artist," Maggie inserted proudly. "She sees color and design that other people miss."

Travis knitted his brows. "What in tarnation is a quilt artist?" he looked at Lisbeth.

"I design and make quilts," Lisbeth answered.

"You mean blankets on beds, like grandmas used to make?"

"Hardly!" Maggie snapped. "She's won dozens of national and international awards for her quilts. She's an artist in every sense of the word. And they aren't blankets, they're quilts!"

Travis held up his hands and took a step back. "Hey, y'all, didn't mean any offense. I just never heard of a quilt artist before."

"No offense taken," Lisbeth responded, a smile cracking at the sides of her lips. "You're not the first person to make the mistake." She glanced at the elevators and, taking the hint, Travis led them to the express elevator where they were whisked up to the top floor.

Travis ushered them into the lawyer's office and said goodbye, promising to see them later. Howard Sheridan got up and greeted the two women. He was a tall, older man with a heavily lined face and a head full of thick silver hair. His dark blue eyes struck her as astute and discerning. When he stepped around his desk, Lisbeth noticed he was wearing the most elegant pair of cowboy boots she'd ever seen.

"Guess it's a Texas thing," she thought, remembering Travis's boots.

"Please, please sit down," he indicated two large leather chairs on the other side of his desk. He buzzed someone outside his office and asked for coffee service. Lisbeth watched him; his gentle eyes comforted her, putting her at ease.

"I trust you both had a good flight?"

"Yes, we did," Lisbeth answered. "By the way, this is my friend, Maggie Bowen. We've known each other since elementary school. She's as close to a sister as I've ever had."

"Nice to meet you, Ms. Bowen, and nice to finally meet you, too, Ms. James. Before we get into the will and its specifics, I'd like to tell you about your birth and your adoption. I think it will help you understand where you came from and why you were put up for adoption. Are you ready?"

Lisbeth swallowed hard and looked at Maggie, who nodded. Lisbeth looked back at the lawyer. "Go for it, I'm ready."

She clasped her hands together, first in her lap, and then placed them under her chin. The lawyer produced a birth certificate and slid it across the desk. It was Lisbeth's birth date, only the name was Savannah Mae McDonald. The certificate named Emma Lisa Clayburne, 17, of Waxahachie, Texas, as the birth mother, and the birth father as Jack McDonald, 17, also of Waxahachie. Lisbeth stared at the birth certificate, chewing on her lower lip, until the lawyer coughed to get her attention. She looked up just as a woman entered the office with a tray of coffees and pastries. She set it down on the desk and handed a cup of coffee to each of them.

"This is my real birth certificate?" Lisbeth asked, her eyes glued to the paper. The lawyer nodded. "And Savannah Mae McDonald is my birth name?" The lawyer nodded again. "You said you handled my adoption, right?" She didn't wait for an answer. "Why did they give me up? Why didn't they want me?"

The lawyer took a sip from his coffee cup and pointed to the certificate. "As you can see from the ages on your birth certificate, your parents were young, in high school," he began. "They came from good families that expected them to go to college and pursue careers. Your parents had other plans. They were in love. They ran away and found a judge out in East Texas to marry them. When they returned and announced their marriage to their families your grandmother, Fannie Lee, threw a conniption.

A couple of months later, Emma discovered she was pregnant. She was elated. Never saw that girl so happy. However, your grandmother wouldn't hear of it. She began pressuring your mother into divorcing Jack and giving you up."

He looked at Lisbeth and saw sadness filling her eyes.

"You must understand that your grandmother's intentions were good. She didn't want your mother to be burdened with raising a child while trying to go to school or start her life as an adult. And though she had no hard feelings against Jack, she felt they were much too young to be married. Your father wasn't happy about Fannie Lee's pressure on Emma but said he would go along with whatever your mother decided. After a great deal of bickering and heartache that went on for weeks, your mother agreed to your grandmother's wishes. I never saw your mother smile again."

The lawyer stopped and took a sip of his coffee. Remembering the cups in front of them, Lisbeth and Maggie did the same, breaking the thick air of sorrow filling the room.

"It feels like only yesterday this all happened," the lawyer continued. "A tremendous rift erupted in the family. Things were never the same after the adoption. Your mother went to school in the Northeast and never came home, even to visit. After graduation, she stayed there—Boston, I think—and cut off all communication with the family. She had two sisters, a brother, aunts, uncles, cousins, and wanted nothing to do with any of them. She blamed your grandmother for taking you away from her. And being a closed adoption, she didn't know how to find you, or I think she might have."

"Mr. Sheridan, how did you find me? I mean, I have a different name than the one given to me at birth."

The lawyer nodded. "Well, that was something both your grandmother and I insisted upon as a condition of the adoption. We required that your adoptive parents inform me of the legal name that they would give you, if they decided to change it. And as you can see, they did."

Lisbeth shook her head from side to side. "This doesn't make any sense. Why did my grandmother, who didn't want me, put me in her will? Why didn't she give the house and money to someone else in the family?"

"I talked to your grandmother about these very questions. After the adoption was finalized and she realized what her actions had done, how she'd lost her daughter over forcing her to give you up, she regretted her actions. But the deed was done and couldn't be reversed. She never forgave herself and lived the last 30 years of her life in a constant state of sorrow. When it came time to write her will, she informed the rest of the family that she intended to leave the home and some of the money to you. Now, you need to understand that the Clayburnes are a very wealthy family—there was plenty to go around. Not one of them argued with her decision—well, except one person, and that isn't important right now, because they had witnessed her grief and thought that perhaps if she gave you the house, their mother would find some peace. They also hoped that it would bring you back to Texas."

Lisbeth sat still, speechless. She looked at Maggie, who reached over and squeezed her hand. She looked back at the lawyer. "Are my parents still alive? My grandfather?"

"Your grandfather died many years ago, long before you were born. Your father is very much alive, as are many other relatives. From what I understand, after the divorce, your parents went their separate ways. Your father remarried, and I believe he and his family live in the area. As far as anyone knows, your mother stayed in the Northeast. However, she seems to have disappeared. I don't know whether she's alive."

Lisbeth leaned back into the cushy leather chair. "It would have been nice to meet her," she said wistfully, longing for someone she never knew, someone she desperately wanted to know, someone she had thought about her whole life. She took in a big breath of air and let it out slowly. "Even so, an inheritance, a house, and a family? This is a lot to take in."

"Yes, I imagine it is," the lawyer responded. "Are you ready to hear the will and learn exactly what you have inherited?"

Lisbeth nodded. "Sure, I don't think I could be any more surprised than I am now."

Over the course of the next hour, the attorney detailed Lisbeth's inheritance. He told her that the home is one of the oldest in Waxahachie, a classic Victorian. She would also inherit all of the home's contents, from personal items to furniture. It was up to Lisbeth if she wanted to share any of the contents with her birth family, but she didn't have to.

"Wouldn't they want the contents, or at least some of them?" Lisbeth asked. "I mean, they're more connected to all that stuff than I am."

The attorney rubbed his chin before answering. "As I said, the family has money. All of your relatives own very nice homes and have more belongings than they probably need. They thought that if you would consider relocating to Waxahachie, that having a home in pristine condition, fully furnished, with a considerable amount of money to live on might entice you to move."

"What about my mother?"

"As I said, we were not successful in finding her, though we are still trying. She, too, has an inheritance in the will. If she is alive and we can find her, she will receive it, and if we can't find her, but we can locate children she may have, they will receive her inheritance. Should those efforts not prove successful within a certain period, her inheritance will revert to you."

Lisbeth shook her head. "I don't even know how to begin to process all of this."

Maggie turned to face Lisbeth and chimed in, "Don't overthink this, Lisbeth. You just got handed an unbelievable gift. Your whole adult life, you've been a renter and you've always said you wish you could afford to buy your own home. Plus, you've always wished you weren't an only child and had a family. Lisbeth, both of your wishes just came true. And it sounds like you'll have enough money to live comfortably and won't need to work. You could turn your quilting into that full-time passion you're always talking about."

Lisbeth smiled. "Yeah, that's true. I'm just a bit overwhelmed is all."

"Are you ready to sign the papers?" the attorney asked, grinning like a proud papa.

After reading and signing all the papers, the attorney handed her a keychain with several keys, a trust statement in her name showing an account balance of $2.2 million, and a statement of how the money was invested, showing a return higher than her monthly salary at her job.

Lisbeth stared at the sum and looked up at him. "Is this correct?"

' "Absolutely," the attorney answered, as he gestured toward the door. "A car—rather a pickup truck—is waiting downstairs to take both of you to Waxahachie, to your house. Oh, and there's this." He handed her a file with the names of all her relatives, their addresses, and their phone numbers. He opened the file, took out three photos, and handed them to Lisbeth. "The older woman is your grandmother, Fannie Lee. The young woman is your mother, Emma. And the young man is your father, Jack."

Lisbeth stared at the photos; a lump formed in her throat as her eyes welled with tears. She looked up at the attorney. "Can I keep these?" He nodded. "Just one more thing, Mr. Sheridan. When you find my mother will you let me know? I don't care where she is, I'll go anywhere to meet her."

The attorney nodded again. "Of course. Don't get your hopes up too high. She may not be alive."

"Mr. Sheridan, I know she's alive, I just know it."

Mr. Sheridan nodded and stood up, signaling the discussion was over, and showed them out of his office and down to the first floor where Travis and the pickup truck awaited them. Travis stowed their luggage in the back, opened the passenger side door, and ushered them into the truck. The women waved to the attorney as the truck pulled away.

"Did everything go well?" Travis asked as they pulled away from the curb.

"Yes, more than well, I'd say," Lisbeth answered.

Travis looked back at the road, staying silent the rest of the trip as the women chatted about what they saw out the windows. A while later, the truck pulled into a quaint town full of gingerbread houses.

"Where are we?" Lisbeth asked.

"Waxahachie," Travis answered. "I take it you've never been here before?"

"No. What a beautiful town," Lisbeth commented, straining her neck to see all the picturesque houses.

"Tell ya what, I'll show you something really interesting before I take you to the house."

Soon he pulled up in front of an old building in the center of town. No ordinary structure, it was tall, several stories high, and built of red stone.

"What is this place?" Lisbeth asked, looking up at the towering, imposing building.

"It's the Ellis County Courthouse, built in 1895 in what's called the Richardsonian Romanesque style. Impressive, isn't it? Step out, I want y'all to see something unusual." They all walked up to the building and Travis pointed to some face sculptures. "Those are called the Unrequited Love Carvings."

"Why?" Lisbeth asked.

"Legend says that a man named Harry Herley, a stonemason, was brought to Waxahachie to decorate the outer walls of the new courthouse. The story goes that Harry fell in love with Mabel Frame, the daughter of the boarding house owner where he stayed during his time in Waxahachie. The first carving, this one here," he pointed upward, "is supposed to be of Mabel's likeness. See how sweet and angelic she looks? Apparently, Mabel wanted nothing to do with him, which made him bitter and angry. Each subsequent carving depicts Mabel with increasingly twisted, evil expressions."

They walked around the courthouse craning their necks to examine each of the carvings.

"Did she ever give him a chance?" Maggie asked.

"Nope, he married another local girl, and they moved to Dallas. Now, not everyone believes this legend. Many say that the heads were carved in Dallas and shipped down to Waxahachie to be installed as you see them today. The nonbelieving camp says they represent twelve faces of traditional European figures, not Mabel."

"Huh!" Lisbeth remarked. "Either way, it's a pretty fascinating story."

They got back in the truck and in minutes pulled up in front of a butter-yellow, three-story Victorian, replete with climbing roses, jasmine, honeysuckle, and wisteria scaling up the sides of a wrap-around porch with a swing. Nestled in the front flower beds, azaleas and gardenias showered the front walkway with vibrant colors and heady scents. Gingerbread decorated the exterior of the home's every nook and cranny, giving it a whimsical charm, echoing yesteryear. Lisbeth stood on the sidewalk, her mouth slightly agape, staring at the home.

Maggie whispered to Lisbeth, "Sweetie, this is the kind of home you've always wanted to live in, and now you will. I can't believe it's yours."

Never taking her eyes off the house, Lisbeth said, "Me neither."

Travis coughed into his fist. "Ladies, may I carry your luggage inside for you?" he asked, standing next to their overnight cases.

"Uh, uh, sure," Lisbeth stammered. "Guess we should make sure the key works before you leave."

"Good idea," Maggie agreed.

The three of them walked through the elegant yard bursting with roses and brilliant orange Pride of Barbados; they stepped up the wide, wooden stairs, onto the porch and stood before an intricately carved red front door. Lisbeth inserted the key; it opened the door immediately. The three of them stepped inside, and Travis placed their bags in the front entrance. Lisbeth started to reach into her purse, but Travis stopped her.

"Unnecessary," he said, raising his hand. He tipped his hat, wished them well, and left.

"Do you think he's the law firm's usual driver?" Maggie asked after Lisbeth closed the door. "I mean, don't big firms use town cars or fancy imports to drive people around?"

"Actually, I think that pickup truck costs more than most luxury cars. And judging from their top-floor offices, I'd say they can afford whatever they want. As for Travis, I don't know about him. He was not your typical town car driver."

Lisbeth and Maggie stood in the foyer, staring, nearly frozen in their tracks. After a few moments of taking it all in, they began walking around the house, checking out every room. After a while, they arrived on the third floor to find a small door at the end of the hall. They opened it and found a narrow, steep stairway going up to a dark room. They both instinctively turned on their cell phone flashlights and climbed the stairs. In the attic, they found old trunks, boxes of photos, and more furniture.

"This is going to take time to go through," Lisbeth said. "Think I'll do that another day."

They turned to leave when they noticed a small door in a back corner. The women glanced at one another and immediately headed for the door. They tried to open it, but to their disappointment, it was locked.

"Is there a little key on that key chain Mr. Sheridan gave you?"

Lisbeth pulled the key chain out of her pocket. There was a small key; she inserted it into the lock. Though it fit, the lock wouldn't budge.

"I think it's the right key; the locking mechanism might be rusted."

"Maybe," Maggie responded. "When you get settled here you can call a locksmith to break it for you. Who knows what might be in there. Maybe a family ghost," she hissed in a haunting voice.

"Thanks a lot, Maggie. Just what I need to hear living in such a big place by myself."

Maggie grinned. "Maybe it'll be a friendly ghost, like Casper."

"Yeah, right."

"You hungry?" Maggie asked. "'Cause I'm starving. I saw some cute little cafes when Travis drove us through town. We're so close to the center of town, we could walk there."

"Let's do it. Inheriting a gorgeous house and a couple million dollars, not to mention a family, has really worked up my appetite!"

Chapter Four

When she returned home, Lisbeth called Dennis and suggested they meet at a local coffee shop.

"How was your trip? Is everything okay?"

"Yeah, everything's great. I just need to talk to you about a few things."

"Like what?"

"Don't be so impatient. Meet me at Jules Cafe, and I'll tell you."

"Well, I hope it's good," he said optimistically.

"Oh, it is," she said, expecting that he wouldn't think it was good at all.

Later that day, Dennis walked into the cafe looking as strikingly handsome as Lisbeth had ever seen him. He wore his dark blond hair tousled in a way that made him look like he'd just rolled out of bed, which she figured that he probably had. She looked away to gather her thoughts without letting his looks deter what she had to say.

"How was the trip?" he asked, sitting down and resting his arm, sporting a designer gold watch, on the table, a watch that Lisbeth figured cost more than her car.

"More than I could have imagined."

"How so?"

"First thing, we were picked up at the airport by a driver, who transported us to the lawyer's office in a fully restored, vintage pickup truck."

"A pickup truck? What kind of law firm picks up their clients in a pickup truck?" he said, a slight tone of derision in his voice.

"Well," she started to say as she noticed how snugly the black silk shirt he was wearing hugged him, showing off his muscled chest. She looked away momentarily to refocus her thoughts. "I'm guessing that the truck cost quite a bit to restore, so it wasn't like he was driving us in a beat-up old farm truck."

"Okay, moving on. What did you learn about your inheritance?"

"It's a long story, but in short, my grandmother forced my mother and father to divorce when she found out that my mother was pregnant with me. It caused a huge rift, and my mother moved away, never to return or even keep in touch with the family. My grandmother regretted her actions and, to make amends, I suppose, she willed the house with all its contents and a financial inheritance to me."

"Why would she do that?" Dennis asked, leaning forward.

"The attorney said she hoped that in giving me the house and an inheritance that it would allow her to die in peace."

"And now you're stuck with a musty old house? Some inheritance."

"No, Dennis, it's not like that. The house is gorgeous, and it's in pristine condition, as is everything in it. In fact, it's exactly the kind of house I've always wanted."

Dennis leaned back in his chair, crossing his arms over his chest. "I've never heard you talk about wanting to live in an old house. Where's this coming from?"

"Dennis, I've mentioned it several times, but you never listened to what I was saying."

He fluttered his hand as though batting away a fly. "Never mind that. What are you going to do with the house?"

She didn't answer right away.

"You're not planning to move to Texas, are you?" Dennis asked. Worry lines creased his brow, and the sides of his mouth darted downward.

"Yes, Dennis, that's exactly what I'm planning to do."

He shook his head. "I don't understand."

"What don't you understand?"

"You're leaving me? After everything I've done for you?"

"Listen, Dennis, I appreciate all that you've done for me, truly I do. However, it's time for me to move on to the next chapter of my life."

"What next chapter?" he asked, with obvious annoyance in his voice. "You're in your next chapter, with me. We've been talking about marriage."

Lisbeth inhaled a big breath of air, and let it out slowly. "If you think about it, Dennis, *you've* been the one talking about marriage, not me."

He leaned over the table and took one of her hands in his own. "Lisbeth, I love you, and I want you to be my wife."

"I know you do. And I know you don't want to hear this, but I'm going to say it anyway. I've never been in love with you, Dennis. I doubt that I'll ever love anyone again the way I loved Scott. He was my soulmate, and no one can take his place. Not you. Not anyone."

"You could at least give me a chance," he said, a slight pleading in his voice.

"Dennis, what have the last three years been? I need to move on, and I'm pretty sure God gave me this opportunity to start over in Texas for a reason. I was born there. My family is there. Dennis, I'm leaving."

Dennis let go of her hand and sat there stunned. "I can't believe this is happening."

"Look, I don't want any hard feelings. And I do want to be honest with you. Surely you can appreciate that."

He looked at her, a stone-hard look chiseled on his face. "Actually, I can't." He got up and walked out of the cafe, not looking back.

Lisbeth sat there nursing her cup of coffee, thinking about his response. She didn't think he would be happy but also didn't expect that he would take it so badly. *"Hmm, maybe this is a wake-up call,"* she thought. *"Maybe leaving is the best thing that could happen to me."*

Within days of arriving home, Lisbeth started on the to-do list she had written up on her return flight. She decided that her move date would be in three weeks. Though she knew it was going to be a tight deadline, she'd made up her mind, and she didn't want to waste one moment.

The next day she returned to work and stepped into her boss's office.

"Got a minute?" she asked.

Her boss looked up at her and smiled. "Of course, Lisbeth. How was your trip to Texas?"

"Beyond anything I could have imagined."

Her boss leaned back in her chair. "That's exciting. How so?"

"In short, I found my birth family and inherited the family home and enough money to live comfortably without having to work."

"Lucky you," her boss responded with complete insincerity. "What are your plans?" she asked, her fingers steepled, her eyes carefully watching Lisbeth's face.

Lisbeth reached into her pocket and handed her an envelope.

"Is this what I think it is?" she asked, taking the envelope.

Lisbeth nodded. "I know it hasn't always been easy, and I know that at times you and I didn't get along very well."

"That's true," her boss responded, her voice devoid of emotion.

"I'm not leaving because of any of that. I'm leaving because I'm going home to where I was born, to be with my family that, until recently, I didn't know existed. Plus, my inheritance will allow me the opportunity to focus on my quilting."

The edges of the woman's lips turned up slightly into a small smile, a facial expression Lisbeth had rarely seen. "Despite our differences, I have appreciated having you here. Lisbeth, you've been through a lot in recent years, more than anyone I know. You deserve a second chance, some real goodness in your life. It sounds like this is your opportunity, so take it, with my blessing. When do you plan to leave?"

"Three weeks."

"Then let me give you a little going-away gift. Consider it my making up for all the grief this place has put you through. To be honest, I don't know why you didn't quit long ago. I've certainly caused other people to quit on the spot and leave. If you can work all this week and complete all your open projects, with Friday being your last day, I will give you next week off, and pay you for both weeks, in addition to any vacation pay you have accrued that will see you through the third week. That will give you two full weeks after you finish here to do all that needs to be done to move halfway across the country."

A few days later, after work, Lisbeth stopped first at the cemetery where her parents were buried, and second, at Scott's grave across town. At each, she laid down a bouquet of flowers. When she bent over Scott's grave to lay down the bouquet, she crumbled and curled up into the fetal position, resting her head against his gravestone. She went numb, feeling as though her soul had left her body. She began to silently weep. Lying on his grave, his death reminded her of all that she had lost.

"Scott, wherever you are, you may know that I'm leaving California and I won't be coming by anymore," she said aloud. "If you don't know, I found my birth family, or rather, they found me. I'm moving to Texas to begin the next chapter of my life. I always thought that we would have a future together. It was my greatest wish. Since God had other plans for you, I am heading into the future alone. I have high hopes for my new life, and I'm really looking forward to it. If I can't be with you, at least I might have a family to spend my days with." She went silent before adding, "I will love you always."

She wiped her eyes, stood up, and carefully arranged the flowers under the headstone, then headed back to her car. She dialed Maggie as she drove out of the cemetery.

Maggie answered after the first ring. "Hey, girl, are you still going to meet the gang for drinks this evening?"

"Of course, I wouldn't miss it," she said, trying to sound cheerful and not relay any remnants of grief. "Are we meeting at the usual place?"

"Of course! Best margaritas in Southern California."

"Okay, see all of you in 20 minutes."

"Lisbeth, you know that in Texas they say 'y'all.' You're gonna have to practice or they're never going to let you into the state," she chuckled into the phone.

"Yeah, right. See y'all soon!" Lisbeth giggled back.

As she drove to her favorite Mexican bar and grill to meet up with her friends, she thought about Scott and their wish to be married to one another. Since his death, she'd come to realize how fragile wishes could be; how life and fate could crush hopes and dreams when a person least expected it. How light could turn into darkness in a moment.

She arrived at the restaurant, wiped away a few residual tears before exiting her car, and stepped inside, craning her neck to find Maggie. A hostess asked her if she was Lisbeth and, when she nodded, directed her to the back room.

It was packed not just with close friends, but with nearly everyone she knew. Loud clapping erupted as soon as she stepped inside. Around the room were balloons, ribbons, and hanging Texas flags. Maggie walked up to her and handed Lisbeth a very large glass cowboy boot filled with what looked like at least a quart-size margarita.

"You know I'm gonna get drunk on this don't you?" she grinned at Maggie.

"Of course, you are. No worries, Lucy, our gang teetotaler, is going to drive you home in your car, and her husband Rodney will follow in their car to take her home. We gotcha covered. Drink up, bestie!"

All week after work, and during the following weeks she diligently went through her belongings deciding what to keep and what to give away. Sophie clearly decided that she should help. Each item Lisbeth picked up brought back memories of the last time she used it. Did she need it anymore? Did she want it for sentimental reasons? She tried holding items up for Sophie to inspect. She figured that if Sophie sniffed it or pawed it, then it was a sure sign that it should go to Texas. The only problem was, Sophie sniffed and pawed everything. Lisbeth had to figure out a better strategy. Finally, she developed a system.

"Okay, Soph, here's how we're going to do this. If an item brings us joy, we keep it. And if we don't care one way or another, it goes in a donation pile. Got it?" she asked, looking at Sophie's face, waiting for a response that never came. Sophie decided to groom herself instead while stretching out inside one of the boxes.

Lisbeth figured she would take her sewing machine, fabrics, and sewing supplies, in addition to Sophie's belongings; photos of her parents, Scott, and lifelong friends; and her clothing, shoes, toiletries, jewelry, and a few personal items. With a fully furnished house, she expected that she wouldn't need to bring much. She began a third pile of items she thought Maggie might want, and when Maggie stopped by and saw everything, she dove through it all like a seasoned estate shopper, cherry-picking what she wanted. Sophie watched Maggie's every move, like a diligent supervisor

Every few minutes she would hold up an item and ask Lisbeth, "Are you sure you don't want this?" Occasionally, Sophie would bat at an item, which Lisbeth told Maggie to ignore.

"Sophie has already gone through everything with me. She had her chance to choose what to keep. At this point, everything left is yours or it goes to the local thrift store."

"Tell ya what, I'll be back a couple of days before you leave, and the two of us will finish packing up everything you're taking in the trailer you're renting. Then you and Sophie can stay at my place and leave from there."

"You're the best!" Lisbeth thanked her.

The next morning, Lisbeth's phone rang and she saw it was Dennis. He had been calling incessantly and she hadn't taken any of his calls. She figured she might as well talk to him and get it over with.

She no sooner answered than he responded quickly. "Why haven't you answered any of my calls?" he asked in an obviously perturbed voice.

Lisbeth took in a big breath and slowly, carefully, chose her words, "Dennis, I told you that I'm leaving. Don't make this hard."

"That's a bunch of bullshit. You can't leave, we're engaged," he said authoritatively, as though that was the only sane scenario.

Lisbeth's jaw dropped. *That went downhill fast,"* she thought.

Lisbeth again took a deep breath. In as calm a voice as she could muster, she stated emphatically, "No, Dennis, you know that we aren't engaged, we never have been. We talked about this at the cafe. I'm sorry if you don't want to accept it, but we're done."

Her phone beeped that the caller had hung up. She stared at her phone. She couldn't recall him ever being so angry.

Half an hour later, the blast of a car horn interrupted Lisbeth's packing. She ran to the window and saw Dennis's Lamborghini in her driveway, horn still blaring, and ran out the front door, being careful to close it behind her.

"What are you doing, Dennis?" she said softly, attempting to tamp down his anger, looking around to see if neighbors were stepping onto their porches to see what the commotion was in her normally quiet neighborhood.

"Get in the car!" he yelled out the driver's side window.

"No, Dennis," she answered calmly.

"I said, get in the car!" he screamed louder.

"And I said I would not," she responded, maintaining her composure, holding her head high. Suddenly, she felt something break inside. All the stress of the emotional roller coaster she'd unknowingly been riding with him rose to the surface. As if she were watching a film racing before her eyes, she began connecting the dots, realizing how he'd been manipulating her.

"My God," she thought, *"he's really exhausting. Why didn't I see this before? How did I let this man, who isn't good for me, into my life? I am done!"* she silently told herself.

Dennis got out of his fancy sports car and walked over to her. "Now listen, honey."

Lisbeth steeled herself and held up her hands straight out in front like a barricade, her eyes boring into him. As smoothly as she could, modulating her voice to stay as placid as possible and not raise his ire any higher than it was, she cautioned him, "Don't come any closer, Dennis. I am not your honey. Don't make this any more difficult than it is. So, I'll say this again. We are done. I don't love you. I never have. I am moving to Texas." Then she raised her voice a notch, maintaining her composure. "Now, please get off this property before I call the police."

They stood watching one another, Dennis poised like a feral dog about to attack, Lisbeth quiet and coolheaded. She'd never seen him behave like this. There was so much bitterness and anger pouring out of him. Though she wanted to make her point by hollering at him until she was hoarse, she quickly decided that an all-out screaming match would do no good. She watched wine-colored blotches bloom all over his face as he stood his ground, and then he took one step backward. A bead of perspiration trickled down his forehead.

"Obviously, you need some time to think this through. I'll come back, but I'm not taking no for an answer. When do you plan to leave?"

Lisbeth looked him straight in the face and calmly said, "Two weeks from tomorrow," fibbing as best she could.

"No, you won't. I will not stand for it. You're going to stay here and marry me. Texas? Yeah, right. Why would anyone move to that hick state? You should think up a better lie."

Dennis got back into his car, backed up quickly, and screeching the tires, sped down the street and out of sight. As soon as his car turned the corner, Lisbeth let out the breath she'd been holding in, bending at the waist to let it all out.

Soon after, Maggie came over to help finish packing and putting everything Lisbeth was taking with her into the rented trailer. Before they took Sophie to the car, Lisbeth went to her bedroom closet and brought out the last item, a gift-wrapped box. She handed it to Maggie who looked at her, surprised.

"What's this?"

"Just open it."

Maggie tore open the box to find a quilted wall hanging of a blond, female surfer riding the waves. Maggie looked up at Lisbeth, her eyes glistening.

"I made it for your birthday. Thought I'd give it to you now. I could not have gotten through this move without you, Mags. Through any of this without you."

Maggie examined every inch of the wall hanging. "You really made this for me?"

"Of course, I did, silly. That's you on the surfboard."

"Yeah, I see you spiked my hair, that's cool." Maggie stood up and gave Lisbeth a long hug. "I'm so happy for you, and I'm really gonna miss you."

"And I'm gonna miss you, too."

"I'm worried about you driving all alone to Texas. Let me go with you," she pleaded.

"Maggie, I told you the last time you brought this up that I'll be fine. Really, I will."

"Promise you'll call me every night when you stop at a hotel and let me know that you're okay?"

"You know I will. In fact, I'll probably call you several times when I'm on the road and tell you about all the interesting stuff I see."

"Promise?"

"Absolutely." After several moments of silence, she added, "You do realize this isn't goodbye, don't you?"

Maggie nodded. "It won't be the same without seeing you all the time."

"The same, no," Lisbeth agreed. "It'll be different. What you and I have had will never change or go away, Mags. Our memories are indelible. Remember when we were kids and we'd find flowers and press them between wax paper in books to keep as mementos?"

"Yeah, I think we pressed some bugs, too."

Lisbeth grinned. "We did, and I found a bunch of them when I was going through books to donate. My point is, our friendship won't ever die because it's based on love and unforgettable shared memories."

"I hope you're right, Lis. I really do. Still, I'm gonna miss you."

"We're going to create new memories from new experiences when you visit me in Texas. And I'm telling you right now, we have to set up weekly video calls, and every month or every other month, you're flying out to Texas to spend a long weekend with me. Or maybe a whole week if your boss will let you work remotely. So, get that through your head, Maggie, 'cause our friendship is only taking a turn, a really good turn."

Maggie laid the quilt on a chair, turned, and hugged her so hard, Lisbeth felt like her lungs were being crushed.

Chapter Five

Four days after leaving Southern California, Lisbeth rolled into Waxahachie with all her worldly belongings, and Sophie asleep in a carrier on the passenger seat. Lisbeth pulled up to the house to find a group of people standing on the front porch. She got out and trotted up the steps.

"Hello, can I help you?" she asked.

A tall, stately woman with short red hair the same shade as Lisbeth's stepped forward. "Are you Savannah Mae—excuse me, Lisbeth James?" her Texas accent thick as barbecue sauce.

Lisbeth nodded, "Yes."

"I'm Ruth Hanson, your aunt. And this here is my husband, Lyle; our daughter Annabelle, and her husband, Tim. Your grandmother Fannie Lee was my mother."

Another woman, with more than a few extra pounds on her and brilliant red hair, stepped forward, a slight scowl on her face. She held her jaw down, forming two double chins, and narrowed her eyes, scrutinizing Lisbeth. "I'm your Aunt Thelma. And I haven't quite decided how I feel about you inheriting our family home and a good chunk of the inheritance. This home was supposed to pass to me."

"Now, Thelma," Ruth said in a stern voice. "We talked about this, and you promised to be cordial. I'm counting on you to treat our niece with respect."

"I am being cordial," Thelma snapped. "I haven't cussed or yelled at her, have I?" she remarked with a smirk across her face.

Ruth moved closer to Lisbeth. "Please forgive my sister's behavior."

"My behavior is just fine!" Thelma asserted.

Watching the interchange between her aunts, Lisbeth wondered if this was normal. Another man, tall and lean with the same striking red hair as everyone else, stepped forward.

"I'm your Uncle Keith."

"He's the quirky one of the family," Thelma commented without a hint of derision.

Keith looked over at Thelma. "You only wish you were as interesting as me." He turned back toward Lisbeth who, at this point, was feeling a little overwhelmed by the family drama.

"I sure am happy to meet you, Lisbeth," Keith began, then bent down and gave her an affectionate hug. "Always wondered what happened to that cute little redheaded baby. You sure turned out pretty."

"Thank you, Uncle Keith. And just so I know what to expect, why does Aunt Thelma say you're quirky?" Lisbeth asked.

"He thinks he's Sherlock Holmes," Thelma answered for him.

"Great!" Lisbeth responded. "Every family needs their own personal sleuth."

"I think so, too," Keith said, nodding his head. "You know, there's ghosts in this house. If you want, I can tell you all about them."

"Keith!" Ruth exclaimed. "Don't scare her before she even moves in. She won't be able to get a wink of sleep."

Lisbeth smiled. "Ghosts don't scare me, Aunt Ruth." She turned to Keith. "I'd love to hear about the ghosts. Are any of them named Casper?" she asked with complete seriousness.

"I'd have to look that up, but maybe," Keith chuckled.

"You two are going to get along just fine! Now we have two weirdos in the family!" Thelma muttered.

Lisbeth smiled, thinking *"Well, I always wanted a family, and I sure got an interesting one."*

"Please, everyone, come in. I am so happy to meet all of you," Lisbeth waved everyone toward the door.

Lyle stepped forward, "'Scuse me, Savannah Mae. Sorry, Lisbeth. That's gonna take some gettin' used to. Here, let us help you bring in your belongings. Might as well take advantage of some muscle while you got it, right?"

Thelma rolled her eyes. "Get real, Lyle. I've got more muscles in my pinky than you have in your whole skinny body."

Lisbeth liked Lyle immediately and ignored Thelma. "I'm just curious, how did you all know I was moving in today?"

"I called Mr. Sheridan," Ruth said. "He told us he'd spoken with you a few days ago and that you expected you would arrive today about this time," Aunt Ruth said. "We got here only a short time ago and figured you'd be along soon."

Lisbeth walked down to her car, followed by the family, opened the passenger side door of her car, and lifted out Sophie's crate. Sophie bellowed a loud howl. "I should probably get her settled first. She's been a pretty good traveler, but I think she's ready to live in something besides a crate or a hotel room."

"Oh, great! A cat to tear up the upholstered furniture and pee all over the house!" Thelma barked, obviously irritated.

Lisbeth turned to Thelma, a flush of red spreading across her face. "Aunt Thelma, stop it right now. First, my cat is well behaved and doesn't scratch furniture. Plus, she uses a litter box. And second, I'm sorry if you feel you were entitled to the house, but it was Grandma's decision to make and she's the one who gave me the house. Please don't be angry with me. This is no way to get started. If you can be civil, you are welcome in my home, and if you can't, then you can leave right now."

"Well, I never!" Thelma remarked, looking over at Ruth, who was holding her fist over her mouth, suppressing a grin.

"She's absolutely right, Thelma. You start treating our niece nicely or you can leave right now," Aunt Ruth said.

"Ditto," Uncle Keith chimed in.

"I can't, you drove all of us over here," Thelma whined.

"You've got two legs. Start walkin'," Uncle Keith suggested.

Thelma pursed her lips and glared at her siblings.

Tim and Annabelle bent down to look into the crate. "She's beautiful," Annabelle cooed. "Anytime you need someone to cat-sit, call us. We love kitties."

"Okay. Good to know," Lisbeth thanked them.

She took the crate into the house while Tim and Annabelle followed with Sophie's belongings. The cousins helped Lisbeth set Sophie up in the bedroom where Lisbeth planned to sleep. Lisbeth laid a little quilt she made for Sophie on the bed, took her out of the crate, and set her on the quilt so she would know that this was "their" special place. Sophie took a sniff and jumped down, ready to explore the house. Lisbeth filled Sophie's water and food bowls for whenever she ventured back into the room and set up her box in the adjoining bathroom.

"Are you wearing Chanel No. 5?" Annabelle asked.

"Why, yes! You recognize it?"

"It's sort of the family scent. Grandmother wore it, my mother wears it, I wear it, I don't know if Aunt Thelma does, and I'll bet your mother wore it. Did you know that?"

"No, no, I didn't," Lisbeth responded, surprised. *"What are the chances of that?"* she thought.

After everything had been brought into the house, Lisbeth went around and shook everyone's hands, being cautious of Thelma who was still scowling but otherwise quiet.

"I can't tell you how thrilled I am to meet all of you. Until a month ago, I didn't know I had a family. I thought that I was all alone in the world." Lisbeth stopped when she felt herself choking up.

"Oh, you poor thing," Annabelle said, putting her arm through Lisbeth's. "Well, you have a good-sized family now. There're a lot of cousins you'll meet later on. And we can tell that you sure are one of us—you have the family's red hair. Same shade and all."

"You sure do!" Lyle agreed.

Aunt Ruth stepped forward. "Honey, for generations it's been said that our red hair shows the character of our souls."

"You can say that again," Thelma quipped, which everyone ignored.

Lisbeth cocked her head sideways, not understanding Ruth's comment. She looked at Lyle, Annabelle, and Tim, who all nodded.

"Yeah," Annabelle chimed in. "We're a spirited bunch."

"You have no idea," Tim chuckled. "This family is never, ever boring." He glanced over at Keith and Thelma. She stoically looked forward, ignoring his glance while Keith grinned with pride.

"By the way, you'll never spend a holiday or a birthday alone," Lyle said. "We're a tight family, kinda like one of the ticks 'round here that lodge onto you in the summertime. You got us for good."

Lisbeth burst out laughing. "I'd like to think of you all as dear family, not ticks!"

"Just consider us your peeps," Tim chimed in. "I don't come from such a big family, but once I married into this one, I discovered more people than I thought could be related to one another!"

Lyle heaved a hard-sided case with something very heavy inside. "What you got in here? A set of weights?"

"Oh, no, that's my sewing machine. In fact, most of what's in the boxes is my sewing stuff."

"What do you like to sew, honey?" Aunt Ruth asked.

"Quilts," Lisbeth answered. "Let's take these boxes upstairs, and I'll show you," she said, pointing to some boxes.

"Here we go again with quilts!" Thelma mumbled, pretty much to herself because everyone else had already stopped paying attention to her.

Aunt Ruth placed a hand on Lisbeth's shoulder. "You couldn't know this, but your grandmother was a quilter, and she taught my sister, your mother, how to quilt. I used to quilt a little, too, in my younger years," Aunt Ruth said. "There're some quilts in the linen closet you might want to see."

"Seriously?" Lisbeth declared, her eyes wide with surprise. "When I visited the house a month ago, I didn't see them. Quilts made by my grandmother and my mother?" She laid a hand over her heart. "I'll cherish them. Unless you'd like them?"

"Honey, we have more quilts than we need. Your grandmother made us all quilts. The ones here are yours," Aunt Ruth assured her.

"You can have the quilts they gave me," Thelma offered cynically. "I don't like quilts, and I never use them"

Lisbeth slowly turned toward Thelma, trying very hard to maintain her composure. "How very sad. Quilts are comforting, something it appears you could use. If you really don't want them, I'd be happy to take them and give them to a local homeless shelter. I'm sure that someone would appreciate them."

"Hmph!" Thelma responded and plopped down in a chair.

One by one, Ruth, Lyle, Annabelle, Tim, and Keith carried boxes upstairs, Aunt Ruth leading the way. She opened a door and stepped into a room furnished with a few tables and cabinets. "This was Mother's sewing room. You'll probably find fabric in here and all sorts of thread and notions. Honestly, I don't know what kind of shape they're in. They might be too old to be useful."

Lisbeth clapped her hands together in delight, like a kid on Christmas morning who had just opened the best present ever. She bent over one of the boxes. "Here, let me show you some of my quilts."

Aunt Ruth stopped her. "Let's do that after lunch, Lisbeth. Right now, I'll bet you're tired, hungry, and thirsty. We made lunch and have it in our car. We'll bring it in, and we can visit and get acquainted."

"I'd love that," Lisbeth beamed, her heart swelling, and followed the group downstairs.

Watching her new family felt surreal. People she had never known existed were suddenly her kin. Her blood. Her people. Only weeks ago, she thought she was alone in the world, and now, far from it. Here were people who were a part of her and she was a part of them. Her greatest wish had always been to have a big family—people who loved her because they were family, who shared the same heritage, people she could love in return. A part of her wondered if all this was even real or if it was a dream. Then she remembered Thelma sitting downstairs pouting and realized it was quite real because there was nearly always a bad egg in every family.

Annabelle and Tim brought in lunch while Aunt Ruth and Uncle Lyle spread a tablecloth over a large oak table and set it with china from the cabinet, and flatware from the kitchen drawers. Lisbeth picked up a plate and studied the delicate, floral pattern. "These are lovely, they seem a bit too nice for a casual lunch. Did Grandmother have any dishes that she used for less formal occasions?"

Ruth and Lyle looked at one another and chuckled. "Your grandmother insisted on using her fine china every day," Ruth began. "She thought it was ridiculous that most people use their good dishes and flatware only on special occasions. She felt that if you own such beautiful dishes, you should enjoy them every day, not just when company comes to supper or for holidays." Ruth winked at Lisbeth and lifted up one of the plates, looking at it with pride. "I hope that you'll keep up her tradition. She would want you to."

Lisbeth stammered, "I'd be afraid to break one and ruin the set."

Ruth grinned and held up two dishes. "Oh, honey, many of these dishes don't match. See? They're all different patterns."

"Huh, whaddaya know? I hadn't noticed that," Lisbeth said, taking a closer look.

Lyle piped up, "Whenever one would break, your grandmother would go out and find a replacement. She didn't care if they matched or not."

Sitting off to the side, Thelma rolled her eyes. "So ridiculous. I like china to match. Of course, nobody listens to me." And no one did then either.

"Okay!" Lisbeth grinned, just as Annabelle and Tim came in with bags of food. "What's for lunch?" she asked her cousins.

"Fried chicken, biscuits, fried okra, coleslaw, and pecan pie!" Annabelle said, taking the food out of the bags. "Oh, and sweet tea. We thought you should get started right with a good ol' Texas meal."

"Maybe she doesn't like Texas food," Thelma proffered. "She's from California. Just give her a salad with sprouts."

"Thelma!" Aunt Ruth shouted.

"What?"

"Stop it, right now. You are being rude and insolent."

"No, I'm not. I'm just being truthful. And if our young interloper here doesn't like it, she can give the house back."

Everyone ignored her, aware that engaging her would only lead to even more bad behavior.

Lisbeth dove into the food Annabelle heaped on her plate. She didn't think she could eat even half of it. Distracted by the conversation, when she looked down at her plate, only the chicken bones remained.

"Either you like Ruth and Annabelle's fine cooking or you were real hungry," Keith commented as everyone at the table grinned. Except Thelma, who wore a permanent scowl on her face.

"I guess I was hungrier than I thought," Lisbeth replied, a little embarrassed. "I don't normally eat a lot unless something is really, really good, and this," she gestured to the food, "is really, really good!"

After they ate and Lisbeth learned a bit about everyone, except Thelma who refused to talk, and they learned a bit about her, everyone helped clean up. When they prepared to leave, Lisbeth stopped them. "Aunt Ruth, before you go, there are some photos on a wall that I'm hoping you can identify. I saw them when I was here last month."

"Of course, dear," Ruth responded, following Lisbeth to a wall of photos in the hallway. Lisbeth pointed to the oldest photo of a woman who looked as ancient as time, lifelines furrowed on her face that, if they could talk, would tell thousands of stories.

"Ah, that would be Great-Great-Grandma Lillian, she would be your great-great-great grandma. You can't tell in this old black-and-white cracked photo that she had the brightest red hair you've ever seen. We all get our red hair from her."

"And this one?" Lisbeth asked, pointing to an elegant older woman, with deep hollows surrounding mournful-looking eyes peering out at the world.

Ruth reached up and ran her fingers over the glass plate covering the photo. "This would be your grandmother, Fannie Lee. She was a beauty in her younger years and would turn heads just walking through the market. Most people considered her the most beautiful woman in Waxahachie, and had there been a beauty contest, no question, she would have won. After your mama left, never to return, she became so despondent that her grief changed not only her demeanor, but also her face. Her beauty left with her spirit."

Lisbeth rolled her lips inward in contemplation, slightly shaking her head side to side. "And this man?" Lisbeth pointed to a plain-looking man in his thirties, dressed in a simple jacket and tie.

"That's your grandfather, Henry. He died relatively young. Boy howdy, did he love your mama. He would carry her all over the house when she was little, talking to her and making her laugh. And when we all went out, he would push the buggy and coo at her to keep her calm. When she reached toddler age, he would get down on the floor and play with her, which was very unusual for a man of that time. Back then, men left child-raising to the women of the house. But not your grandpa. He loved children. Your mother must have been around nine when he died."

For several moments, they stood looking at the photos until Ruth broke the silence. "Lisbeth, it's about time we left you to start your new life. Besides, you must be awful tired."

"Oh, but I haven't shown you my quilts yet," Lisbeth said.

"My dear, we now have a lifetime to spend together. Let's do that in a week or two after you've had time to rest from your journey and get settled."

Lisbeth smiled and stifled a yawn. "Before you leave," she spoke just above a whisper, "is Aunt Thelma always in such a bad mood?"

"My sister is not a happy woman and is often grumpy. We tolerate her because she is family, and she really does like to be included in family gatherings, though if you asked her, she wouldn't admit it. By the way, you handled her just fine. She needs to know she can't step on your toes or get under your skin. Eventually, she will calm down and become much more agreeable. Till then, ignore her outbursts."

They walked to the front door and, before exiting, Ruth stopped and turned back to Lisbeth. "I almost forgot," she said, digging around in her purse. She handed Lisbeth a slip of paper folded in half.

"What's this?"

"Your father's phone number. He lives a couple of miles away, here in town. I called and told him about your moving here. He was speechless at first, then couldn't stop asking questions. He can't wait to meet you."

"You have no idea what this means to me, Aunt Ruth. I can't ever recall being this happy. It's more than I could have wished for."

"Even with a sourpuss aunt?" she smiled.

"Yes," Lisbeth grinned. "Even with the sourpuss."

Ruth gave her hand a squeeze. "Welcome to the family, sweetheart."

Lisbeth stood on the wide porch and bid everyone goodbye, waving and watching them drive down the sycamore- and oak-lined street, canopies of leafy branches stretched against the cloudless sky. Though she was beyond exhausted, she couldn't fathom taking a nap. She skipped up the stairs and began unpacking her boxes and putting away her meager belongings.

After a couple of hours when exhaustion forced her to stop, she leaned back on her heels and took a moment to breathe, to inhale the air around her, and that's when she noticed it. The house seemed to be breathing, too. She closed her eyes and listened carefully. She was sure she could hear a low, barely discernible inhale and exhale. She opened her eyes, stood up, and walked through the house. It felt as though the walls expanded as she passed through each room. It wasn't foreboding or frightening. On the contrary, it felt as though the walls and the house knew her. She wondered if that was even possible. She ran her fingers over the walls, over the dozens of photos, along chairs and tables and items all over the house. She wondered about everything she touched. About their history and her connection to them. In every room she wandered into, she heard the breathing, and an ever-so-slight sighing coming from upstairs. Stopping to listen, she heard an occasional creaking in the over hundred-and-forty-year-old floorboards and the sounds of wind whistling through sashed windows rustling the curtains. She wondered if she was imagining the sounds, but she knew she wasn't. For a moment, she thought they might be ghosts, then decided that if they were, she was probably related to them and they meant no harm. They were family, and they, like her new family, were welcoming her home. She made a mental note to ask Uncle Keith about them.

Finally, fatigue caught up with her. She knew that if she didn't lie down, she might take a nap right on the floor. She headed toward her bedroom, her legs moving as slowly as jam dripping down the side of a glass canning jar. She lay on top of the bed, grateful that someone had made up the bed for her. Too tired to get under the covers, she felt herself drifting off to sleep just as Sophie jumped onto the bed and snuggled up next to her. Lisbeth fell into a deep sleep, dreaming of found things. During the night, she was awakened by the raspy screech of a barn owl, calling for its mate. "Probably lives in that old sycamore tree," she told herself as she fell back to sleep.

Chapter Six

Lisbeth woke the next morning just after dawn, surprised that she had slept so long. She laid there for several minutes listening to rumbling thunder, tempered by the prairie. Outside, birds chirped and branches swayed in a light breeze, whispering, beckoning her to rise. She swung her legs over the side of the bed and stepped barefooted onto the hardwood floor, which squeaked under her weight. She stumbled downstairs to the kitchen. After fixing herself some hot tea, she took one of the leftover biscuits out to the backyard where she sat at a filigreed iron table; listening and taking in the garden, thick with fragrant flowers and bushes, with trees shading every corner. The garden shimmered in the morning light, the heat of the day rising with the morning sun. The day before it had been hot enough to burn the wings off dragonflies, and she figured it would be much the same today. She moved over to a chaise lounge covered in a thick cushion, shaded by a large pecan tree. She leaned back, closed her eyes, and nodded off to sleep again.

She awoke an hour later astounded that she'd fallen asleep. She felt a tickle on the top of her hand and looked down to see a multi-colored butterfly resting on it. Gently moving her fingers, she woke the insect and lifted her hand to get a better look at the luminous butterfly before it took flight. Lisbeth shook her head to clear her mind and felt something in her pocket. She took out a folded piece of paper and opened it to find the note with her father's phone number and address. She dialed the number, and after the first ring, a man answered.

"Hello. Is this Jack McDonald?" she asked.

"Yes," the man answered. "Who is this?"

Lisbeth swallowed hard. "This is your daughter, Lisbeth James." Silence. "Are you still there?"

"Yes, yes," he said slowly as though pondering what to say next. "I don't have a daughter named Lisbeth. I have one named Savannah Mae. Are you Savannah Mae?"

"Yes, I am, but, as you know, I was adopted. My adoptive parents named me Lisbeth."

"Of course, I'd heard that, just didn't remember your adopted name. Your Aunt Ruth told me you were moving to Texas. Young lady, it's time we got reacquainted. Haven't seen you since you were born."

"That's why I'm calling. I can't wait to meet you."

"Tell ya what, are you free this Sunday afternoon to come to supper and meet the family? You have several sisters and a brother who want to meet you, too."

His words burst through the phone like candy-coated bullets. *"Siblings?"*

"Whaddaya say, Savannah Mae, uh, Lisbeth?"

"Oh, yes! Of course. You live here in Waxahachie, right? Name the time and what I can bring, and I'll be there."

"You just bring yourself and a good appetite. We'll take care of the rest. See you Sunday afternoon around two o'clock."

Lisbeth hung up the phone and felt a rush of overwhelming affection that nearly crippled her. Growing up, she had always wished for a sibling—someone to share joys and friendship, secrets and sibling rivalry, and the sorrows when her parents passed. But knowing that her mother couldn't get pregnant, she accepted that she would never have one. And now, she had "several" siblings? Sunday might as well have been a year away—she could hardly wait.

She showered, got dressed, and decided to tackle the task she was anxious to start—setting up her sewing room. She entered the room and immediately began going through the drawers in the sewing table. She found a small key that looked like the key that wasn't able to open the mysterious locked door in the attic. She held it up to the key she had tried when she and Maggie toured the house. The key in the drawer was a little different and newer. She scampered up the stairs to the attic and headed for the little door. As soon as Lisbeth inserted the key, the lock clicked open. She stepped inside and pulled on a string attached to a ceiling light. The old bulb illuminated the ceiling rafters, a long cardboard box, and what looked like a sewing machine case. Lisbeth took both downstairs to the sewing room to see them in a better light.

Just then, the doorbell rang. She dashed downstairs and opened the door to find Travis standing on the doorstep holding a bouquet of wildflowers. Stunned, she didn't say a word. She just stared at him.

"Uh, hello?" he said, cracking a slight smile. "Did I come at a bad time?"

"Bad time? Oh no, sorry. I'm just surprised." She felt her cheeks turning crimson. "I didn't expect to see you again."

He turned slightly, "I can leave ..."

"Oh, no, please come in," she opened the door wide. Travis stepped inside, took off his cowboy hat, and handed her the flowers. "Just a little housewarming gift. Picked them outside my house."

"Aww, thanks." Lisbeth grinned and could feel a little flutter in her chest. "You didn't have to do that."

"I figured it would be a good excuse to see you again."

Lisbeth blushed, realizing that the pickup truck driver was interested in her. *"What the heck,"* she thought to herself, *"it's kinda sweet."*

"Come on," she waved him toward the kitchen, "I need to find a vase for these, and honestly, I have no idea where to look."

"Lemme help, darlin', I'm pretty good at finding things. Well, mostly lost calves, but how hard can it be to find a vase?"

As they began opening up cabinets, she looked over at him. "Did you say lost calves?"

"Yep."

"Um, where would that be?"

"On my ranch. It's between Waxahachie and Maypearl."

Lisbeth stopped and looked at him. "You're a rancher? I thought you were a driver for the law firm."

Travis suppressed a chuckle. "A driver, really?"

"Well, yeah, you picked me up at the airport and drove me here to the house...."

"That's true. I was doing the law firm a favor."

"Oh," Lisbeth said awkwardly and began going through another cabinet. "There's one," she said, pointing to a cut-crystal vase on a high shelf.

Travis reached up, took down the vase, and carried it over to the sink. He filled it with water and arranged the flowers.

"You're really good at that," Lisbeth marveled, watching him deftly arrange the flowers as well as any florist. "Do you raise flowers, too, on that ranch of yours?"

"Naw," he chuckled. "Well, not intentionally. These are wildflowers. They grow all over Texas. Bet you didn't know that Lady Bird Johnson made it her life's work to protect and help wildflowers thrive throughout the state."

Lisbeth's eyes grew wide in awe of Travis. He was proving to be something of an enigma. "No," she shook her head. "I didn't know that."

"Yeah, now that you're a Texan, you should read about her sometime. She said something really profound that my mother used to say. Let me see if I can remember it ... oh, now I remember: 'Where wildflowers bloom, so does hope.' Mom often reminded me that wildflowers are proof that even though life ends, it will return because splendor perseveres and survives."

Lisbeth leaned back on the counter, her mouth slightly open. "Wow. I never thought about flowers like that. Sounds like your mama is a wise woman."

"She was," he looked down at the floor, then back at Lisbeth. "Lost her a while back."

Lisbeth's smile disappeared. "I'm sorry. It's never easy losing a parent."

"Hey, how 'bout we go have some lunch?" he asked, steering the conversation to something more upbeat. "I know a real good place about an hour from here that I think you'll like. You game for a drive into the country?"

"Well, actually, I was doing some unpacking and should get back to it."

"Come on. You have to eat, don't you?" he flashed his pearly whites. "Besides, you've got a lifetime to unpack."

That smile, that face. Maggie described him as the kind of effortless handsome that some men aren't aware they possess, yet one smile like that could make a woman's knees weaken if not downright buckle. Lisbeth could feel her knees start to do just that. She had to distance herself physically from him immediately. Otherwise, she was afraid she would end up on the floor.

"Uh, sure, but I'm not going out like this," she pointed to her old worn sweats full of holes and rips. "Give me a few minutes to change." She ran upstairs just as Sophie was coming down. She bolted into her room and caught her breath. "What is happening to me?" she mumbled to herself. By the time she got back to the kitchen, Travis was holding Sophie, who was purring as though he was her best friend.

"That's a first," Lisbeth observed. "She doesn't usually take to strangers."

Travis chuckled. "I've got a few cats on the ranch, mostly barn cats to catch the mice and rats. She probably smells them on me. Or dogs, cattle, or horses. Who knows?"

"She's pretty much an indoor Southern California girl. The only dogs she's ever seen were at the vet's office and, as far as I know, she's never seen, much less smelled, a cow."

"Well, she's in Texas now. She's gonna smell all kinds of new things. Come on, let's go. I'm starved."

They drove out into the country to a small place with a simple weathered sign over the door that read "Barbecue." Travis's boots crunched the gravel as they walked across the parking lot and through a door barely hanging on its hinges. Inside, a burly, bald man with biceps as wide as Lisbeth's thighs was standing over a searing hot pit, turning meat. An older woman with deep lines etched into her face hunched over the counter. Her face lit up when she saw Travis.

"Hey stranger, where ya been? Haven't seen ya since, when? Tuesday?" she laughed a deep guttural cackle. "What's it gonna be? The usual?"

"Naw, how about a little of everything? My friend here needs to taste real Texas barbecue." He turned to Lisbeth. "You haven't had real Texas barbecue yet, have you?"

"I've had barbecue back home, but no, I haven't had barbecue here yet."

"Red, I don't know where home is but if you ain't had Texas barbecue, then you ain't had barbecue, period!" the counter woman declared. "And considering we have the best barbecue in the state, you're in for a real treat." She bounced her eyebrows up and down.

Lisbeth looked at Travis, no one had ever called her "Red" before. She was a little put off by the woman.

"She's absolutely right," he said. "Hope you're hungry. What'll you have to drink, a Dr. Pepper or a Shiner Bock?"

"I don't know," Lisbeth answered. "What's a Shiner Bock?"

"Oh my!" a throaty laugh rolled out of the counter woman. "Travis Sheridan, where'd you find this woman?"

Travis lowered his head and quietly asked. "You like beer?"

Lisbeth nodded, looking at him curiously.

"Make it two Shiners, Gracie."

He took Lisbeth's arm and steered her to a table. He placed his hat on one chair, pulled out one for Lisbeth, and sat down on a third wooden chair. Gracie came up behind, delivering a stack of white bread slices and two bottles of Shiner Bock beer. After Gracie left, Lisbeth looked Travis straight in the eye.

"She called you Travis Sheridan."

Travis nodded.

"So, you're related to Howard Sheridan, the attorney at the law firm?"

Travis nodded again, taking a swig of his beer.

"How are you related to him?"

"He's my father."

For a moment Lisbeth didn't say anything. She took a swig of her own beer. "Why didn't you mention this before now?"

Travis shrugged his shoulders. "Wasn't relevant, was it?"

"Well, no, but you portrayed yourself as the driver for the firm."

"Actually, I never said I was the firm's driver, I just picked you up and transported you around. You assumed that I was a paid driver."

"True. Ya know, you sound a lot like a lawyer yourself."

"That's because I am. I'm a partner in the firm."

"I thought you were a rancher."

Travis chuckled. "That, too. I mostly work the ranch, and one or two days a week I come into the office and handle a few cases."

Lisbeth leaned back in her chair, crossed her arms over her chest, and stared at him.

"What's wrong?" Travis asked, knitting his dark brows together.

Lisbeth shook her head. "Nothing's wrong. I just thought of you as a driver, and now I find out you're a rancher, a lawyer, and the son of my attorney."

"That's bad?" he cocked his head sideways.

Lisbeth shook her head. "No, not at all. It's just me being naive. I guess people here can wear a lot of hats."

Travis nodded. "It's pretty common 'round these parts."

Gracie laid out the biggest spread of barbecue fixins Lisbeth had ever seen, mounds of brisket, beef ribs, baby back pork ribs, smoked chicken, pulled pork, two kinds of beans, potato salad, and coleslaw. Lisbeth's eyes teemed with awe and surprise. She helped herself to small amounts of everything, and then as she finished each sampling, she took seconds, something she never did.

She wasn't ravenous when they started, but the more she ate, the more famished she felt. *"What is it about barbecue?"* she wondered, ignoring any signs of satiety her body was trying to tell her. Finally, Lisbeth pushed herself away from the table.

"Don't you like it?" he asked looking at her half-eaten plate.

"It's wonderful, it's just that this is more food than I normally eat in a week, much less in one meal."

"Oh, come on."

"Seriously, Travis, I can't eat another bite."

"What about dessert? Gracie makes the best buttermilk pie around."

Lisbeth shook her head and raised her hands. "No, no, no. Not one more bite of anything."

Travis got up and returned with a box and a large serving spoon. He put all the leftovers into the box and handed it to Lisbeth. She looked up at Travis with confusion.

"Supper or breakfast tomorrow or whenever you're hungry. Can't let this go to waste."

"Whenever I'm hungry? Are you kidding? I don't think I'll ever be hungry again," she picked up the box and carried it out to the truck.

An hour later, Travis pulled up in front of Lisbeth's house. Lisbeth stared at the front steps.

"I don't know if I can walk up the stairs. I've never been this stuffed!" Lisbeth moaned, regretting how much she'd eaten, her hands on her stomach.

"Do you want me to carry you up the stairs?" Travis asked. "Your neighbors might talk."

"Ha! I don't know any of my neighbors. No, thanks. I need the exercise. Think I'll run up and down all the stairs 20 times and try to work off some of lunch."

Travis glanced down for a few moments, then back at her, focusing with a razor-sharp intensity. "See you again?"

"Maybe," she mused, a smile cracking at the sides of her lips.

"Why maybe?" he pulled his head back to get a better look at her.

"Because if you take me to any more places like that barbecue joint, I won't be able to fit into any of my clothes. I'll see you again only if you promise to take me to a salad place."

"A salad place? What's that?" he comically scratched the top of his head.

Lisbeth slapped him on the arm. "You know darn well what it is," she scoffed at him.

Travis shook his head. "Naw, don't think I do. Does it involve vegetables?"

"You're incorrigible!" Lisbeth laughed again, picked up the box of leftovers, got out of the truck, and ran up the stairs as best she could. She turned before going in the front door and waved goodbye.

As soon as she stepped inside and closed the door, Lisbeth walked into the kitchen and placed the leftovers box in the fridge. Before leaving the kitchen, she unzipped her jeans and let out a sigh of relief as she ran up the stairs to her room to put on a pair of comfortable and roomy leggings and a loose-fitting T-shirt.

"Much better," she exhaled and headed for the sewing room.

Returning to the task she had started earlier; she opened the cardboard box she'd found in the locked room upstairs and discovered an elegant wedding dress. She carefully lifted it out and laid it across a table. She ran her fingers over the dress, discovering that it wasn't made of just one fabric, but many different exquisite silks. She found brocade, charmeuse, and dupioni, all accented with lace and an overlay of tulle on the skirt. She had been to countless weddings and could not recall ever seeing such an exquisite dress. She scavenged around for a note or something that would reveal whose wedding dress it was. No such luck.

Next, she opened the sewing machine case and let out a little yelp when she discovered a Singer Featherweight sewing machine that appeared to be in pristine condition. Like those of a child on Christmas morning, her eyes came alive, glistening at her newfound treasure. She pulled it out and saw the distinctive medallion, this one commemorating the machine's production in 1951 for Singer's centennial. She knew that while they were common throughout America back when they were made, ever since Singer had ceased production, the machines had gone from being a household essential to a collector's item. She had quilting friends who accumulated so many of them that they built special shelves to display them or bought large freestanding cabinets with glass doors to store and display their Featherweight gems. Though a hot collector's item, she knew just as many people who used them for making quilts and clothes. She had always wanted one of the small machines, but because collectors drove up the market, she'd never been able to afford one. She ran her fingers over the precious machine, figuring it belonged to her grandmother. As she sat marveling over the little machine, she wondered why it was locked away, forgotten.

Lisbeth set it on the sewing table next to her own electronic sewing machine. She pulled out the owner's manual she found in the box and used it to go over the machine's functions. Next, she took out a spool of her own thread and threaded it. She threaded a new bobbin and replaced the old one. Then she plugged it in, inserted a piece of folded fabric under the needle, and said a little prayer. She gently applied pressure to the foot pedal. At first, the machine groaned; then it hiccupped and died. Lisbeth waited a moment and tried again. Nothing. She looked upward.

"Grandma, if you can hear me, and if you can do anything from wherever you are, would you please help me out here? I promise to take your precious machine in to be serviced. Really, I will. I just want to see if it works. Okay?"

Lisbeth took a deep breath and tried again, and this time it worked. She grinned and glanced up. "Thanks, Grandma."

She sewed a few stitches, then a few more, marveling at how well the machine worked considering that it probably hadn't been used in quite a while. She bent over and hugged the little machine like it was a doll.

"Little machine, I'm gonna name you Fannie to honor my grandma who made it possible for me to come here and find you. We're going to be great friends," she murmured at the machine, aware that anyone watching her would probably think she was short a few brain cells. She didn't care. Lisbeth had named every sewing machine she'd ever owned. Her large, electronic one that she bought in California was named Joyce, for her adoptive mother, who encouraged her to pursue her love of sewing. Lisbeth went back downstairs, poured herself a glass of sweet tea, and sat down at the kitchen table. She dialed Aunt Ruth's number and told her about her conversation with Jack McDonald and the Sunday supper invitation.

"Oh honey, that's wonderful," Aunt Ruth responded.

"Funny thing is, he kept calling me Savannah Mae."

"That's to be expected. All these years we thought of you only as Savannah Mae, the name your parents gave you. After you were adopted, we didn't know your new name because it was a closed adoption. It's just a little hard to start thinking of you as Lisbeth. Don't worry, we'll all get used to it."

"Hmm. It is a sweet name. Maybe I'll grow into it," she mused. "Oh, before I forget, I found a Featherweight sewing machine in an attic closet, and it works!"

"I'm surprised! It's been years since anyone has tried to sew on it."

"And I found something else. A wedding dress. The most beautiful wedding dress I've ever seen. Do you know anything about it?"

"Oh, yes, the dress," her voice lowered. "I forgot it was up there. The story is a bit of a sad one, Lisbeth. You sure you want to hear it?" Aunt Ruth asked, her voice taking on a somber tone.

"Yes, I do," Lisbeth assured her, leaning back in her chair.

Aunt Ruth told her what she already knew, that her mother wanted to keep her, even though her grandmother Fannie insisted she give Lisbeth up for adoption. What she didn't know was that Emma had sewn herself a wedding dress for a proper wedding later on when she and Jack could afford it. Fannie discovered the dress and insisted Emma stop and forget about Jack McDonald. After Emma gave birth and went away to college, never to return to Waxahachie, the dress was put away in a closet. Years later, when it was apparent that Emma was never going to come home, even for a visit, Fannie put it in a special box manufactured to preserve the fabric and stored it away in the attic closet, under lock and key.

"Why didn't she do something with it?" Lisbeth wanted to know.

"Oh, Lisbeth, it was too distressing for her. Anything Mother made from the fabric would be a constant reminder of the mistake she had made," Ruth sighed. "That's why she tucked it away in that box you found. In her later years, she told me that her biggest regret was that she didn't allow Emma and Jack to stay together and keep you. It was a heartache she took to her grave."

"Aunt Ruth, what happened to my mother? Do you know where she is?"

"No, I don't. She wanted nothing to do with any of us, even me. We had been so close," Aunt Ruth's voice began to crack. "Excuse me, dear, give me a moment." After several seconds she continued. "Mother was not the only one brokenhearted. I lost my sister."

"Do you think she's still alive?"

"Honestly, I don't know," Ruth answered sadly, trying to hold back the crack in her voice.

Lisbeth slumped back in her chair. "I want to know. I feel like I must know. Otherwise, there's this big hole in my life. If I still have a mother out there, I want to find her. I want to show her that I turned out okay and that I want her in my life."

"Oh, sweetie, that would be so nice, but are you sure you want to find out? She might not be the person you're expecting."

"I don't have any expectations; I just want to know what happened to her."

Aunt Ruth let out a long, slow breath. "Whatever you decide to do, I'll support your wishes."

Lisbeth returned to the sewing room to look over the wedding dress again. As dusk fell, the moon rose in the sky, casting long shards of moonlight and shadows across the room. She ran her fingers over the fabric, fingering every stitch as a stab of melancholy crept into her heart. She wondered how her life might have turned out if her grandmother hadn't interfered and her mother and father had stayed together raising her in Texas. A sadness began to seep through her body. She could feel it engulfing her. She shook her head to clear her mind, to think about something else. She left the room and went downstairs to feed both herself and Sophie.

Chapter Seven

Lisbeth puttered around the house on Sunday until she glanced up at the clock and remembered she was going to meet her father and family in an hour. She rushed to get ready and headed out the door for the McDonald home.

She stepped up onto the wide porch and knocked on the towering wooden door with a stained-glass insert. A tall man, with gray at the temples and a wide smile opened the door. Behind him stood several people.

"Hi, I'm Lisbeth," Lisbeth began, holding a bouquet of roses.

Jack McDonald bent over, embraced her and didn't let go.

"I'm sorry, I didn't know that I would be this emotional. I've been waiting a long time for this day," he told her.

Lisbeth smiled. "Me, too, Dad. Oh, may I call you Dad? That was kind of presumptuous of me."

Jack smiled, his emerald eyes bright and alive with admiration. "Of course," he paused for a moment. "Only if you let me call you Savannah Mae. It's how I've thought of you all these years."

Lisbeth smiled. "Then Savannah Mae it is, Dad. Here," she handed him the bouquet. "These are from my garden." She peered around his side. "Who are all those people behind you?"

"Dad, introduce us to our sister. We've been waiting forever to meet her," piped up a girl with waves of blond hair cascading down her back, her eyes the same emerald green as her father's and Lisbeth's.

"Come, come in," Jack beckoned Lisbeth into the house.

The girl who'd spoken first stepped forward. "Hi, I'm your sister, Dixie." Before Lisbeth could respond, Dixie enveloped Lisbeth in a big hug. "I'm 16, and I'm so glad to have you as my big sister."

The next girl to step forward stood quietly in front of Lisbeth, smiling sweetly. "My name is Hattie. I'm 21. I was named after a great-aunt, and I can't wait to get to know you. I hope we can be great friends." She, too, sported blond hair, twisted into a French braid. Like her sister, her eyes glowed emerald green, with a hint of tenderness and affection.

A third daughter stepped forward, not waiting to introduce herself. She wrapped herself around Lisbeth and wouldn't let go. A woman pulled her off Lisbeth.

"Honey, tell her who you are," the woman instructed her.

"I'm your sister," the girl piped up, staring up at her with the same family emerald eyes. "I've been waiting to meet you since I was born," she said with an enthusiasm that surprised Lisbeth; she felt a lump forming in her throat. Her eyes were almond shaped and slanted up slightly. There was something different about this sister, something special, and she wasn't sure what it was.

"My name is Honey," the girl added. "I'm 10, and I have Down syndrome," she announced proudly, turning to look at her parents. Her mother and father nodded.

A young man who looked like a young clone of his father stepped forward. "I may be last, but you'll soon learn that I am not the least. I'm your big brother, Zachariah, but everyone calls me Zach. Oh, and I'm probably closest in age to you. I'm 24."

Lisbeth grinned. "That's quite a compliment, Zach. Actually, I'm 30 which makes you my baby brother, but if you want to be my big brother, I'm okay with that. You're certainly taller than me," she remarked.

"Just so you know, I'm no baby," Zach responded, an obvious irritation in his voice. Dixie and Hattie rolled their eyes upward.

"Really, Zach?" Dixie commented.

"Be nice," Hattie added.

The older woman who'd peeled Honey off of Lisbeth moved to the front. She took Lisbeth's hands into her own. "Savannah Mae, I'm your stepmother, Bonnie Ada, and I've been waiting a lifetime to meet you, ever since Jack told me about his little girl." She reached over and gave Lisbeth a tender hug. She stepped back and held Lisbeth at arm's length. "Welcome to the family, dear."

Without warning, silent tears seeped out of Lisbeth's eyes. Honey stepped forward and linked her arm through one of Lisbeth's. "Why are you sad?" the girl asked. "Did we do something wrong?"

Lisbeth turned to her, wiping her eyes. "Oh no, Honey. These are tears of joy. Until very recently I thought I was an only child. I didn't know that I had a family here in Texas."

Honey cocked her head sideways and pinched her brows together. "Why not? We've always been here waiting for you."

Bonnie Ada sidled up and took Lisbeth's other arm. She looked at Honey. "*La fille,* would you help me escort your sister to the table? I'll bet she's hungry."

"Well, if she isn't, I am!" announced Zach coming up on the rear.

"Oh, Zach, that's because you're always hungry," Dixie said. "You have the appetite of a gator!"

The family filed into the dining room; the table had been set with fine china. Lisbeth sat and looked down at the plates. Bonnie Ada caught her studying them. "These have been passed down in my family for several generations, going back to pre–Civil War times," she explained. "Just as I inherited them from my parents who received them from my grandparents, so will our children inherit them."

"Yeah, but who gets them?" Zach interjected, an impertinence feathering his voice.

"Young man, I can assure you that it won't be you if you don't mind your manners," Bonnie Ada admonished him sternly. "We not only have company, but we are also introducing your sister to our family, so you best put on your most polite behavior."

Zach looked down. "Yes, ma'am. Sorry."

Lisbeth watched the interaction with awe. Never had she witnessed such manners and children who understood proper etiquette, even if they didn't like it. Respect seemed to be rampant in Texas, something missing in California. She smiled inwardly; she liked it.

"Now," Bonnie Ada said, *"Laissez les bons temps rouler."*

Dish after dish arrived: chicken-and-sausage gumbo with fresh-baked French bread, crawfish étouffée, maque choux (a creole specialty of corn, bell pepper, onion, garlic, celery, and tomato), and seafood-and-sausage jambalaya.

Lisbeth looked at Bonnie Ada. "Did you make all of this?" she asked.

Bonnie Ada nodded.

"In case you can't tell, Mom came from New Orleans—well, they call it N'awlins there," Hattie chimed in. "She's the best

Louisiana cook in Waxahachie, probably all of Texas." Bonnie Ada looked adoringly at her daughter.

"I've been to New Orleans only once," Lisbeth said, "and I can't think of a single meal there that compared with this. This is extraordinary."

"Oh, just wait until dessert," Jack interjected. "No one makes a doberge cake like Bonnie Ada. No one."

"Oh, no, no, I couldn't eat another bite," Lisbeth protested, holding up her hands and shaking her head from side to side, tossing her red curls.

"But it's Mama's pride and joy, isn't that right, Mama?" Honey asked, looking at her mother, then back at Lisbeth. "You have to eat Mama's cake. She made it special for you."

Lisbeth sucked in a big breath of air, realizing she wasn't going to get out of dessert. It occurred to her that this scenario of food overload in Texas seemed to be a constant theme. Everyone cleared the dishes, and Bonnie Ada told Lisbeth and Jack to stay seated.

Lisbeth looked at her father, her eyes wide. "Does your family always eat like this?" she asked.

"Oh, good Lord, no, Savannah Mae. This is a very special occasion, and we wanted it to be exceptional for you. As you probably noticed, your stepmother is an excellent cook and wanted to make today memorable so you would understand how much you mean to all of us. In fact, the whole family sat down and figured out the menu together. The kids picked out their mother's favorite recipes."

"That's sweet."

"You have to understand that they were very excited that they were finally going to meet you and wanted to make sure that you enjoyed the meal so much that you'd come back."

"Are you kidding?" Lisbeth exclaimed. "Of course, I would come back. Wonderful as this meal has been, it's all of you who brought me to your table. The fine cooking is simply the proverbial icing on the cake."

"Speaking of cake, ta-dah!" Dixie sang, carefully carrying a multilayered cake on a pedestal crystal cake stand into the dining room. She gingerly set it down on the table, while Hattie and Honey placed dessert plates and forks next to it. Zach laid a large serving knife by the cake stand. Lisbeth's eyes bulged, staring at the half-chocolate, half-caramel ganache icing.

Finally, she looked up at Bonnie Ada. Lisbeth did a double take at the cake and Bonnie Ada. "You made this?"

Bonnie Ada smiled. "What can I say? I do like to bake. I thought that maybe it would be something new for you. In N'awlins, where my people are from, this is what we would call a lagniappe. A little something extra."

"I'm grateful, but honestly you didn't have to go to all this trouble."

"*Cher,* I would not have it any other way," Bonnie Ada responded. "Hattie, please hand me a plate, so I can cut the first slice for Savannah Mae." As Bonnie Ada cut the slice, Lisbeth watched her slide it onto a plate. She sat counting the layers and trying to figure out what they were as Bonnie Ada cut everyone else's slices. After a few moments, she felt everyone's eyes on her. She looked up.

"What are all these layers?"

Hattie said, "The doberge cake is traditionally filled with chocolate and lemon or caramel. We like all three, but for this cake, Mom alternated the layers with chocolate and caramel."

"This is incredible," Lisbeth sighed.

"Oh, just wait until you taste it," Jack said, politely waiting.

Lisbeth looked around and realized that everyone was waiting on her. She pushed her fork into the cake and lifted a bite to her mouth. She closed her eyes and let the velvety cake slide down her throat. She opened her eyes to find everyone staring at her.

"Well?" Honey asked. "Do you like it?"

"Do I like it? Honey, if I died this very moment and this was the last thing to cross my lips, I would die very, very happy."

"Oh, don't die!" Honey yelped. "We just met you!"

Lisbeth chuckled at Honey's innocence. "Don't worry, Honey, I'm not about to die. Not with a cake like this in front of me." Even though Lisbeth wasn't sure she could get down one more bite of food, she uncharacteristically wolfed down the cake.

"Tomorrow," she thought to herself. *"I won't eat a thing tomorrow, and maybe the day after, too."* Then as an afterthought she wondered if, in fact, she had died, and this cake was her reward.

After they'd finished supper and Lisbeth had bid everyone goodbye, Jack walked Lisbeth to the door and stepped out onto the porch.

"Don't be a stranger, Savannah Mae. You have family here, both on your mother's and my side, and we want you to be a part of our lives. I mean that."

Lisbeth stepped back and looked at him. "Thanks, Dad. I will." She leaned back on the porch railing. "I can't tell you how much your welcome means to me. I had no idea I had sisters and a brother." She looked toward the front garden and back at Jack. "My adoptive parents were wonderful people, and I will be grateful to them as long as I live, but I always felt like I missed out being an only child. You and Bonnie Ada have given me what I always longed for—siblings. I can't wait to get to know them, you, and Bonnie Ada better. As soon as I'm more settled, I want to have you all over for dinner at my house. And I want all of you to feel free to drop in any time."

"Be careful what you ask for," Jack grinned. "You could find yourself with a house full of sisters and an ornery brother wreaking havoc if you don't watch out."

Lisbeth chuckled. "I doubt that. You and Bonnie Ada have raised them well. Bye, Dad. See you soon."

She tiptoed up, kissed him on the cheek, and walked down the stairs toward her car as the evening swallowed the day. She recalled the slight anxiety she felt earlier approaching the house. What would they be like? Would they accept her? A gentle breeze rose up and quieted her mind. Thinking of yet more new family, now a part of her life, any worries she had in anticipation of visiting her father's house disappeared with the setting sun.

Chapter Eight

On her way home from Jack's house, Lisbeth picked up a Sunday newspaper at her local market. When she got home, she retreated to the living room to read the paper. In the features section, she found an article about a local quilt show coming up the following month. *"Bingo,"* she thought, *"this'll be a good way to find some other quilters."* She picked up her phone and called Maggie for their weekly phone date.

"Hey girlfriend," Maggie answered. "How's it going?"

"Amazing," Lisbeth responded. The previous week she'd told her about meeting her mother's side of the family, including the sourpuss aunt and the quirky uncle. "Earlier today I met my father and my sisters and brother."

"You have siblings?" The shock in Maggie's voice reverberated through the phone.

"Yes! Plus my stepmother is one of the best cooks I've ever met. She made an entire Louisiana-style lunch. She is so talented that I'm sure she could open her own restaurant and have a packed house every night."

"Ooooh, lucky you!" Maggie cooed. "Tell me about your siblings."

Lisbeth grinned thinking about them. "Well, Zach is a typical mid-20s guy with an ego. Even so, I like him. Hope he grows out of it."

Maggie laughed.

"What's so funny?"

"I was thinking that maybe he and that nasty aunt could hang out together."

"Oh, that is funny!" Lisbeth giggled. "Other than a 40-year age difference, they're well suited to one another."

"And your sisters?"

"Oh, my goodness, so sweet. All of them epitomize the perfect Southern belle with gorgeous silky blond hair and eyes the same color as mine. The oldest is 21, the next one is 16 and very mature, and the baby is 10. She's the most extraordinary of all."

"How's that?"

"She has Down syndrome. She knows it and wears it like a badge of honor. Her parents have obviously taught her not to hide or be ashamed of it."

"And your dad?"

"Everything I hoped he would be. Kind, gracious, intelligent, loving. He kept calling me Savannah Mae because that's how he remembered me from when I was born."

"Wow! All your dreams have really come true."

"Yep. Now you gotta plan a visit to come out here. Can you get a few days off of work?"

"Probably! My boss said I can work remotely whenever I like. When are you thinkin'?"

"There's a quilt show going on near here next month. I haven't been to one yet in Texas. It wouldn't be real big, and it would be a nice way to meet some local quilters. You up for it?"

"Sure."

"Okay, I'll send you a ticket."

"Lis, you don't have to do that. I can pay my own way."

"I know you can but as often I'm going to ask you to come out here, with my inheritance I can pay for your tickets. You shouldn't have to fork over your money for it."

"I don't want you using up your inheritance on me."

"Don't worry, that won't happen. The money is invested and each month I receive a dividend of more money than I can use."

"Okay, if you're sure."

"I'm positive, see you next month. Oh, and if there's something in particular you want to do or see while you're out here, let me know."

"Got any good beaches where I can do some surfing?"

Lisbeth burst out laughing. "In your dreams! The nearest beach is four or five hours away down on the coast. How ya feel about waterskiing? There's a lot of lakes around here."

Maggie chuckled. "Uh, thanks, but no thanks. Gotta go, Lis. See you soon."

Lisbeth woke early on Monday morning, got ready to take a shower, and discovered that she had no water. She looked up the number of the Waxahachie Water Department on her phone and called. When a woman answered Lisbeth explained that she didn't have any water. The woman asked her name and looked up the address, then told her that someone had the water turned off.

"What? Who turned off the water?" Lisbeth asked.

"You did," the woman said.

"No, I didn't."

"I beg to differ with you. It's right here on the digital record. Three days ago you turned in a request to have the water stopped as of today."

"This is ridiculous. I didn't stop in and request for the water to be turned off."

"I don't know what to tell you. We have the official record of the request, with your signature."

Lisbeth groaned. "How do I get it turned back on?"

"Come to our office with your identification and something showing that you live in the house, and we'll try to get this straightened out."

As soon as Lisbeth got dressed she headed out to the Water Department. The clerk showed her the form that she supposedly filled out. Lisbeth scrutinized the signature. While it was similar to hers, it was slightly different, and she pointed it out to the clerk.

"Here," the woman passed her a piece of paper and asked her to write her signature. When Lisbeth did, the woman compared the two signatures, got up, and went into another office. Lisbeth could see her showing the document and the piece of paper she just signed to a man at a desk. The man looked from paper to paper and asked the clerk a question. She pointed to Lisbeth. The man got up and walked to the window where Lisbeth was waiting.

"Miss James?" the man began. "Did you bring your identification with you?"

Lisbeth handed him her identification and the form she filed after she arrived changing the account to her name. He scrutinized everything, then looked back at the printed copy of the water cancellation and the piece of paper Lisbeth had just signed.

"This is highly irregular," the man said. "Are you sure you didn't come in and cancel your water service?"

"Absolutely. And as you can see, the signature on the request to turn off the water is slightly different from mine."

"Yes, I see that," the man nodded, and scratched his head. "This is a first. Never had this happen before. Well, clearly you didn't request to have your water shut off so we will turn it back on as soon as possible. Usually, it takes three days."

"Three days?!" Lisbeth squealed.

"Okay, okay, I'll put in an emergency request to turn it on as soon as possible. I can't promise it will be today, but we'll try."

"Thank you," Lisbeth said wearily. She picked up her paperwork and the printed digital copy of the order to turn off the water, stuffed them in her purse, and walked out of the building.

She was still shaking her head in disbelief when she drove by a corner coffee shop. Realizing that she didn't have water to make coffee, she stopped in, bought a cup of coffee to go, and headed home. Late in the day, she saw a Water Department truck in the alley behind her house. As soon as the truck drove away, she ran into the kitchen, turned on the faucet, and after it sputtered a bit, a full stream of water poured out. She ran upstairs to take the shower she didn't get to early that morning.

She had just finished showering and getting dressed when the doorbell rang. She went downstairs, still toweling her hair, and opened the door to find Aunt Thelma standing there holding a big plastic bag.

"May I come in?" she asked quite civilly.

Though surprised to see her, she opened the door wide. "Of course."

They stood in the foyer. "Would you like some sweet tea or coffee?" Lisbeth asked.

"Yes, sweet tea would be nice," she answered quietly. Lisbeth headed for the kitchen, Aunt Thelma right behind her. She poured them both a glass of sweet tea and motioned to Aunt Thelma to sit down at the kitchen table.

"So, to what do I owe this visit?" Lisbeth asked.

"I owe you an apology," Aunt Thelma stated matter-of-factly. "You are my niece, my sister Emma's daughter. You are family and I had no business treating you the way I did the day you moved here."

Lisbeth didn't know what to say. She just sat there, stunned.

"Yes, I was angry that you inherited the house," Thelma continued. "But that wasn't your fault. Mother chose to give you the house, because quite frankly, I already own a beautiful home, as do all of us. I suppose I was being greedy and sentimental. I would like to start over by telling you that I am deeply sorry for how I treated you. Can you forgive me?"

Lisbeth sat there blinking. She could see what looked like both sincerity and anxiety on her aunt's face as she waited for an answer.

"Yes, of course," Lisbeth finally said. "I accept your apology, and I would like to start over, too."

"Thank you," Thelma said. "I brought you something." She held up the big plastic bag. "Remember the quilts I mentioned that I'd received over the years?"

Lisbeth nodded.

"Well, I got to thinking about what you said, that quilts can be a source of comfort, something you said I seemed to be in need of. I realized that you are quite right. So I pulled out all the quilts and picked out my favorite one and laid it on my bed. The rest I packed up in here," she held up the bag. "I think it would be quite nice if you donated them somewhere to people who can use them. It would be selfish of me to keep them when there are people who need them more than me."

"Thank you, Aunt Thelma. I have an idea. Let's donate the quilts together. We can go right now."

"Oh, no, I wouldn't feel right doing that. You should go to the shelter. You should get the credit."

"Aunt Thelma, it's not about getting credit, it's about helping other people. Come," she gestured to Aunt Thelma to stand up. "Let's go."

Lisbeth tossed her towel over her chair and grabbed her keys and purse. Aunt Thelma followed Lisbeth out the door with the bag of quilts and down to her car. A short while later they arrived at a shelter with a sign that read "Genesis Women's Shelter and Support."

"Is this shelter only for women?" Thelma asked.

'It's for women and children who need a safe place to live."

"There are no men here?"

"No. These women and children are at great risk for domestic violence."

Thelma stared at the front door. "I had no idea such a place existed."

"Unfortunately, places like this exist all over."

"Thank goodness they do," Thelma said. "Let's go give these women and children some comfort," she said as she hoisted the bag of quilts out of the car. Lisbeth followed behind her, a grin plastered across her face because there was hope, even for a sour-puss aunt.

A few weeks later, Maggie flew into the Dallas Fort Worth airport, and Lisbeth picked her up at the curb. As soon as Lisbeth saw

Maggie emerge, she jumped out of the car and wrapped her arms around her. "I have missed you so much."

"Me, too," Maggie said, just as an airport security officer walked up to them.

"Move along ladies, or I'll have to write you a ticket."

Not waiting for him to make good on his threat, they jumped in the car and Lisbeth whisked Maggie back to Waxahachie to have lunch at the Dove's Nest. As they entered the old vintage building, they meandered through a store full of clothes, jewelry, kitchen knickknacks, home decor, and other items to entice patrons waiting to be seated at tables at the restaurant in the back.

When they began reading the menu, Maggie asked, "Have you been here before?"

Lisbeth shook her head. "Aunt Ruth has. Said it's one of the best-hidden gems in Waxahachie. She always orders the chicken apricot salad, so that's what I'm ordering."

"Think I'll try the smoked turkey and ham panini with bacon and Havarti cheese. That looks really good!"

"Save room for dessert. Aunt Ruth said that their desserts are fantastic."

"Lisbeth, have you ever in your entire life known me to pass up dessert?"

"No. Point taken."

When they finished lunch, including one slice of buttermilk pie and one slice of pecan pie, Lisbeth said, "Now I have a surprise for you."

"Okay, any hints?" Maggie looked at her cautiously.

Lisbeth shook her head. A few minutes later, Lisbeth pulled up in front of a very ornate 19th-century-style home. "Does it look familiar?" Lisbeth asked.

"Kinda, I suppose. It looks creepy actually. Like it's haunted. Is it?"

"I don't know, it might be."

"So, why are we here looking at a possibly haunted, creepy-looking house?" Maggie asked.

"Look real hard at it. Does it remind you of any house you've seen? Maybe one on TV?"

"The only creepy houses I've seen on TV are reruns of *The Addams Family, The Munsters,* and a few newer series like *The Haunting of Hill House* and *American Horror Story.*"

Lisbeth pressed harder. "Does this house look like any of the houses on those shows?"

"What are you getting at, Lis?"

"I just want you to figure out what it is."

Maggie got out of the car and stepped up to the tall iron gate, where she stared hard at the house. Lisbeth came up alongside her.

"Well?" Lisbeth asked.

"It's the Munster Mansion, isn't it?" Maggie said.

"Bingo! You got it!"

"Wasn't that hard," Maggie said pointing to a sign that said "The Munster Mansion."

Lisbeth nodded, smiling.

"Okay," Maggie said, "I gotta ask, what is the Munster Mansion doing in the middle of Texas?"

"Apparently, the owners got old footage from the show and used it to design and build every aspect of the house. They've also collected items from the show and placed them throughout the interior. Anything they couldn't buy, they had custom-made to look just like it did on the show."

Maggie stared in disbelief at the home. "Incredible! Is there any chance we can go inside?"

"Yep, I booked a tour for later today. I've been wanting to go and thought it would be something fun to do when you visited."

"I never expected this!" Maggie snickered with excitement. "This is going to be awesome!"

The next morning, they stopped into a nearby bakery, had coffee and croissants, and then headed for the Creative Quilters Guild of Ellis County Quilt Show.

As soon as they stepped into the hall, Maggie looked all around at the swath of colorful quilts adorning every vertical surface of the hall. "This is so cool, Lis."

"Isn't it?" Lisbeth agreed, feeling instantly at home. "I think I've found my peeps."

They walked up row after row, fingering fabrics and checking out new tools and quilting machines. They came to a booth that encouraged "test-driving" various models. Lisbeth looked over the machines, oohing and aahing over each one.

"Do you have a mid or longarm?" asked a friendly woman working in the booth.

Lisbeth shook her head. "I've always wanted one. Until recently I was working at a pretty intense job and didn't have much time to quilt."

"And you have more time now?" the woman pressed.

Lisbeth looked at Maggie, smiled conspiratorially, and looked back at the woman. "I sure do now."

"Then today is your lucky day. These are all shop models that we're selling at 30 percent off. None of them has over an hour of sewing time on them. It's like getting a new machine that's been broken in for you."

Lisbeth's eyes fluttered. In the past, she could never have afforded such a machine. It had always been a pipe dream, and now she realized she could do it; she could buy one. She could refine her quilting skills with more intricate stitch designs, as well as quilt larger tops, something she hadn't been able to do on her small domestic machine.

"Okay," Lisbeth responded. "Please show me all the models and explain their capabilities. I'm definitely interested." Over the next hour, Lisbeth test-drove every machine in the booth while Maggie stood nearby and watched. Finally, Lisbeth turned to the woman and pointed to a mid-arm, "This is the one. Definitely."

The woman wrote up the sale, Lisbeth handed her a credit card, and they made arrangements for the machine to be delivered and set up at her house.

Next, they continued meandering up and down the rows of booths. She stopped at the one for the guild sponsoring the quilt show. A bright-eyed woman with an infectious smile asked if she knew about the guild.

"No, I read about the show in the paper and thought I'd stop by. I'm new to the area."

"Then you've come to the right place. We're a real friendly bunch. Do you know how to make a quilt or are you looking to learn?"

Lisbeth grinned widely, as Maggie lightly jabbed her in the side. "I already know how to sew quilts. Mostly I hand-quilt, though I do quilt on my domestic machine, too. And I just bought a mid-arm from that booth over there," she said, turning to point at the booth along the back wall.

"Woo-hoo!" the guild woman said. "Congratulations! You said you're new to the area. Where'd you come from?"

"Southern California."

"We've got a few guild members from California. I'm Gloria Kucherovsky, the guild president," she said, reaching over, taking Lisbeth's hand, and shaking it. "What kind of quilts do you like to make?"

Maggie was itching to blurt out Lisbeth's talents but held her tongue when Lisbeth shot her a look that cautioned her not to.

Lisbeth pulled out her phone and began showing Gloria photos of her quilts, each one more exquisite than the last. A second woman entered the booth and leaned over to look at the photos.

"Hi, I'm Yolanda Marquez, the vice president," she said to Lisbeth. "What are we looking at here?"

"My quilts."

"This nice lady recently moved here from California," Gloria told Yolanda, who had taken Lisbeth's phone and was scrolling through all the photos.

Yolanda looked up at Lisbeth. "I recognize some of these quilts. Did you enter them in the Road to California Quilt Show?"

"Yes."

"And you won a boatload of ribbons, didn't you?" Yolanda asked.

Lisbeth smiled shyly and nodded.

Yolanda turned to her friend. "Gloria, remember when I was visiting my sister in California and I texted you from that show with photos of some of these very quilts and told you how extraordinary they were?"

"Yeah, now I remember. No wonder they looked familiar."

Both women looked straight at Lisbeth. "What's your name?" Yolanda asked.

Maggie couldn't contain herself any longer. Suddenly she blurted out, "She's Lisbeth James, an award-winning art quilter!"

"Well, I'll be!" Gloria exclaimed.

"Ditto," Yolanda said. "What are you doing here at our little quilt show?"

"Yolanda, I just told you that she recently moved here."

"That's right. Are you living here in Ennis?" Yolanda asked.

"In Waxahachie."

"You must come to our next meeting. Everyone will be beside themselves to meet you," Gloria said.

"I just had an idea," Yolanda stated. "Gloria, on my way in here I found out that next month's speaker had to cancel, and we have an opening." She turned to Lisbeth. "By any chance, are you free? Can you be our speaker?"

"Uh, sure," Lisbeth answered, figuring it would be a good way to make a lot of quilting friends real fast. "Just give me the date, time, location, and what you want me to talk about. Here's my number, please text it to me."

"You are a blessing, Lisbeth," Gloria declared. "I know I speak for the whole guild when I say what a pleasure it is to have you living here."

Yolanda spoke up. "I handle the programs. If you want to bring quilts to show, members can hold them up while you talk about them or, if you prefer, put together a PowerPoint presentation, and you can show them on our screen. Or do both! And one last thing, we'll want to hear all about you, how you got into quilting, and how you ended up in Texas. Here's my phone number. Call if you need anything or have a question about the area. I'm sure you must be lost being so far from home and family."

Lisbeth smiled. "Actually, I have a lot of family in Waxahachie. I don't have any family left in California."

Gloria reached out again and took both of Lisbeth's hands into her own. "Well, you've got a lot of quilting family here. I'm so glad you've chosen our area to call home."

As soon as Lisbeth and Maggie got into the car, Maggie turned to Lisbeth. "That was absolutely amazing!"

"You liked the quilts?"

"Yeah, of course. I'm referring to those women. You've found your tribe. Now I know that I don't need to worry about you."

"Maggie, you never did. I'm really okay here."

"I know that, but I still worry about you."

"Well, if you're so worried about me, you could move to Texas," Lisbeth suggested, knowing full well that Maggie couldn't survive without a nearby coast.

"I wish that you'd chosen to live in a town on the coast. Because if you had, I'd seriously consider relocating."

"Waterskiing on a lake won't do it for you?" Lisbeth joked.

"Hardly!"

"Well, you know ... you could move to a town on the coast and do all the surfing you wanted. While we wouldn't be living in the same area, we wouldn't be so far from one another the way we are now."

"I doubt there are any good surfing beaches here," Maggie dismissed the idea.

"Actually, there are. I looked into it before you got here. There's a bunch. South Padre Island, Matagorda, Corpus Christi, and Port Aransas are some of the best."

"Hmm. Maybe next time I visit we can go see some of them," Maggie mused.

"Seriously, you'd consider moving here if you found a place you liked to surf?"

"Maybe. I'm just saying it's worth looking into."

Lisbeth squealed with joy. "Okay, when we get back to the house, let's plan out your next trip!"

The following week, a delivery truck arrived with Lisbeth's mid-arm sewing machine and frame. Two women carried the machine and a box of frame parts into the house. "Where do you want us to set this up, ma'am?" a young woman sporting a ponytail asked.

"Follow me," Lisbeth waved them up the stairs to her large sewing room. She pointed to the empty half of the room.

In under an hour, the women set up the machine and frame. Afterward, they familiarized Lisbeth with the basics of operating her new machine, then handed her a booklet to learn more.

"Your purchase includes two private lessons on your machine. All you gotta do is call the shop to set them up."

"Thank you, I'll probably be okay on my own."

The women glanced at each other and looked back at Lisbeth. "If I had $100 for every customer who said that I'd be stinkin' rich," Ponytail said.

"Is it that difficult?" Lisbeth asked, now a bit concerned.

The second woman, who was older, with a mop top of curly salt-and-pepper hair piped up. "It's not particularly hard. It's just that mid- and longarm machines are a bit different from a domestic sewing machine. You have to practice a lot before you start using it to quilt anything important."

Lisbeth nodded. "Gotcha. I'll call the shop later today and set up my sessions."

She escorted the women out and waved goodbye. She walked back upstairs and into the quilting room; she stood looking at her new machine for several minutes. The women had shown her the basics and left the sample fabric in the machine. She sat down on a stool, turned on the machine, and started to practice, figuring she'd give it fifteen minutes or so. "Or so" turned into three hours. She changed fabric and thread several times to get used to the machine's mechanics. Even though she already felt fairly comfortable with the machine, she called the shop and set up her two free sessions, figuring she had already paid for them with her purchase, so why not take advantage of them?

Chapter Nine

As Lisbeth settled into her new life, she began researching people who specialize in finding long-lost relatives. She started with Howard Sheridan who gave her several names. She also phoned Maggie, who had proven her super-sleuth skills countless times. When she explained what she needed, Maggie interrupted.

"No worries, girlfriend. I'm on it!"

Over the next few weeks, Lisbeth called and interviewed countless people on both Maggie and Howard Sheridan's lists. She asked for their track records and documentation of their successful efforts, as well as those they couldn't find and why. She sat back in her chair, threw her head back, and ran her hands through her hair. The task wasn't just daunting and overwhelming; it was beginning to feel impossible. How was she going to determine who would be the best person for the job? Should she fly all over the country and interview these people in person? Was she on a wild goose chase that would never result in finding her birth mother? Just then her phone rang.

"Hello?"

"Hey, California girl, whatcha doin'?" Travis asked cheerfully.

"Oh, hi, Travis. You don't want to know. Just driving myself a little crazy."

"You wanna talk about it?"

"Not really," she sighed. "I think I need to take a break and come back to it with a fresh perspective."

"Well, I'm just the man to help you do it. Put on some jeans you don't mind getting a little messy, a T-shirt, and a pair of cowboy boots. I'll pick you up in a half-hour."

"Whoa, whoa, hold it. First, I don't have any cowboy boots, and second, where are we going?"

Silence filled the air. "Travis?"

"Yeah, I'm here. You really don't have any cowboy boots?"

"Nope. Why would I? I used to live near a beach."

"Okay, then, we'll stop and pick up a pair on the way. If you're going to live in Texas, cowboy boots are an essential item."

Lisbeth laughed. "How come? Are we going two-stepping or something?"

"That's not a bad idea," Travis mused, "but not this time. I've got something better in mind."

"Stop being so secretive. Where are we going? It's not another barbecue restaurant, is it?"

"No," he smiled into the phone. "See you in a half-hour," and he hung up.

Lisbeth was changed and ready when he pulled up in front of the house. She scurried out before he had a chance to ring the doorbell. "Hey, I found some boots. No need to go buy any," she pointed to her feet.

Travis looked down at the sophisticated, spike-heeled suede boots and let out a deep belly laugh. "Sorry, those won't do. You need real boots."

"These are real boots. I paid a little fortune for them," Lisbeth pouted.

"And they're real pretty, but they won't work for what we're going to do. Come on, let's go shopping."

Lisbeth moaned, shaking her head.

A few minutes later, they pulled up in front of a Western store and walked inside. "Hey, Travis, how's it goin'?" a man about his age asked.

"Good, good," he answered. "My friend needs a pair of boots."

"Sure 'nuff." He reached over and shook Lisbeth's hand. "My name is Carson, and you are?"

"Lisbeth."

"Nice to meet you, Lisbeth. What style are you interested in?"

Lisbeth's eyes widened. "Um, not sure. Didn't know there's more than one style."

Carson grinned and pushed back his cowboy hat. "You're not from around here, are you? No, don't answer that. It's fine. We get outta-staters all the time. Follow me."

Lisbeth looked at Travis and hunched her shoulders as she followed Carson. Travis grinned and placed a hand on her back, guiding her along.

After what seemed like hours but was only 60 minutes, Lisbeth had tried on 25 pairs of boots in every color from hot pink to baby blue to purple—some with bling, others intricately embroidered. Travis kept steering her toward more basic colors with a functional design. "Remember, you won't be using the boots for honky-tonkin'; they should be practical."

"Maybe if you told me what we're going to be doing, I could make a better decision."

Travis shook his head and grinned at Carson. "No can do." He pointed to a pair of dark brown boots with a rounded toe and low heel made by a Texas manufacturer. Carson helped Lisbeth put them on.

"Are they comfortable?" Travis asked.

"Yeah, they feel like slippers, but they aren't very cute," she said.

"Trust me, cute isn't what you need today," he winked at Carson. "You need basic sturdy boots. Keep 'em on, then you don't have to change later."

"Okay, but I sure wish you'd tell me where we're going," she said.

"You'll know soon enough," he said, handing Carson his credit card.

"You don't have to do that," she grabbed the card from Carson and handed it back to Travis. Travis handed it back to Carson who darted over to the cash register.

"It's my treat," Travis said.

Lisbeth grimaced, pursing her lips and wrinkling her nose.

"Look, you wouldn't normally be buying boots like these," Travis stressed. "And since I'm asking you to wear some sturdy boots, it's only right that I pay for them."

"Well, you've got a point. They are nice and comfortable, so I may get more use out of them than just today. I could use them for gardening."

Travis grinned. "Gardening? Well, if you say so. And when you're ready, you can come back here and buy yourself a pair of those girly boots with all the rhinestones," he smirked, trying to hide his amusement.

"I will!" Lisbeth smirked back. "They were cute, weren't they? Hey, I just thought, we could go dancing sometime, and I could wear the rhinestone boots. What do you call it? Honky-tonkin?"

Travis nodded, suppressing a smile.

After leaving town they hit a backcountry road that meandered for miles alongside vibrant fields of corn, sorghum, and cotton, and pastures dotted with cattle, horses, goats, and sheep. They passed farmhouses that looked like they'd been standing since the 19th century, fat and round white grain silos, and charming red barns dotted with what she recognized as barn quilts, painted to depict classic quilting blocks. They turned down a drive and passed under a black iron arch with a sign that read "Outlaw Creek Ranch." Several stock tanks of water flanked the side of the road. A few cattle stood in the water, while others lounged under large oak trees shading them from the afternoon sun. In the next field, horses of every color meandered alongside weathered wooden fences, neighing as Travis drove by. The drive rose up and around a small hill and ended at a large, two-story house built of limestone and wood, an expansive porch gracing the front. It faced a barn nearly as large as the house; several riding rings and acres of lush grasslands and pastures stretched to infinity.

"I take it this is the ranch," Lisbeth said, scanning the view. "Why is it called Outlaw Creek Ranch?"

Travis pointed out toward a hill. "There's a creek way past that stand of trees. Legend has it that many of the West's most notorious outlaws used to hide out there," Travis answered. "I'll show it to you. It's one of the most peaceful places on the ranch. In fact, it's where I go when I need to clear my mind. Hopefully, it will take your mind off what's bothering you." He planted his Stetson hat on his head, walked around the truck, opened the passenger door, and helped her out of the truck. "Do you know how to ride a horse?"

"A horse? Yeah, though it's been a while. I used to ride when I was a teen. In fact, I had a Morgan horse named Choppo. He was a sweet boy."

"A Morgan?" Travis widened his eyes. "That's a fine horse."

"Actually, I used to ride English, though I occasionally rode Western, too."

"We saddle up Western here. You up for a ride?"

Lisbeth beamed, her eyes fluttering. "I'd love to. I can't remember the last time I rode."

Travis pulled out his cell phone and called someone named Tyler. "Hey, I've got a friend up here with me. Could you saddle Doc Holliday and one for the lady? She hasn't ridden in a while, so don't give her Butch Cassidy. Maybe Annie Oakley, she'd be good. Great. We'll be down in ten. Thanks."

Lisbeth grinned all the way down to the barn. "Travis, this is the best surprise ever!" He reached over, put his arm around her shoulders, and gave her a squeeze.

They arrived at the barn to see a lanky ranch hand leading two horses out of the barn, a soaring chestnut horse whose coat glistened in the sun, and a medium-sized palomino that radiated kindness. They were saddled up and ready to go.

"Oh my!" Lisbeth exclaimed, covering her mouth with her fingers.

Travis looked over at her.

"They're beautiful, just beautiful." Lisbeth walked up to the palomino and stroked her neck. "This is Annie Oakley, right?" she looked over at Travis.

Travis nodded. The horse reached around and nosed Lisbeth, blinking her long lashes and staring at her with deep truffle brown eyes. Travis walked over, placed his hands on Lisbeth's waist, and lifted her up onto Annie. He stepped over to Doc Holliday, swung up, and hoisted himself onto the saddle.

"Ready?" he asked.

Lisbeth nodded. They headed out, side by side, toward the stand of trees, a light breeze at their backs. The sun shone down on Lisbeth's hair, making her red locks shimmer like embers. When they reached the pasture, Lisbeth caught Travis's attention.

"How's Annie at galloping? I'd love to see what she's got."

"You sure? You said you haven't ridden in a long time."

Lisbeth nodded. "We'll see, won't we?" Lisbeth laughed and gave Annie a gentle nudge. She bent down and whispered, "Let's go, girl, show me what you can do."

She had barely finished speaking when Annie took off at a sprint faster than Lisbeth had anticipated. "Woo-hoo!" she yelled, her hair flying behind her, looking like her back was on fire.

Travis gave the chestnut a slight nudge and took off after her. When he caught up, Doc Holliday charged past Lisbeth and Annie, taking the lead.

"Come on, Annie," Lisbeth bent low on her horse's neck and whispered, "you're not gonna let them beat us, are you?"

Lightning quick, the horse charged ahead, soaring past Travis and Doc.

"You wanna race, huh?" Travis called to Lisbeth. "You're on!"

He gave Doc a slight nudge, which was all the majestic horse needed; he bolted to catch up with Lisbeth and Annie. The pair raced through the pasture, laughing as they went, looking over at one another and grinning. As they neared the stand of trees, the horses deliberately slowed to a walk. Travis looked over at her, observing the fiery spirit that he saw smoldering in her eyes.

"You okay?" he asked her.

"Oh my gosh, more than okay! That was incredible."

"Not bad for someone who hasn't ridden in years," he grinned, his dimples stealing the show on his rugged face.

"I guess it's kind of like riding a bicycle, something you don't forget," she beamed back at him.

Travis guided them over the undulating terrain, chiseled by long-ago dried-up creeks, through the stand of trees and out the other side, meandering through hip-high yellowed grass until they came upon a tranquil creek. Across the water, an escarpment of rock and sandstone rose against a lapis blue sky. He stopped his horse by a sycamore tree with a massive trunk, slid off, and stepped behind the tree. Lisbeth dismounted from Annie just as Travis brought around a picnic basket. She raised her brows.

"Where'd that come from?"

"This?" He held up the basket, pushing his hat back on his head and grinning. "These things grow on the sycamores."

"Yeah, right, cowboy. Seriously, what's it doing out here?"

Travis hunched his shoulders as though he didn't know, a good-natured smile etched on his face. He led the horses to the creek, came back, and opened the basket. He took out a blue checkered picnic cloth, laid it on the ground, and patted the cloth. When he took off his hat; his dark hair rippled in the light breeze while his striking silver-gray eyes flashed at her. Lisbeth got the hint and sat down as Travis took out wine glasses, a bottle of wine, and an opener. She smiled as he opened a bottle of white wine, poured two glasses, and handed one to Lisbeth.

She held up her glass, "To a great day full of surprises."

"I'll second that. Had no idea you could ride like that," Travis remarked.

Lisbeth took the bottle and looked at the label. "Hmm, a 2017. Carter Creek Winery Plateau White. I've never heard of this winery."

"It's down in Hill Country. This particular wine won best in class at this year's Texas International Wine Competition. Thought you might like it since you're from California."

Lisbeth glanced at him. "What's California got to do with it?"

Travis ran a hand through his nearly shoulder-length hair. "Livin' out there, I'm pretty sure you've had more than your fair share of great wine."

Lisbeth beamed and took a sip. "This one is really good. Honestly, I didn't think that anyone here was making this caliber of wine. I'm kinda astonished."

Travis bowed his head and sipped his wine. "As you said, it's been a day full of surprises." He reached back into the basket and pulled out a couple of plates, several cheeses, sausages, crackers, pastries, and cloth napkins. "Hungry?"

"Starved!" she replied and began filling her plate.

When they finished eating, Travis handed Lisbeth one of the pastries. "These pastries are as Texan as bluebonnets."

"They look like a Danish. What makes them so special?"

"Take a bite and you'll see."

She no sooner bit into it than her face lit up like a child's on Christmas morning when she discovered that what lay in a package was just what she wanted. "What are these things? They're wonderful and quite different from a Danish," she said while chewing.

"Kolaches," Travis answered, devouring his and reaching for a second. "They're made by descendants of Czech immigrants who settled in Texas in the mid-19th century. You can buy them all over, but the best ones come from towns with a significant population of Czech immigrant descendants. These came from West."

"Out in West Texas?"

"Naw, it's a small town north of Waco that has several bakeries and a Czech restaurant. Hey, look!" he pointed to the other side of the creek; a female spotted deer and her fawn were grazing on young shoots of green grass. They flicked their ears and looked over at Travis and Lisbeth. The deer watched them for several moments, then bolted up the escarpment; above them, a hint of sapphire blue pushed through the pastel midafternoon sky, heralding the evening to come.

"I've never seen deer that close before, or with a spotted coat like that. They're simply beautiful."

"Yep, that they are," Travis winked at Lisbeth. "And good eatin', too."

"Seriously? Who would eat a stunning animal like that?"

"Me for one. A lot of people do. They're axis deer and not regulated like whitetail deer."

"Why not? I'd think that the authorities would want to protect an animal that beautiful."

"Pretty as they are, unfortunately, they aren't native to Texas and they're an invasive species."

"Why does that matter?"

"Axis deer occupy the same grazing areas as whitetail deer and compete with them for available resources. Whitetail deer are native to Texas, and hunting them is regulated so that overhunting doesn't wipe out their herds. Nonnatives, like axis deer, are fair game any time of year.

"Do you hunt?"

He chuckled. "Am I a Texan?"

"I guess that means yes."

Lisbeth laid back on the picnic cloth and gazed skyward, watching the clouds quickly moving across the expansive sky. A pair of hawks with four-foot wingspans soared above them, circling and gliding on the air currents.

"What are those hawks doing?" Lisbeth asked. "They seem to be watching us."

"It's not us they're watching. They're looking for prey."

"What kind of prey?" she asked, mesmerized, watching the raptors dive and arc across the landscape.

"Rodents, snakes, small mammals, like squirrels. They do a good job of keeping the snake and rodent population at bay."

"I could take a place like this for granted anytime. It's easy to quiet the mind here," Lisbeth murmured, sitting up.

A tranquil silence unfolded between them. They sat quietly for several minutes, listening; breathing in the musky, heady scents of the countryside; and watching the wildlife until Travis broke the stillness.

"I suppose that's why I'm drawn to this place. It soothes my soul and gives me what I need to live my life," Travis responded.

"If you don't mind my asking, what exactly is that? What is it that you need that this place gives you?"

He looked over at her. "Peace of mind and the ability to live a good and honest life, for me to decide how I will live my life. You know that I'm a lawyer and a rancher. I've never told you that I used to be in law enforcement. It took me several career changes to discover what suits me best. Even though I occasionally work a case at the law firm, it doesn't give me near the satisfaction of taking care of this beautiful piece of land and the animals here."

"Have you ever considered giving up on law entirely and just running your ranch?"

"I have. But I think it's important to help out my dad at the firm. He came to my aid when I was dealing with a tragedy and didn't know which way to turn. It was the first time in my life where I was lost, paralyzed actually. He stepped up and offered me a way through the darkness. I will forever be grateful to him for that. So, no, I won't give up law entirely. It's the only way I can truly repay him for pulling me out of the gutter."

"Do you want to talk about it? The tragedy?" she asked.

"Today? Not really. I'll tell you about it some other time. Today I'd like to just ride my horse and try to outrace a pretty woman who is a much better rider than I thought ..."

"Oh, yeah?" she teased. "Well, I may have been a little rusty riding out here. Watch out, I might just win the race back to your corral."

Travis looked up. "Then we should get started. The clouds are moving fast. We better ride back."

"You think it's going to rain?"

"I don't think it, I know it. We need to get going, the storm is close." He pointed toward the dark clouds bearing down on them. Thunder rolled; its harsh flanks tempered by the distance.

They packed up the basket and scampered down to the water's edge to retrieve the horses. A strong wind hurried across the creek, churning the formerly passive water into sharp whitecaps. Lisbeth pulled herself up onto Annie while Travis left the picnic basket behind the sycamore tree.

"Shouldn't we take the basket back with us?" Lisbeth asked.

"Nah, one of the ranch hands will retrieve it. Let's ride," he said as he mounted Doc and looked at the clouds. "It looks like the sky is gonna crack open any minute." He clucked at his horse who took off, Lisbeth right behind them.

Just as they entered the group of trees they'd ridden through on their way in, strobes of light ruptured the clouds like fireworks, followed by deafening thunder. The skies opened up with torrential rain, pouring with biblical force and pounding the dry earth with the strength of an angry spirit seeking retribution. The old trees creaked, sounding like screams. The deluge soaked Lisbeth and Travis in moments. Lisbeth broke out in choking laughter that made her hiccup. Travis looked over at her, water cascading off the brim of his hat.

"What's so funny?"

"Isn't this wonderful?" she laughed. "I love rain. Whenever a downpour began back home, I'd run outside and stomp through puddles, holding my face up to the sky. There's something magical about rain, don't you think? Somehow it has an uncanny ability to wash away troubles." She grinned with exhilaration, her eyes dancing.

"You spinnin' a yarn?" Travis asked.

Lisbeth shook her head, rain flinging off the ends of her hair. "I kid you not. I love rain."

It poured down hard for fifteen minutes, finally tapering off to a slow, steady shower, dropping like thin, cotton threads. When they emerged from the stand of trees, he turned to Lisbeth.

"I take it that the rain took your mind off whatever was bothering you earlier today. You looked pretty distressed."

"It wasn't just the rain that helped, it was this whole day, Travis. The ride. The surprise picnic. And yes, I was pretty stressed out, but I'm okay now."

"So, what was bothering you?"

Lisbeth explained her quest to find her birth mother and how both Travis's father and Maggie found scores of investigators.

"What I thought would be a simple task feels overwhelming."

"Why?"

"Because I don't know if a phone interview would suffice or if I should fly all over the country interviewing the best ones in person."

"You should've asked me for a recommendation. I know a good one with an exceptional track record."

"Really, who is he?"

"She, actually. And she's local, in Fort Worth. I think you'd like her."

"Oh, Travis, thank you. A local person would be a huge relief."

The rain came to an abrupt halt. Though the earth was muddy, they gingerly picked up their pace and rode leisurely back to the ranch as dusk fell, wet but content. After giving the horses to Tyler, they traipsed up to the house and, as Travis instructed, left their boots outside the front door. Travis showed her the guest room with its own bathroom. He took a large fluffy green towel out of a cabinet and handed it to Lisbeth.

"You might want to wash some of that mud off of you. Lay your clothes on the bedroom chair, and I'll put them in the dryer. And I'll get your old boots out of the truck to wear home. When you're finished showering, there's a white robe hanging on the bathroom wall."

"Oh, Travis, that is sweet of you, but honestly, you don't have to go to all that trouble."

"Sure, I do. I wouldn't take you home lookin' like a drowned rat."

When Lisbeth emerged from a long, hot shower she wrapped herself in the robe, walked into the guest room, and found her purse and dry clothing lying on the bed; her high-heeled boots on the floor. A note next to her clothes told her to meet Travis on the back patio. She dressed and meandered through the house until she found the French doors to the outside. She found Travis in clean clothes, his hair still wet. He was sitting next to a stone ring, a small fire blazing, blue and orange flames dancing to a fire song. She sat in the chair next to him; he handed her a mug of something hot, and she took a whiff.

"How did you know that hot cocoa is one of my favorite things in the world? "A smile spread across her face that made her eyes do a little jig.

"You had a hot cocoa air about you."

"I don't know what a hot cocoa air is," she said. "For future reference, I'll never turn down a mug of hot cocoa, anytime or anywhere." She took a sip. "By the way, what's in this cocoa? It's really different."

"There might be a little whiskey in there."

"Hello!" she said in between sips of her drink. "Cocoa with whiskey ... hmm, this might very well suit my new identity."

Travis looked over at her, a question mark on his face. "And what new identity would that be?

"My birth name is Savannah Mae McDonald. I didn't know that until your dad showed me my birth certificate."

Travis cocked his head sideways, sizing her up. "I can see you as Savannah Mae."

"I like it. Even though I have always been Lisbeth James, I've never felt like my name is a good fit. Then the second your dad showed me my birth name, the strangest thing happened. This is going to sound off the wall, but it was as though the stars aligned in some strange way. It just felt right."

"Are you thinking about going back to your birth name?"

"Thinking? Yes. Am I ready to take a big step like that? No. At least not yet."

Travis reached over and gently placed her hand in his. As tendrils of steam rose off their mugs, curling into the fading light, they watched the sun slowly make its way toward the horizon, casting orange, lilac, and crimson scattered fragments of light on the clouds. Night consumed the day, the stillness of the twinkling night crept over them, bathing them in tranquility as the stars came to life, poking through the night sky, illuminating the darkness.

Lisbeth looked over at Travis. "Is it always like this here?"

"Like what?"

"This still, this calm, this beautiful?"

He nodded. "Every day."

They sat watching the sky and listening to the quiet for several minutes. A tiny dust devil, stirred up by a warm breeze, spun around them. She watched the spinning leaves as though they were alive. Travis broke her reverie.

"Hungry?" Travis asked.

"You cookin'?" Lisbeth's eyes widened.

"Not unless you want to eat around midnight. We can stop at Campuzano's in Waxahachie on the way to take you home. Have you eaten there yet?"

Lisbeth shook her head.

"Best fajitas and margaritas in the area."

Lisbeth stood up. "Let's go, cowboy. I could put down a whole platter of fajitas by myself."

As she predicted, Lisbeth ate nearly the whole platter of fajitas. When Travis realized they should've ordered two platters, he started to laugh and put his fist in front of his mouth.

Lisbeth looked up at him. "What's so funny?"

"You."

"Me? Why?"

"You constantly surprise me."

"How?"

"I have never seen a woman as lean as you put down as much food as you do. I'm not criticizing. It's refreshing actually, to be able to eat with you 'cause you don't worry about every calorie on your plate."

"Well, I do watch what I eat."

"No, you don't. Like I said, it's refreshing."

They left the restaurant and walked toward Travis's truck in the parking lot. They both came to an abrupt halt.

"Oh my God," Lisbeth remarked, looking over the truck.

"That's an understatement!" Travis said angrily. He walked around the truck and examined the deep scratch marks someone had carved into his truck. He discovered a few choice words that he assumed the perpetrator wrote referring to him and Lisbeth.

"Who would do this?" Lisbeth asked. "Do you have any enemies?"

"Not that I know of," he answered, his eyes skimming the truck. Then he noticed that the hood was slightly ajar. He walked over to it, raised it all the way, and using the flashlight on his phone, he examined the engine. Though not a mechanic, he knew enough about his truck to notice the fuel lines leaking gasoline.

"Shit!" he bellowed.

"What's wrong?" Lisbeth walked up to the front of the truck.

"Not only did some jerk destroy the paint job, the miscreant really messed with the engine." He pointed to the fuel lines. "See this?"

Lisbeth looked where he was pointing.

"These fuel lines are old and rotting. I had new fuel lines installed recently. Somebody removed the new ones and replaced them with these old lines."

"Why would someone do that?"

"Good question!" Travis walked around the truck and looked underneath, where he discovered a pool of liquid. He reached under the truck and touched the liquid, brought it up to his nose, and took a whiff.

"What is it?" Lisbeth asked.

"It's fuel, probably caused by those old rotting fuel lines."

"How dangerous is it?"

He turned toward her. "Very."

Lisbeth's face went white as memories of the accident that killed Scott came to mind. Travis saw her pale. "Don't worry, nothing's going to happen as long as I don't turn on the engine."

Lisbeth felt her heart beating faster and faster. She didn't know what to say, what she could say.

Travis dialed someone on his phone. "Hey, Luke, this is Travis. I hate to bother you this late, but could you have someone tow my truck over to your shop? Some idiot did a real number on it. Scratched it all over and tampered with the fuel lines. Yeah, the jerk replaced the new lines you put in last month with some old rotting ones that are leaking fuel. I don't want to take a chance driving it. Hey, do you have a vehicle I could borrow to take my friend home and get back to my house? That'd be great. Thanks."

Travis turned around and saw how upset Lisbeth had become. "Hey, it's okay," he said, putting his hands on her shoulders. "It's all fixable."

"Good, that's good," she said nervously, trying not to think about Scott's accident. She looked up at him. "Who could've done this? Who would want to harm you or us?"

"Your guess is as good as mine. Don't worry about it. We're all right and Old Nellie here," he pointed to the truck, "will be fine."

A short while later, a tow truck arrived along with Luke driving an SUV. Luke immediately surveyed the outside of the truck and then looked at the engine. "Damn!" he cursed. "Travis, you were absolutely right. If you'd started the engine, this whole thing would've exploded. I'm real glad you called me."

Travis arched his eyebrows. "Yeah, me, too."

Luke handed him the keys to the SUV. "Here, you take this car, and I'll go back to the shop with Chase," he pointed to the tow-truck driver.

"Thanks, buddy," Travis said. He turned to Lisbeth and guided her over to the big black Ford Expedition. He opened the passenger side door, and she jumped in. He got in the driver's side. "You okay?"

"Yeah, just a little unnerved. I don't think I'll ever forget this date."

Chapter Ten

The next day, Lisbeth packed up several quilts, both hand- and machine-quilted, and gathered her laptop with the slideshow she had made for her talk at the quilt guild meeting. The slides featured photos of every quilt she'd ever made, starting with the first one when she was a kid. She looked around the sewing room wondering what else she should take. Satisfied that she had everything she would need, she carried it all downstairs and packed the car. She drove over to the Waxahachie Bible Church, where the guild held their meetings. The parking lot was packed, but she found a space near the back. As she began unpacking the car, two petite women approached her.

"Hello," a gray-haired woman spoke first, her voice wispy and childlike. "Can we help you carry in your stuff? That looks like a lot to carry. By the way, I'm Merry Abernathy and this," she pointed to her friend with white hair streaked with highlights of purple and pink, "is Debra Garcia."

"Nice to meet you both," Lisbeth said. "And yes, I'd love some help."

"Are you a new member or thinking of joining? Usually, new people don't bring a bunch of stuff to their first meeting," Debra commented.

Lisbeth grinned. "I hope to become a member. Today though, I'm the speaker."

The two women's eyes went wide. They turned to look at each other and then back at Lisbeth. "You're Lisbeth James, our speaker?" Merry asked.

Lisbeth nodded, handing them several quilts encased in protective plastic coverings.

"Welcome," Merry said, grinning so wide her lips went all the way to the edges of her narrow face.

"We're so glad to have you," added Debra.

After meeting dozens of women in the hall, she set up her presentation and then sat down. When the guild finished the regular meeting agenda, Gloria, whom she'd met at the show, invited her up to the podium. Lisbeth stepped up to the microphone, launched her presentation, and spoke for three-quarters of an hour, stopping periodically to ask volunteers to hold up one of the many quilts she had brought with her. She no sooner finished than guild members began raising their hands.

"Do you quilt on a domestic machine or a longarm?" a woman in the front row asked.

"Until now, I've been either hand quilting or quilting on my domestic. I just recently bought a mid-arm and I'm still learning how to quilt on it," she said.

Gloria asked if any of the quilts that she had brought were quilted on her new machine. Lisbeth nodded and pointed to two of them.

"I'd say you got the hang of it," one woman shouted from the audience. "I've had a longarm for three years, and my quilting doesn't look half as good as yours."

When she finished the presentation, Yolanda helped her take her quilts and laptop to her car. "I hope you don't mind," she started to say, "I have some friends in other quilt guilds. When I told them how lucky we were to have you come speak to our group, they asked for your phone number. They want to have you come speak to their guilds, too. I hope it's okay that I gave them your number."

Lisbeth blinked and quickly nodded. "How many guilds are we talking about here?"

"Oh, not too many. A dozen or so."

Lisbeth gasped. "Wow!"

Catching her reaction, Yolanda's cheerful face fell. "I'm so sorry, I should've asked you first. Never mind, I'll call them back and say that I made a mistake."

"Don't even think about it, Yolanda. I'm just a little surprised, that's all. As long as I can spread out the talks, it'll be okay. I'll never get any quilting done if I'm driving around giving talks all the time."

"Okay, if you're sure," Yolanda said.

Lisbeth smiled and nodded. "I am."

"On the bright side," Yolanda continued, "you'll make a little money giving the talks. Which reminds me," she put her hand into her pocket. "Here's your fee for speaking tonight. And I hope that since you live so close, you'll consider joining our guild."

"I'd love to. And thank you for this," she held up the envelope with the check. "See you next month." She turned to get into her car. "Oh, one more thing, Yolanda. Please warn anyone else that you refer to me that I now have a waiting list for lecturing. You have just made me busier than I ever expected to be. Thank you. I mean it."

The recent storms had cleared the air of the oppressive summer humidity that had been hanging over the town like a damp veil. Lying in bed before getting up one morning, Lisbeth realized that several months had passed since she had moved to Texas. She had been so busy settling in that she was a little astounded that time had passed so quickly. She loved her life; every day she learned something about her new state and her new extended family. She saw them at least once a week. Between running over to Ruth's house and Jack's house and her family coming to Lisbeth's, she was pretty sure that she and her family had carved a rut in the road between their homes.

One day, Aunt Ruth took out a small wooden recipe box and handed it to Lisbeth. She explained that, in it, were all of Fannie's recipes handed down to her from her mother and her mother's mother.

"These recipes are part of your heritage, Lisbeth," Ruth said. "Your grandmother would want you to have them."

Lisbeth's eyes widened. "I couldn't, Aunt Ruth. You should have them, not me."

Ruth took her hand and looked deep into her eyes. "Dear Lisbeth, don't you think that I know these recipes by heart by now? Thelma knows them all, too."

"I see ... what about Annabelle, wouldn't she want them?"

Ruth chuckled. "She scanned them and downloaded them onto her laptop years ago. You're the only one who doesn't have our treasured family recipes. You definitely should have them." She reached over and gave Lisbeth's hand a squeeze.

A few days later Ruth and Annabelle showed her how to make the family recipes for chicken-fried steak, fried okra, cheesy grits, greens, and black-eyed peas. Annabelle demonstrated the finer points of making pecan pie. Ruth told her that there was a family secret to making the perfect crust.

"Mother taught us something that's been passed down by the women in our family for generations. The belief is that everyone is born with a special innate ability that gives them strength and stamina. Much like this pie dough, when handled properly, both the pie crust and the essence of a person's being becomes something wondrous."

Lisbeth studied her aunt's face. "And if the dough isn't handled properly?"

"If you don't handle the dough perfectly, just like not properly caring for yourself, the dough won't come together and become a fine crust, and a person's spirit will get sick."

"Did Grandma make a good pie crust?" Lisbeth asked.

"Yes," Ruth answered sadly. "That is, up until your mother left and never returned. After that, your grandmother couldn't make a decent pie crust to save her life. We think it was because her spirit was sick."

Annabelle saw the look of sadness on Lisbeth's face. "You master these recipes, cousin," Annabelle interjected cheerfully, steering the conversation in a different direction, "and you'll be able to call yourself a real Texan."

"Deal!" Lisbeth responded. "I'm gonna go home and start practicing right away."

"Thatta girl!" Aunt Ruth said. "Technically, you are a real Texan already, since you were born here. We're just going to help you become an even better one."

"Thank you both," she said as she turned to leave. "Oh, I forgot something."

The two women looked at her.

"Do you have a family tree that I could have, showing everyone from as far back as possible up to the present?"

Annabelle said, "Sure do. I scanned one that I found a few years ago and updated it. I'll email it to you."

When Lisbeth got home and fired up her laptop, she found Annabelle's email with the attachment. She opened it and, scrolling down, found her own name, Savannah Mae, with her birthdate at the bottom under Emma's and Jack's. She saved the family tree on a thumb drive, slipped it into her purse, and headed out to a local copy and print shop. She asked the shop owner if he could print it onto a sturdy piece of muslin measuring approximately four feet long and three feet wide.

"Sure, you bring me the muslin, and I can print it." He looked down at the thumb drive. "What's on here anyway?"

Lisbeth answered proudly. "My family tree."

"And why do you want it printed on muslin? You gonna hang it up or somethin'?"

She nodded. "Yes, but first I'm going to embroider the tree, its branches, and all the names by hand and then appliqué a border around it."

"I don't think I've ever seen anything like that," the elderly store owner scratched his head. "I would love to see it when you finish, young lady. Will you bring it by?"

"Of course!"

"If you bring me the muslin today, come back tomorrow afternoon, and I should have it done by then."

The next day, after picking up the muslin printed with the family tree, Lisbeth called the woman in Fort Worth whom Travis had recommended. Not only had she been a police detective who had helped find numerous people, but she also sounded like the kind of person Lisbeth could trust to do the job right. There was something in her tone that told Lisbeth this was a person who could do the job. A week later, Lisbeth met with the private investigator in her office near the historic Fort Worth Stockyards and told her everything she knew and all that she had gleaned from Howard Sheridan and Aunt Ruth. The investigator told her that she would try, but to be patient, and that it would take some time. She warned Lisbeth not to get anxious if she didn't hear back from her right away.

When Lisbeth returned home, she called Travis and asked if he could drop by for dinner the next evening. "I have a little surprise."

"Uh, okay, any hints?"

"Nope," she said emphatically. "Drop by around six-ish?"

"Sure, and just so you know, it's not called dinner," he said.

"Huh? What do you mean it's not called dinner?"

"We call it supper," Travis stated.

"Supper, dinner … what's the diff?"

"Well, here in Texas we don't call the evening meal dinner, we call it supper."

"You gotta be kidding."

"Nope."

"Well, if the evening meal is supper, what meal is called dinner? Lunch?"

"No, lunch is called lunch and breakfast is breakfast. We don't call anything dinner."

"Well, whaddaya know. Never heard of that. See you later for s-u-p-p-e-r," she said slowly drawing out the word.

Lisbeth spent the afternoon baking the pie that Annabelle had taught her and prepping all the dishes she was going to cook the next day. She was so happy baking and prepping that she didn't notice a burning smell. When she did, she looked all around the kitchen but didn't see any smoke. She looked out the kitchen window and saw smoke wafting across the backyard. She ran out the kitchen door and saw smoke billowing from the garden shed at the back of the property. She pulled her phone out of her pocket and dialed 911 to report the fire. The fire department arrived quickly and came in through the garden gate pulling their long hoses to the back of the garden. They put out the fire in short order. The captain approached her as they were wrapping up.

"You're the homeowner?" he asked.

"Yes."

"Any idea what started the fire?"

"None at all. I rarely go into the shed. And honestly, I can't think what's in there that could combust."

"Do you keep fertilizer in there?"

"Yes, but only the garden variety that's already mixed into bags of soil."

"That shouldn't have caused it. Fortunately, we caught the blaze in plenty of time so that it didn't spread. I think you're going to need to build a new shed though. It's in pretty bad shape." He rubbed his chin as though he were thinking. "Normally we wouldn't bother to send out an investigator, but given the questionable circumstances, I think we will."

"What questionable circumstances?"

"There's no reason why your shed should have combusted like that. Plus, one of my men thought he smelled barbecue lighter fluid. Do you have a grill?"

Lisbeth shook her head.

"So, no reason to have lighter fluid in the shed?"

"None whatsoever."

"Then we'll definitely send out an investigator."

"Well, okay, if you think it's necessary."

"It is in cases where the source of the fire is uncertain. One of the inspectors will stop by tomorrow."

"Okay, thank you for getting here so quickly and putting it out."

He nodded and left.

The next day when Travis arrived and stepped through the front door, he stopped and took a whiff of the aromas coming out of the kitchen. "Do I smell chicken-fried steak?"

Lisbeth smiled and led him to the dining room, where she'd set the table with Fannie's china, cloth napkins, and platters of food covered in plastic wrap. He removed his hat and laid it on a chair. Lisbeth walked back into the kitchen, took two bottles of Shiner Bock out of the fridge, opened them, and handed one to Travis.

"I had planned to have a little picnic in the backyard, but a weird fire broke out in the shed yesterday, and it still reeks of smoke out there, so I thought we'd eat in here."

"What do you mean by a 'weird' fire?" he asked, his brow creased.

"Well, it happened quite suddenly. One minute I was baking the pecan pie, and the next I smelled smoke. I saw it coming from the shed, so I called 911. By the time the fire department got here, it was engulfed in flames. They sent out a fire inspector today who determined that it was started by lighter fluid. But it gets weirder still. I don't own a grill, and there was no lighter fluid in the shed. At least I didn't think there was. There was no reason for lighter fluid to be in there. The inspector found traces of it inside and around the outside."

"Did the inspector give you a summary of what he found?"

"Yeah, it's over here." She stepped over to a kitchen desk, picked up the summary, and handed it to Travis. He quickly read it over.

"Lisbeth, it says the fire was deliberately set."

"I have no idea how that was possible. I was in the house, and the garden gate was locked. No one could've gotten back there. Besides, why would someone want to burn down my shed?"

"To scare you."

"Travis, that's crazy. I don't know enough people in Waxahachie to have accumulated any enemies. Why would anyone want to scare me?" she shrugged it off.

"I don't have any enemies either, but that didn't stop somebody from trying to destroy my truck and kill us both."

She stood and blinked, giving it some thought. "You do have a point. It is a little scary, the uncertainty of it. I really don't want to think about any of this right now. Let's just have a nice time, shall we?"

As he took a swig of his beer, she uncovered the platters. His eyes bulged.

"Where'd you get the chicken-fried steak?"

Lisbeth planted her hands on her hips and gave him a stern look. "I didn't get it anywhere. I made it. In fact, I made everything on the table."

"I wasn't under the impression that you knew how to cook."

"Oh, that's ridiculous! Of course, I know how to cook! I just didn't know how to cook things like this," she pointed to the table. "Now that I have my granny's recipes and Aunt Ruth and Annabelle showed me how to make them, I'm becoming quite the Texas cook. You're my first guest, and you can tell me if I hit the mark or missed it."

"Are you saying that I'm your guinea pig?" Travis asked, trying not to laugh.

"You are so bad!" Lisbeth narrowed her eyes and smirked at him, as she gently shoved him into a chair. She placed a large piece of chicken-fried steak on a plate and asked him if he wanted black-eyed peas.

"Yes, ma'am."

"Collard greens with bacon?"

"Yes, ma'am!"

"I assume you want grits, too?"

He nodded, his eyes growing wider and wider at the food Lisbeth heaped on his plate. They dug in as soon as she dished up her own. When they'd finished eating, Lisbeth took the plates into the kitchen and told Travis to stay put. She brought out a pecan pie, a pie cutter, fresh plates, and forks.

"Don't tell me you made the pie, too?"

"Yep, from the pecans off the trees in the yard,"

He stared, watching her carefully cut into the pie with a knife, neatly cutting a slice and laying it on a plate in front of him. He lifted the plate up to his face, closed his eyes, and inhaled the confection's sweet aroma. He set it down and took a forkful, bringing it up to his lips. He closed his eyes as the bite slid across his tongue, nearly melting in his mouth. The filling slipped down his throat, followed by the delicate buttery crust. Lisbeth watched him, intrigued. He opened his eyes and rolled them upward.

"Does that mean you like it?"

"I think so, let me take another bite to be sure." He took a second bite and a third and a fourth and finished it with a fifth bite. He leaned back and patted his stomach. "Lisbeth, that is one of the finest pecan pies I've ever eaten. Seriously. That's your grandmother's recipe?"

Lisbeth grinned. "Yeah, but I tinkered with it a little. I added a little bourbon and a few chocolate chips."

"You know that's considered a desecration here in Texas, right? You don't mess with classic pecan pie. Tell ya what, give me a slice to take with me and I won't give away your secret."

Lisbeth beamed. "Actually, I baked a second pie for you to take home. It's in the kitchen. You didn't say anything about the rest of the meal. Was it okay?"

"Okay? It was more than okay. It was outstanding, I mean it. In fact, you should think about giving up all that quilting you do and instead open a cafe here in town."

Lisbeth stood up, leaned down, and gave him a light kiss on the cheek. "Thanks, cowboy, that means a lot."

Travis shot up out of his chair, took her head into his hands, bent down, and kissed her passionately, deeply. When he let go of her, Lisbeth stared up at him. "It's been a long time since anyone has kissed me like that," she said quietly.

"Sweetheart, you keep cooking like this, and there will be a whole lot more where that one came from," Travis said, looking at her tenderly.

"Please don't take this the wrong way ... I don't think I'm ready."

"Ready? What do you mean?"

Lisbeth looked away, then back at him. "Ready for anything more than a friendship."

Travis nodded and leaned back. "Sorry. Guess I got carried away with your cooking."

"And I appreciate that, Travis. I really like you. I do. Forgive me if I'm a bit skittish."

"No apologies necessary. I get it. We barely know each other."

"True, but it's not that. I've been through some trauma that really turned my world upside down. Moving to Texas has helped a lot. But let's not talk about it now. I'll tell you about it some other time. Ya wanna help me with the dishes?"

No sooner had they carried everything into the kitchen than the doorbell rang. Lisbeth asked Travis to answer the door while she rinsed the dishes. He opened the door to a man wearing a black suit, black silk shirt, and an extravagant pair of leather shoes, out of place in a small Texas town. Though tall, Travis towered over him like he did most everyone.

"Hey, I'm Dennis," the man said, stepping inside. "I'm Lisbeth's fiancé. Who are you?"

Travis turned around as Lisbeth walked up to the door. She stood back, too shocked to say anything. Though standing several feet away, she felt a heat emanating from him, and one she didn't find attractive. Silence hung in the air like kudzu draping the trees in the East Texas bayous.

Travis turned and looked at her. "Savannah Mae, do you need me to stay?"

She smiled ever so slightly. "I'll be fine, Travis. I can handle this."

"Handle what?" Dennis demanded, irritation in his grating voice. He turned to Travis. "Why did you call her that? What kind of lame name is that? Look, I don't know who you are," he said, his nostrils flaring, "but you need to leave."

Lisbeth stared at Dennis's profile, at the tension in his jaw. And Travis saw it, too. Silently, Travis stared down at Dennis, holding his gaze, not backing down, until finally he turned to Lisbeth and arched a brow.

"It's okay, Travis," she assured him.

"I'll call you later, Savannah Mae," Travis said slowly, giving her a discerning look. She could hear a thread of affection braiding through his voice as he turned toward the door. And she was pretty sure that Dennis heard it, too, which made her simper inside.

"Don't bother, dude," Dennis called after him. "I don't want you to come back here or call her. Like I said, I'm her fiancé."

Travis grinned and turned back around. Dennis saw the holstered pistol on Travis's hip. "Is that so? I imagine the lady will have something to say about that," he berated Dennis, whose jaw dropped at the sight of the firearm.

"Wait a sec," Lisbeth turned and ran to the kitchen, grabbed the second pecan pie, and saw Travis out onto the porch, closing the door behind her.

"Are you all right?" he asked, frowning. She could see that he was hesitant to leave her with Dennis, his eyes narrowing as he searched her face for a clue.

She stammered as her cheeks flushed, mortified and angry at Dennis for bursting into her home and claiming to be her fiancé. Though she was grateful that Travis was there, she was also embarrassed that she needed rescuing. Regaining her composure, she smiled sweetly and handed him the pie.

"Oh, more than okay, cowboy," she responded, trying to stay calm. "This has been a long time coming. And I am so ready to take it on." She stood on her tiptoes and kissed him on the cheek. "I'll call you later."

Travis walked down the steps and got into his truck. He drove it around the block and parked it across the street two houses down where he could watch the house. Lisbeth stepped back into the house, where Dennis was waiting for her. He stood fast, his arms folded over his chest. As she had seen so many times before, he seemed to fill the space, her space. She felt her chest tighten, as though he were sucking all the available oxygen out of the air. This time she also saw something she hadn't noticed about him before: for a few brief moments, glints of madness in his eyes. Then it was gone, replaced by his usual arrogance.

"Did you see that?" he pointed toward the door. "That guy threatened me!" His anger was abrupt and unexpected. It hung in the air so thick, she could almost touch it.

Lisbeth placed her hands on her hips and gave out an exasperated sigh. "What are you doing here, Dennis? And why did you say you're my fiancé?"

"Because I am, sweetie, and I came all this way to take you back home."

"Get a grip, Dennis," she said as she rolled her eyes. "This is my home. I live here. I own this house. I'm not going back to California, and I'm certainly not marrying you." She could feel her insides straining. The air between them tightened like a stretched rubber band about to break.

Dennis shook his head and blinked. "What are you saying? We talked about this."

"Really, Dennis, are we going to have this discussion again? May I remind you that you're the one who talked about marriage, not me. You never asked if I wanted to marry you, and if you had, I would have told you 'no.' All this time, you've assumed that whatever you said I'd jump to it. I told you when I packed for my move out here that we were done. Don't you remember that, or have you suddenly developed a case of amnesia?"

His shoulders slumped slightly. "I thought you were kidding or that you needed a little time, which is what I gave you, time." He glanced away and back at her, aware that she was scrutinizing him. He wasn't sure what was going on, so he reverted to the only way he knew how to handle her.

"I insist you stop all this nonsense," he stated in his most authoritative voice.

"What?!" she smiled. "You insist? Who do you think you are?"

He quickly changed his tone and smiled sweetly, saccharin and insincerity infusing every word. "Now, don't get all riled up, honey. Look, I'll help you put this old clunker on the market and get it sold so we can go back to L.A. and get married. A city girl like you shouldn't be living in a dump like this."

Rage welled up inside her, bordering on an explosive fury that she didn't know she possessed. Instead of caving into him, as she had done in the past, she felt a rod shoot up her spine, emboldening her.

"Dennis, you aren't listening," she leaned in and hissed at him. "First, don't you ever call me 'honey,' because I am not your honey. And second, news flash, I'm not going to sell my wonderful house, which by the way, is my family home. And I'm certainly not going back to L.A., nor am I going to marry you. Ever!" She stopped and sucked in a big breath of air. "You need to leave now," she barked at him, on the verge of an all-out scream. He didn't budge. She shot a finger sideways and pointed to the door.

He stepped forward, and his demeanor changed. "Now look, sweetie," he said, his voice soft and affectionate. He reached for her. "I love you. I want what's best for you."

"Don't you dare touch me!" she snapped at him, stepping back. "You don't want what's best for me. You never have. You've always wanted what's best for you, which is to have a woman you can control. I may have let you get away with it before, but not now. I am not that woman, nor will I ever be again. Now get out of my house, or I swear, I'll call the police."

"Are you serious?" He looked at her, a mild look of shock crossing his face. Seeing the expression on her reddened face, he realized that she was. He held up his hands in surrender. "Okay, okay, fine," he said. "I'll be back in the morning to give you time to calm down so we can discuss this rationally."

She let out a protracted moan. "There's nothing to discuss, Dennis. Get out, and don't come back!" she hollered at him, pointing to the door again.

He slowly turned and walked toward the entrance. He opened the door, trudged across the threshold, and stopped to look back. She slammed the door in his face and locked it. Only after Dennis had gotten into his rental car and driven away did Travis pull out of his parking space and turn toward home.

After Dennis left, Lisbeth retreated to the wooden swing on the front porch. A weight thick as black gumbo soil bore down on her chest, making it hard to breathe. After several minutes, she managed to inhale the scents of the climbing jasmine, honeysuckle, and roses scaling up along the railings. Slowly, the sweet-smelling scents calmed her mind. The front garden shimmered in the early evening light, as heat waves rose from the damp earth, tenacious as the mint growing in the front corner. Noisy cicadas shrilled their song. Here, time moved slow as molasses. It was her favorite spot overlooking the front garden, a place she retreated to when she needed tranquility, a spot that would ease her troubled mind. She sat on the swing, closed her eyes, and inhaled the fragrance of

Cecile Brunner roses climbing up the porch. A pair of cardinals entered the garden, playing hide-and-seek, their melodic trills dancing through the air. In moments, Lisbeth felt her heart rate lower and the heaviness lift off of her chest. She called Travis, got his voicemail, and left a message saying that everything was fine. And it was.

She sat on the swing for a while thinking about how, her whole life, she'd felt that there was something missing. It wasn't until she moved to Texas and met her extended family that she realized what she'd been longing for. Family, connections, history. Being adopted, she had no idea who she was, who her birth family was, her place in the world. Everything and everyone now in her life filled that void and answered the questions she had shouldered for as long as she could remember. She nodded to herself and whispered aloud, "This, this is where I'm supposed to be."

She took several long, deep breaths, oblivious to the waning light. Then she noticed how the air had grown still, how she could hear the slightest sounds of leaves rustling in the breeze and birds settling into their nests for the oncoming night. Suddenly, Sophie jumped on her lap and began pawing her, meowing loudly.

"How'd you get out of the house?" She looked toward the front door and noticed it slightly ajar.

"Dinnertime, huh? No, no, we've been saying it all wrong, Sophie," she chuckled. "It's called supper," she smiled, stroking the kitty. Sophie responded with a loud, resounding meow, jumped down, and skittered back into the house, Lisbeth right behind her. She no sooner set down Sophie's plate of food than her phone rang.

"Sisters, sisters, never before have there been such devoted sisters," Dixie sang.

"Ah, you're a fan of *White Christmas*," Lisbeth said.

"You bet," Dixie responded. "We watch it as a family every Christmas."

"Now I know that we're blood. I have the DVD and watch it every Christmas, too."

"Well, this coming Christmas you have to watch it at our house because Mom makes all the treats from the movie and a few of her childhood favorites. You'll love it."

"I'm sure I will now that I've tasted your mom's cooking."

"Speaking of movies, Zach and I are going to see a movie tonight and wondered if you'd like to join us."

"Cool!" Lisbeth chirped. "Which movie?"

Dixie laughed. "Does it matter? I don't know. We thought we'd get an early dinner at Panza's on North Rogers, then catch a movie after. Have you had their pizza?"

"Uh, no. I'm game. But I gotta tell ya, I'm really full and probably won't eat much. Had a late meal."

"Your appetite will come back real fast when you taste it. Best pizza in town."

"Sounds good, shall I come over to your house?

"Naw, we'll pick you up, say, in a half-hour?"

"See you then," Lisbeth agreed.

After a meal of pizza with a crazy array of toppings, as good as anything Lisbeth had ever eaten, they drove over to the Galaxy Theater in Ennis, the next town over.

"A drive-in? Really?" Lisbeth asked.

"Yep," Zach nodded. "It's ancient. Dad says it hasn't changed since he was a kid. You okay with a drive-in?"

"Oh yeah," Lisbeth remarked. "I love drive-ins. It's really sad that most of them have closed. What kind of movies does the Galaxy show?"

"Let's see," Zach said as he looked up at the board, glancing at the day's features. "Looks like it's Humphrey Bogart night. *Casablanca.*"

Lisbeth faked a swoon. "I can't tell you how many times I've watched that movie. It's one of my all-time faves."

Zach and Dixie looked at Lisbeth and chuckled.

"What? Did I say something funny?" she asked.

"No, Lisbeth, it's just that you're so, so old school," Dixie responded.

Lisbeth cranked her head to the side. "And that's bad?"

"No!" Zach and Dixie said in unison.

"Even though we're young, we're old school," Dixie said. "It's so kickin' that you are, too. Guess it runs in our genes."

As soon as they found a good spot in the parking lot, Zach jumped out of the car. "I'm going for snacks. Y'all want anything?"

Lisbeth looked at Dixie, then back at Zach. "We just ate!"

Dixie grinned. "That makes no difference whatsoever to Zach's stomach. He's hungry all the time."

Lisbeth looked back at Zach, who was nodding, an impish expression on his face. "Thanks, Zach, but I'll pass."

A few minutes later, Zach returned with a tray of food—hot nachos covered in melted cheese and jalapeños, caramel corn, a huge bag of M&M's, a big box of Junior Mints, and three extra-large drinks. "This should hold us for a while," he quipped, setting the tray down between them.

Lisbeth stared bug-eyed at the food.

"Told ya," Dixie said.

"Sheesh," Lisbeth declared. "Wish I had your metabolism!"

Chapter Eleven

The next morning, Lisbeth's phone rang early. She looked at the number, let out an irritated sigh, and took her time picking up.

"What is it now, Dennis?"

"I'm coming over. We need to talk," Dennis said sternly into the phone.

"No, we don't. I made it perfectly clear yesterday that I don't want to see you, and you are not welcome in my home."

"Lisbeth, we're engaged. We have a lot to talk about."

Lisbeth had lost all patience with him. "For goodness' sake, Dennis, are you deaf or just stupid?" She got out of bed and paced around her room. "What part of 'We're not engaged,' and 'I don't ever want to see you again,' don't you understand?"

"Now, settle down. I thought that, once you had time to get a handle on your emotions, we could have a reasonable conversation."

If Dennis had been in the room, she was pretty sure she would've slapped or choked him.

"Do not insult me, Dennis. My emotions are just fine. Don't you dare show up at my door."

"Or what?"

"You really want to find out?"

"You going to have that fake cowboy threaten me again? Or sic those kids on me that you went out with last night?"

She felt her heart skip a beat. It was one thing for him to be watching her, which was bad enough, but even worse that he was now aware of her brother and sister, even if he didn't know who they were. "You were watching me?"

"Of course, I was watching you, sweetheart. I care about you, and I don't want you getting mixed up with dubious people."

"How dare you! You're a piece of work, Dennis, you know that? I'm warning you. Don't come near me or my house. Go back to California!"

"No can do, sweetie. I'm not going back to L.A. without you." He hung up the phone.

Lisbeth dialed Travis as fast as she could.

"Hey, California, how ya doin'?"

"Sorry to be abrupt, but can you get me a restraining order?"

"That serious, huh?"

"Yeah."

"I can do it, but it'll take some time. Text me the guy's info. Meanwhile, get out of the house. Go over to your aunt's house or your dad's. Dennis doesn't know who they are, does he?"

"No, well, yes, sort of. When he called this morning, he said he saw me go out last night with some kids. He didn't know that they were my brother and sister. They picked me up and we went out to a movie. Travis, he was watching me and my house!"

"Go over to your aunt's and drop in like it's a casual visit. Meanwhile, I'll get the restraining order and go to your house with the sheriff. Don't worry, we'll take care of this."

"Thanks, cowboy. I really don't mean to put you out. I just didn't know where else to turn."

"Hey, don't thank me. I'm just glad you called and I can help. Now get out of there. I'll call you when it's all taken care of."

Lisbeth dressed quickly and left the house, making sure that Sophie was indoors. A few minutes later, she knocked on Ruth's door.

"Oh, Lisbeth, I'm so glad you dropped by," she said, opening the door and waving her inside. "I was going to stop by your house and show you some photos. You saved me the trip."

"I knew that!" Lisbeth chimed.

"You did?" Ruth raised her eyebrows.

"No, I was joshing you. I just needed to get out for a bit. I love that we live so close."

"Me, too. Can I offer you some sweet tea and cookies? I baked them this morning."

"Of course! What kind did you bake this time?"

"Soft raisin cookies."

"Lead the way, Auntie! I'm yours," Lisbeth sang, under her breath silently thanking Travis for urging her to leave the house.

For a couple of hours, they looked over photos Ruth brought out showing Emma and Ruth as children and teens. Other photos featured Fannie Lee and countless other relatives. Lisbeth picked up a photo and said, "I think this one is my favorite."

Ruth leaned over to see which photo she was holding. "Why?"

"Aunt Ruth, those hairdos, the makeup, those clothes. You and Mama were quite the fashionistas, weren't you?"

Ruth smiled. "Well, yes, we were," she said, a fond memory crossing her face.

Their conversation came to a slow end. Lisbeth wondered when she should go home. Would Travis call? Then she remembered something.

"Aunt Ruth, there's something really important that I've been thinking about and I want to run it by you."

Ruth nodded. "Go on."

"I'm seriously considering changing my name."

Ruth's eyebrows bolted up her forehead.

"Even though Lisbeth is the only name I know, it's strange ... I never felt like the name fit me. Sort of like wearing someone else's clothes, you know what I mean?"

Ruth nodded.

"When I found out my birth name, I loved it the second Mr. Sheridan told me. It's a beautiful name, and it felt oddly familiar. I can't imagine that I remembered it from being an infant, but maybe I did." Lisbeth saw Ruth smiling, an endearing smile.

"Since getting over the shock of finding out who I am, I've thought about the name a lot. When I met all of you the day I drove into Waxahachie and you called me Savannah Mae, just as my father did, it felt comfortable, normal. Everyone has been very gracious about calling me Lisbeth, which I appreciate. Really, I do. Somehow though, Lisbeth doesn't feel right anymore. I'm Savannah Mae, not Lisbeth."

Ruth reached over and clasped Lisbeth's hand, looking her straight in the eye. "Honey, that's because none of us ever forgot you. Over the years, we've talked about you, wondered where you were, how you were doing, what kind of person you'd become. We've called you Savannah Mae for 30 years. When we found out you were Lisbeth James, it was a little bit of a shock. We're adjusting, though. I'm sure it's the same for your father."

Lisbeth nodded. "Funny thing is, Dad and his whole family call me Savannah Mae." Lisbeth looked down at her hands before looking up again. "What do you think? I mean about switching my name back to Savannah Mae? Even though it would be a huge change for me, somehow it seems like the right thing to do."

"Right for who?" Ruth asked.

"For me. I've had a while to think about this. Yesterday something happened that made me take stock of the last few months. Initially, I didn't know how I would adjust to living in Texas. It seemed so foreign to me in the beginning, but now I can't imagine living anywhere else. I've realized that while I left Texas as a baby, Texas never left me. Texas and my family fill my heart, my very soul. It's who I am. This is home, and not just now. It's always been my home."

Ruth gave Lisbeth's hand a squeeze.

"Aunt Ruth, there is one thing that I want to know, something that doesn't make sense."

Ruth nodded, urging her to go on.

"Why name me after a city in Georgia? It seems odd."

Ruth smiled. "There is definitely a story there. When your mother, Thelma, Keith, and I were children, your grandparents took us to Georgia on a road trip. Of all the places we visited, Savannah captured your mother's heart. She truly fell in love with the town, and she said that if she ever had a daughter, she would name her Savannah Mae. At the time, we all laughed, but your mother never forgot. Then, when she and Jack eloped to get married, they spent a weekend honeymoon in Savannah. It was where they cemented their marriage. Nine months later, she gave birth to you, and of course, there was no question, and your father agreed that Savannah Mae would be your name."

"I knew there was something deeper going on here, much more than looking up baby names in a book. This explains a lot," Lisbeth said. "As I've thought this through, I've realized that I've always been Savannah Mae, even if I didn't consciously know it. Subconsciously I think that I did."

Ruth's eyes widened. "Are you sure about this?"

"I think so. There's just one thing. I feel like if I change my name, I'm going to dishonor my parents who adopted me. They gave me everything—not only love and a home, but their name, and without other children, I'm the only one who can pass on their name, their history."

Ruth watched Lisbeth's face, the twist of her mouth, the disquiet in her eyes. "It is of course your choice. Know that whatever you decide, we will all love you whether you decide to stay Lisbeth or use the name Savannah Mae. You are loved regardless."

Lisbeth nodded. "Thank you, Aunt Ruth. That means a lot to me." Lisbeth stayed quiet for several minutes. Realizing that her aunt was staring at her, she piped up, "Ya know, Travis was over at my house yesterday. I made him a lot of the dishes you and Annabelle taught me and a couple from the recipe box. Before he left, he called me Savannah Mae."

"How did that feel?"

Lisbeth smiled modestly, her eyes wistful. "I liked it."

"That's because you are Savannah Mae, my dear. May I offer you one bit of advice?"

Lisbeth nodded.

"There's no deadline here, no one is pressuring you to change your name. You are still adjusting to this new life, to a whole new family, to a new future. Take your time. This new life of yours is here to stay."

Lisbeth reached over and gave Ruth a hug just as her phone rang. She saw it was Travis. She looked at Ruth, grinned, and answered. "Hello, this is Savannah Mae."

"Well! Hello to you, too, Savannah Mae," Travis said, amusement in his voice. "The deed is done. Ya want me to pick you up? We can go get a beer and I'll tell you all about it."

"I'm at Aunt Ruth's. I'll be waiting for you out front." She stood up, kissed Ruth on the cheek, and said, "Thank you, Aunt Ruth. I gotta run."

Chapter Twelve

A short while later, Travis and Lisbeth walked into a bar in downtown Waxahachie and sat down at a table. As soon as their Shiner Bocks arrived, Travis leaned back in his chair.

"First, I have to ask you, 'cause I need to know who I'm dealing with here. Are you Lisbeth or Savannah Mae?"

She smiled. "What do you think, Travis? You called me Savannah Mae at the house yesterday."

He nodded. "It suits you."

"I think so, too. In fact, I'm seriously thinking of legally changing back to my birth name."

Travis nodded slightly. "When you're ready, call me. We have someone at the firm who can do that for you."

"Good to know," she responded.

"Now for the most pressing matter," he began. "We have a saying here in Texas for guys like that Dennis—he's slicker than a slop jar."

Lisbeth snorted and quickly covered her mouth. "Oh, that's a new one for me. It fits him perfectly. What happened at my house? Tell me!"

"Now, I didn't get to know the guy. It seemed to me that he thought he was some big shot who had some God-given right to control you, that he knew better how you should live your life than you do."

"I'd say you figured him out to a tee."

Travis leaned back in his chair and stared at Lisbeth for a few moments. "I'm not sure how or why you got involved with him, but I have a feeling that it wasn't your choice to start something with him. Am I right?"

Lisbeth nodded. "No, it wasn't."

"Just so I can better understand that guy, can you tell me what happened and why he seems to think he owns you?"

"Yes, you deserve an answer," she said, as a weight, dense and thick as the humidity hanging in the air, pushed down on her shoulders. For the next half-hour, she told Travis about Scott, their planned wedding, the tragic accident on the way to the ceremony, and how Scott died but Dennis wasn't even injured.

"As Scott's best friend, Dennis felt he had a responsibility to step in for Scott and take care of me," Lisbeth added. She ran the tip of her tongue over her top lip. "In my grief, admittedly, I let him. I was distraught and felt lost. Then before I knew it, he was running every aspect of my life. Or at least trying to."

Her throat constricted as she described how she felt like she had no control over her life. She stopped and took a deep breath. She described how she didn't know how to stop him, couldn't stop him. She paused and looked away, then back at Travis.

"Go on," he said in a hushed voice.

"His possessiveness was making me nervous. Then he started talking about marrying me. That was it, I told him no ... only he wouldn't listen. I really thought that if I broke up with him I could move on with my life. And I thought I had. It's been nearly six months since I've seen or heard from him. I honestly believed that by moving to Texas the problem was solved until he showed up at my house yesterday and marched in acting like he did in California. I was so shocked because I thought we were done and this whole thing was over. That's when I realized that he hasn't accepted that we're through."

"Moving to Texas didn't stop him, did it?"

Lisbeth shook her head. "I told him when I left L.A. that I was leaving for good and that I never wanted to see him again. I should have known he wouldn't give up so easily." Her throat tightened again; barely whispering, she continued. "He laughed."

Travis crossed his arms over his chest and shook his head from side to side. "This is worse than I thought. I wish you had confided in me sooner."

"Oh, Travis, I didn't want to bring Dennis up and get you involved in this mess. It wasn't your concern. Besides, I hadn't heard from him since I left California. I seriously thought he had given up."

Travis scowled, his eyes boring through her. "The guy is a scumbag, and scumbags don't give up. Their egos can't handle it."

Lisbeth nodded and took a big swig of her beer.

"For the short term, he isn't going to bother you. The sheriff and I met him at your front door and served him a restraining order. He balked, said something about being from a wealthy family with connections, and that he would have his lawyers contest the restraining order. Then he began ranting that this was harassment and that as your fiancé he had a right to be there. Said he wouldn't stand for it." Travis let out a belly laugh. "Darlin', don't worry. We informed him otherwise. The sheriff told him that if he was seen within 500 feet of your home, he would be arrested. Then the sheriff escorted him to the county border."

"Really?" her eyes brightened a little.

"Yeah, come here," he said, leaned over, and held her in a tight embrace.

His strong arms wrapped around her momentarily reassured her, though she didn't think it would last long. Back in California, she'd often felt a knot in her stomach whenever Dennis became overbearing. Since moving to Texas, the painful knots had disappeared. And now, a particularly painful one was back. She knew it was the old familiar uneasiness she'd been living with for the past several years. She knew that Dennis would not give up so easily, restraining order or not.

"Now I'm going to make three suggestions that you might not like, so I'm just going to ask you to mull them over, and then we can talk about them now or later."

"I'm listening."

"My first suggestion is that you get a dog specially trained for protection, like a German Shepherd, Doberman, or Rottweiler. There are other breeds, too."

Lisbeth blinked and stammered. "Uh, I don't think Sophie would do well with a guard dog in the house. She's never been around any dogs, much less a guard dog. She's not a young cat. I couldn't do that to her."

"I figured as much. Don't discount it just yet. My second suggestion, and I hope you'll agree to this because it's very important: you need to install hidden cameras all around your property and inside."

Lisbeth was watching him intently. "Cameras? Travis, is that really necessary?"

He nodded. "Right now, near as I can tell, this guy is a loose cannon. There's no telling what he might do. If it comes to a worst-case scenario, having footage is key to charging him if he commits a crime against you."

"I appreciate your concern, Travis, really, I do, but honestly, I doubt he would harm me. Plus, I really hate the idea of cameras all around the property and inside. They would take away from the charm of that lovely old house, and my privacy."

"Hear me out. We have a guy who we use at the firm. He's a pro. When he's done with his installation, you won't be able to tell that there's a camera anywhere on site. Plus, all the footage is transferred electronically in real time back to the server."

"How does he do that ... hide the cameras, I mean?" she asked, her mouth slightly twisted, a habit she fell into whenever she felt stressed.

"He's very clever. Tell ya what. I'll send you a link later today that shows a video demonstration of how he discretely hides the cameras. In gardens, they look like flowers or part of a tree stump. In the dining room, you think they're china cups. In a kitchen, part of an appliance."

Lisbeth leaned back in her chair and shook her head a little, her locks jiggling on her shoulders. "Wow, guess I don't know much about this stuff. He doesn't install them in the bathrooms or bedrooms, does he?"

An amused expression crossed Travis's face. He knew what she was thinking. "No, not usually, unless there's a reason to. Will you consider the cameras? I think this is necessary."

Lisbeth sat and mulled it over. She looked at her beer, up at Travis, and back at her beer. She glanced sideways and looked at him out of the corner of her eye, then turned back to face him.

"Okay, let's start with your sending me the video and I'll consider it. What's the third suggestion?"

"Since I doubt that Sophie could do much against an intruder, I recommend that you take some professional training and get your LTC."

"My what?"

"License to carry."

"Carry what?"

"A gun. You need to be able to protect yourself."

"Holy Mama! Are you serious?" Lisbeth's hands flew up to the sides of her face.

"Deadly. The sheriff and I tossed him out for now, but he's going to come after you again and you need to be prepared. Having a guard dog would be your best deterrent, but if you won't get a dog, then you definitely need to be able to defend yourself."

Lisbeth could feel the hair rise on the back of her neck and goosebumps run up and down her arms. She rubbed her arms to calm down the goosebumps, to no avail. "Travis, I couldn't shoot him, no matter how much I loathe him."

"Even if he was coming after you with a knife? How about if he broke into your house and attacked you? Because that's what guys who are intent on controlling and intimidating women do. The behavior doesn't die down. It escalates because it's the ultimate act of domination."

Lisbeth's eyes grew big and round.

"Look, I'm not trying to scare you. I'm just suggesting you be prepared in case he comes back with extreme force. He obviously doesn't like guns. You saw his reaction when he caught sight of the pistol in my holster. He got even more upset when he saw me again today. He stared at my hip."

Lisbeth stuttered, "I-I-I did see how he reacted yesterday, but honestly, I just can't see him hurting me."

"That's exactly how people like him catch their victims. Because most women want to believe in the best of a man. Many men know this and know how to prey on their vulnerabilities. Dennis wants you, and he is clearly going to do whatever is necessary to get you back. Please trust me, I know what I'm talking about. I handled dozens of cases like this when I was in law enforcement."

They sat for a few minutes staring at their beer bottles.

"I have an idea," Travis added. Lisbeth looked up at him. "There are some good women-only gun clubs around. Their sole purpose is to train women on using firearms for protection, so they're prepared in case of an attack."

She pinched her brows together. "Women only?"

"Travis nodded. "I'll text you the names of the groups in this area. You can check them out and see which one you're most comfortable with."

"You shoot," Lisbeth said. Travis nodded. "Why can't you teach me?"

"I could, but it might be better for you to learn from other women. What they tell you may have more impact than me."

"I have confidence in you, Travis."

"Consider that the women-only clubs might have insight and perspectives that I can't offer."

Lisbeth nodded. "Okay, I'll check into them. Wait, wait. I would need a gun. I don't have a gun. I don't even know what to buy or where to get one." She started shaking her head. "I don't know about this."

Travis reached over and held her hand. "Don't worry. In the beginning, you can use the club's guns until you figure out what you want to buy. Then, when you're ready, I'll take you shopping."

She cocked her head sideways and raised a brow. "You mean like when you took me boot shopping?"

He grinned. "Yeah, but this time you're going to make the decision on what to buy."

"How will I know what's right for me, Travis?"

"That's why you should join a club and try out different guns. In short order, you'll know, and I have a feeling that once you start practicing with your own firearm, you're going to be pretty good at it."

Over the following days, Lisbeth watched the video on residential security camera installation. Satisfied that the cameras would not be intrusive she texted Travis and asked him to send his guy out to her house to begin the process. Next, she looked online at various women-only gun clubs. She made calls about visiting the clubs. Finally, she decided to do something less stressful, something she could do without thinking too much.

She opened the box containing the wedding dress, removed it, and ran her fingers over every inch of the fabric. She felt the texture, fingered the seams, and inspected the handiwork. She was in awe of the craftsmanship. She laid the dress on the table and began thinking about how it could be reused. It didn't take long for her to imagine it as a double wedding ring quilt.

Even though double wedding ring quilts were often made of various colors, with the many tones of white she thought an all-white double wedding ring would work, and it would be elegant. First, using a seam ripper, she carefully removed all the stitches, then, using the lowest heat setting on her iron, pressed the fabrics. Finally, she fused lightweight interfacing on the backs to stabilize the fabrics and keep them from fraying. She knew that the very lightweight interlining would permanently meld the fabrics, giving them stability without adding volume. After she completed the fusing, she carefully began cutting and laying out the design. She decided that she would quilt it by hand, not by machine. Though it would take longer, she felt it deserved hand quilting, a nearly lost art. It was a complicated design, not for inexperienced quilters. Even though Lisbeth had never before attempted the design, she felt confident that she could do it. She worked carefully, one small section at a time. Each time she completed a block, she held it up and caressed it, thinking about how it was her mother who made the dress. She imagined that a bit of her mother's soul was embedded in each stitch.

Her phone rang. She looked down and saw it was from Yolanda Marquez, the guild vice president.

"Hey, Yolanda!" she answered. "How are you?"

"I'm doing great. Listen, I'm calling because I want to show you some interesting quilts that might be something new you haven't seen before. And I thought that if you're not busy, you could come for supper tomorrow night."

"How nice of you to think of me. I'd love to come to supper if you let me contribute."

"No, no, you don't need to bring anything. I'm making a Mexican meal from recipes my grandmother brought with her from Mexico when the family immigrated in the 1950s."

"Real Mexican food, not Tex-Mex?"

"Yes, the real thing. Do you like Mexican food, on the spicy side?"

Lisbeth let out a moan. "Oh, you have no idea how much I've missed real Mexican food. There were a lot of great Mexican restaurants near where I lived. When we craved something even more authentic, my friends and I used to go down to Baja California and hit one of our favorite restaurants south of Tijuana. Tex-Mex is okay, but it's not the same as the real deal."

"You're right about that!" Yolanda agreed. "Is there anything you don't eat?"

"I don't mean to be picky, and I don't want you to leave out a food your family really likes ... but I don't like menudo."

Yolanda chuckled. "Really? You're not a fan of cow's stomach?"

"Uh, no," Lisbeth answered, trying to sound diplomatic.

"No worries, I'm not a fan either so I never make it. How about tamales, posole, chicken enchiladas, beans with jalapeños, Mexican rice, and tacos al pastor? I make my tacos with pork that I marinate. My family loves it."

"You're making me hungry, Yolanda!"

"Okay, come by about six o'clock. We'll have supper, and I'll show you the quilts afterward."

"Can I bring dessert? I make a mean tres leches cake."

"You do?"

"Yeah, a friend back in California taught me her family recipe. It's pretty good."

"That would be great, though I'll warn you that between my husband and kids, they will devour it. That happens to be one of their favorite desserts. They're always complaining that I never make it except on special occasions."

"Well, this is a special occasion, I'm coming to your house!" Lisbeth responded. "See you tomorrow evening."

After putting the final touches on the tres leches cake, Lisbeth headed over to Yolanda's house. As soon as she stepped inside, her senses were assaulted with the heady, savory aromas of the Mexican meal Yolanda had made. She about fell over inhaling the pungent smells, and she could feel her taste buds start to water. Yolanda did a double take at Lisbeth's cake.

"Is it okay?" Lisbeth asked, a little worried when she saw the expression on Yolanda's face.

"Of course, it's more than okay," Yolanda remarked. "Most people who aren't Hispanic don't know what a tres leches cake is, much less how to make one. This is beautiful. I'm going to put it away where they can't see it, or they'll want to eat it first," she laughed.

Over supper, Lisbeth devoured Yolanda's cooking while l earning about her family. The children were extremely well-behaved until Yolanda brought out the cake. They squealed with exuberant happiness. "Mamá, you made our favorite cake!"

Yolanda gestured to Lisbeth. "Our guest made it." The children and Mayo, Yolanda's husband, did a double take looking at Lisbeth. Yolanda cut the cake and gave slices to everyone. Silence prevailed as everyone took a tentative first bite.

"Oh, Lisbeth, you have made this hombre very, very happy," Mayo murmured. "This is as good as my wife's cake."

"Thank you, but I'm sure that can't be true. Yolanda is a phenomenal cook."

"He's absolutely right, Lisbeth. Your cake is as good as mine," Yolanda said as her children nodded while wolfing down their slices.

"Well, thank you. That's quite a compliment."

Upon finishing supper, Yolanda asked the children to clear the table and rinse the dishes while she took Lisbeth to her sewing room.

Yolanda opened a closet, took out a pile of quilts, and stacked them on her large sewing table. Lisbeth helped her unfold the quilts.

"Oh, Yolanda! I've never seen such exquisite quilts. They remind me of the Talavera tiles and Dia de los Muertos designs that are common in Southern California."

"Since you're from there, I thought that you might be familiar with the designs."

"I couldn't not be. Many homes in Southern California feature Talavera tiles in the kitchens, bathrooms, and patios. And personally, Day of the Dead is one of my favorite Mexican holidays."

"I'm surprised. How do you know about it?"

"There's a large Mexican community in both the Los Angeles and San Diego areas. Every year, there are parades and festivals commemorating it. When I was a kid, my parents took me to one of the parades. I instantly fell in love with the colors, the vibrancy, the painted skulls on everyone's faces, and of course, the idea of loved ones coming back to life for one day a year. Ever since my parents and fiancé died I've thought how wonderful it would be if they rose from the dead and I could spend time with them again. I've heard that there are parades and festivals here in Texas, but I don't know where they are."

"Tell ya what, you can go with my family and me to San Antonio. We attend every year. It's really something to see. But I warn you that we go in costume and paint our faces. You up for that?"

Lisbeth nodded her head enthusiastically. "It can't get here fast enough."

Lisbeth stayed and helped Yolanda clean up the kitchen. As she went to leave, she turned to Yolanda. "Thank you so much for this incredible evening. As much as I love all things Texan, I've missed eating authentic Mexican food and being around Mexican culture."

"I'm glad you've enjoyed it. You know, I have a feeling that you and I are going to become very good friends."

"And I have a feeling that you are absolutely right!"

Chapter Thirteen

A few days after researching the women-only gun clubs, Lisbeth attended her first gun club meet. She had barely stepped out of her car and was zipping up her jacket to ward off the cold air when two women approached her and asked if she was there to attend the shooting meet or watch. She explained that she wanted to learn about guns, for self-protection, adding that she didn't own a gun and was hoping that the instructor could advise which one would be most suitable.

"That would be me," offered a dark-haired woman, "I'm Julie Mynar, the instructor, and this is Brenda Hurtick, my assistant." The two women reached out and shook Lisbeth's hand.

"And you are?" Brenda asked.

Lisbeth paused. "It's a little complicated. I've been Lisbeth James my whole life, given to me by my adoptive parents. I recently moved to Texas and met my birth family. Soon I will be legally changing my name, returning to the name given to me at birth. You might as well call me Savannah Mae. I'm getting used to it."

"When will your name change become legal?" Julie asked. "It's important because once you qualify and file for your LTC, it will have to bear your legal name."

"Oh, good point. I'll need to check with my attorney."

"That's fine," Julie responded. "Meanwhile, you can get started learning about gun safety and trying out different handguns to see which ones are most comfortable for you."

"Is there a big difference?" Lisbeth asked.

Julie and Brenda nodded in unison. "Some women can't handle a big caliber like a 45 or 357. For other women, the larger calibers are easy," Brenda said. "Come into the office and we'll fill out some paperwork to get you started."

Two hours and a sore hand later, Lisbeth practically danced to her car. She had no sooner sat in her seat than she dialed Travis's number.

"Hey, cowboy!" she said, not giving him a second to even say hello.

"Hey, yourself! What's up? You sound cheerful."

"I am! I took your advice and went to my first women-only gun club meet."

"How'd it go?"

"Oh, my goodness. Travis, I can't thank you enough for encouraging me to do this. I really liked the women in the club, the instructor, and her assistant. I think this will be the club for me. I don't feel like I need to check out the other club over in Temple."

"That's great. Did you get to handle any guns?"

"Yeah, I did. And I found that I had a really hard time with the higher-caliber ones. I don't have the hand or wrist strength to shoot them properly. They advised me to get some soft rubber handballs to increase my strength and flexibility. They said with time I'll be strong enough to handle the big boys."

Travis chuckled.

"What's so funny?"

"Nothin'. I was just thinking that's true—literally and figuratively. Hey, I'm real proud of you."

"Really?"

"Yep. You took this bull by its horns even though I think you were scared half-witless at just the idea of handling a gun."

"That's true. Meeting those women really did make a big difference, just like you said it would. They asked me why I wanted to do this, and I told them. They said to always remember one thing."

"What's that?"

"That I am worth protecting. I never thought of it that way before. They said that many of the women who join the club come for the same reason. Oh, and there's one other thing."

"And what would that be?"

"I need to move ahead with filing my name change because—"

Travis cut her off. "Your LTC has to properly reflect your legal name."

"Yeah, of course, you would know that. So, can we get the process started?"

"Sure. Come into the office on Monday and we'll get it going. Have to warn you, though, it's not a quick process, it usually takes months. You have to be a Texas resident for at least six months. And you've been here since. ..."

Lisbeth interrupted. "Just a little over six months actually."

"Okay, then. We'll get it started. I'll text you a list of documents you'll need to bring with you."

"Got it."

"One last thing," Travis added.

"Yeah?"

"Remember, tomorrow night I'm taking you honky-tonkin'."

"Oh, that's right! In all this excitement I almost forgot. You're picking me up at eight o'clock, right?"

"Nope, I'll pick you up at 5:30. It's a bit of a drive and we gotta get there early before they run out of smoked brisket. They also have the best ranch beans, cornbread, and mac 'n' cheese. No, let me correct that. Nothin's as good as yours, but they sure are pretty fine."

Lisbeth rolled her eyes. "Okay. I'll be sure to wear my jeans with a stretchy waist."

"You have a pair of those?" he asked.

"No, but I will by tomorrow. I'm gonna need 'em!"

"No, you won't. You'll burn up every calorie, dancin' every song with me."

One afternoon, while Lisbeth was working on the wedding dress quilt, the doorbell rang. She was both surprised and delighted to see Uncle Keith standing there holding a round, covered container.

"Hello, Uncle Keith. How nice to see you! Please come in," she beckoned him inside. "What's that in your hands?" she gestured to the container.

"My special pie."

"Did you say pie?"

He nodded. "I did."

"Well, let's go into the kitchen and take a look at that special pie."

As soon as Keith set it down on the kitchen table, he removed the cover and dramatically swept one hand over it in a flourish.

"Voilà!" he sang.

Lisbeth's eyes bugged out looking at the light yellow-green pie decorated with whipped cream.

"Uncle Keith, did you really make this yourself?"

He nodded. "I did. Learned it from a college girlfriend eons ago. She was from Florida. Though we broke up after graduation, I'll always be indebted to her for teaching me how to make her key lime pie. Have you ever tasted one?"

"I've had commercial ones, which I don't think are anything special. I've never had one homemade," Lisbeth slowly answered.

"You're about to be surprised. There's nothing like a homemade key lime pie. If you'll hand me a knife, pie server, and a couple of plates, I'll cut us slices."

"Deal! We certainly need something to wash it down. What'll you have? Milk? Coffee? Tea? Something stronger?"

"That's the spirit, Lisbeth. How about something stronger? This pie is rich, like a prize-winning bull rich, so we'll need something that can stand up to it. Besides that, I have lots of things to tell you about this house."

"Okaaaay, are you a whiskey man, vodka, gin, rum, wine, or beer?"

"What kind of whiskey do you have?"

"Irish, because that's my favorite. But I also have Jack Daniel's and Maker's Mark and Angel's Envy and Four Roses Small Batch bourbons."

"Four Roses! Never took you for a barkeep," he grinned at her.

"There's probably a lot you don't know about me," she grinned back. "Let's see where Grandma stored her best glasses," she said as she began opening cabinets.

"I'll get them," Keith offered. "She had so much glassware, she spread them out all over the kitchen." He opened a cabinet on the far end of the kitchen, reached up, and took down two elegant cut-crystal glasses. "Do you prefer your whiskey neat or on the rocks?"

"Neat, of course. Why dilute good whiskey?"

"That's my girl!" Keith said. He poured each of them a shot in the glasses, Redbreast Irish Whiskey for Lisbeth, and Four Roses for Keith. While Keith tended bar, Lisbeth cut two slices and slid them onto the plates.

She carried the plates into the living room, and Keith followed her, carrying the glasses. They sat down on the big comfy chairs, Uncle Keith opposite her. No sooner had they sat than they both took a forkful of the pie.

"Oh my God!" Lisbeth exclaimed, her eyes bugged out.

"What's wrong?" Keith asked.

"This," she pointed to the slice of pie. "This is ... is ... is, I don't know what word can properly describe it. Incredible!"

Keith bent his head toward his right shoulder. "You like it, then?"

"You were right. This is nothing like the commercial key lime pies I've had. Did you really make this? Come on, tell me the truth."

"Yeah, I told you, an old girlfriend taught me how to make it. The key is to use fresh squeezed key lime juice, not the reconstituted stuff. It's nearly impossible to find real key limes here in Texas, so I use very small Mexican limes, which are essentially the same thing. You can't use regular larger limes, though, it has to be the small ones 'cause they have a distinct flavor. That's why this pie tastes so different from the commercial ones you've had. For years, it's been my contribution to family get-togethers and parties."

While trying not to eat it like a starving person, she looked up at him. "I never took you for such a talented cook. What else do you make?"

"Oh, just the usual stuff. Brisket, ribs, pork, barbecue stuff. Shrimp dishes of all kinds. I really like shrimp."

His eyes twinkled as he looked at her, and took a sip of the bourbon. "Ya know, there are ghosts in this house."

She took a sip of her Irish whiskey before answering. "I know."

"You do?"

"Of course. A person can't live in this house and not be aware of them. They made their presence known on my first night."

Keith leaned forward after he swallowed a bite of pie. "Really? How?"

"Oh, little things, like I could hear the walls breathing. It felt like they were expanding and opening up as I walked down hallways. Floorboards creaked loudly, even when I was alone in the house," she said matter-of-factly.

"Were you scared?" he asked.

"No," she shook her head. "I figured that they were family, welcoming me home. I thought that maybe they even remembered me from when I was a baby."

"Extraordinary!" Keith remarked.

"What do you mean?"

"You and I are the only people in the family who can sense them, who can experience them just as you related to me."

"You feel them, too?"

"Have since I was a young boy."

"Do they ever present themselves in some kind of form?" Lisbeth asked.

"They did when I was very young. They were like hazy images that floated around. I heard them talking, too, though I never sensed they were talking to me. Actually, I think that they'd become so comfortable around me that they didn't remember I was there and just carried on with their ghost lives."

"Uncle Keith, are the ghosts capable of shenanigans?"

He sat back in his chair and looked at her thoughtfully. "What do you mean by shenanigans?"

"For example, I was living here hardly any time at all when the water went out. I contacted the water company and they said that 'I' had filed a requisition to have the water turned off."

"And did you?"

"No," she shook her head. "I had to take them my identification and a copy of my application for water service, plus a bill showing my name at this address. I also gave them a sample of my signature, which was different from the signature on the requisition. Only then did they turn the water back on."

"And you're wondering if the ghosts did that?"

Lisbeth nodded.

"I highly doubt it. I don't think they're capable of that kind of thing. Has there been anything else?"

"Yeah, the shed caught fire recently. Sort of a sudden combustion. I hadn't been back there and the front gate was locked, so no one could have gotten access to it. The firemen found evidence of it being set intentionally with lighter fluid."

"Oh, no, that is definitely out of their abilities. Our ghosts are quite benign. They're family. They don't want to harm us. This is very disturbing, Lisbeth." He shook his head back and forth. "I don't like this at all. It sounds like the work of someone very much alive. Is there anyone who would want to cause trouble or hurt you?"

Lisbeth shrugged. "Not that I can think of. It was all so weird."

"Well, whoever is behind these shenanigans, as you call them, hopefully they're over playing pranks."

"Me, too. You want a little more bourbon?" She held up the bottle.

"I thought you'd never ask," he said, holding up his glass.

Chapter Fourteen

As she waited for the name change to become legal, Lisbeth continued practicing at the gun range with the women in her gun club. Her confidence soared with each outing. Terrified at first, remembering that she was worth it kept her focused and going to the range on a regular schedule. Soon her practice sessions became as easy as making one of her now popular pecan pies.

When she was home, she worked on the quilt, a little bit every day. After weeks of work, Lisbeth finally finished it, held it up, wrapped it around her shoulders, and closed her eyes. It felt as if the quilt embodied her mother's soul. It radiated love, sheer love. She laid it over one of the living room wingback chairs, so she would see it every day. And any and everyone who visited would see it, too. She thought of it as her finest work. Each time she passed it, she would stop and run her fingers over the fabric and muse over who touched it, who made it, whose soul was embedded in the fabric.

Early one morning, her phone rang with the ring tone she set for Travis's number, "Ride Me Back Home" by Willie Nelson. It reminded her of the ride with Travis on his ranch. She picked it up right away.

"Hey, cowboy, how ya doin'?"

"Not bad, Savannah Mae. You sittin' down?"

"Uh, no, do I need to be?" she asked. "What's up?"

"You know how I told you it would take several months to legally change your name?"

"Yeah," she said slowly.

"Well, I don't mean to disappoint you, but there's been a change in the timetable."

Lisbeth could feel her heart sink. She was afraid to hear what he had to say. "Okay, spill it. What's wrong?"

"You're not sitting down, are you?"

She let out a sigh, a long one, and plopped into a chair. "Okay, I'm sitting down."

"It's done," he stated matter-of-factly, without a hint of emotion.

"What's done? What are you talking about?"

"You are now legally Savannah Mae McDonald."

"W-h-a-a-a-t? You said it would take months!"

"Yeah, I did, but because we were simply returning you to your original name, we were able to get it expedited."

"Oh, my goodness! Travis, are you sure? Is this real? You're not joking, are you?

"Oh, it's real darlin', it's very real. May I be the first to congratulate you, Miss Savannah Mae."

Suddenly, she let out a sob.

"Are you crying?" Travis asked.

"Y-y-y-e-e-s-s," she whimpered.

"Why? I thought you wanted this."

A few moments passed while Savannah Mae composed herself. "I'm sorry, I didn't expect this to happen so soon. I am happy, thrilled, and overwhelmed, all at the same time."

"You know, I'm thinking we need to celebrate. I'll pick you up in an hour."

"Uh, okay. See you soon."

"And wear those boots of yours."

"Which ones?"

"Your riding boots, of course."

She grinned, knowing that could mean only one thing, a few hours riding Annie Oakley on Travis's ranch. It was turning out to be a spectacular day.

As soon as she hung up with Travis she called Ruth, then Jack, and told them the good news. She was so giddy she could barely get it out.

"That's great news, honey," Jack said. "This calls for a real big celebration. Mind if we use your house?"

"Uh, sure," Savannah Mae answered.

"Don't worry about a thing. It will be at two o'clock, on Sunday. I'll call Ruth and Lyle and let them know to bring their gang, and I'll call everyone on our side. If you have any friends you want to invite, call 'em. We are going to celebrate you in style!"

"Oh, Dad, you don't have to go to all that trouble."

"Don't you worry, this day has been a long time coming. Well, gotta go. Bonnie Ada's gotta figure out a menu, and I gotta call Ruth to coordinate."

"Seriously, Dad, you don't have to make a big deal of it."

"Of course, we do. You're a big deal. Gotta go. See you Sunday."

On Saturday afternoon, Savannah Mae's phone rang. She recognized it as her cousin Hattie's number.

"Hey, Hattie! How are you?"

"Great, sister. I know this is sudden ... could you please help me pick out a new dress for a wedding I'm going to next month?"

"Sure, that would be fun. When? Next week?"

"Actually, I want to go tomorrow morning."

Savannah Mae ran her fingers through her hair as she often did when she felt a stressful moment coming on.

"Oh, I'd love to, but tomorrow afternoon is the party at my house and I gotta get things ready."

Hattie's voice turned sweet and syrupy. "Don't worry about that, Savannah Mae, you know that our parents and your Aunt Ruth are going to take care of everything. This will be just a little pre-party girl time." Dixie and Bonnie Ada were standing next to Hattie listening in.

"I don't know, Hattie, I have some last-minute stuff to do."

"We won't be long, I promise."

"Well, okay. What time?"

"Eleven o'clock. There's a special store I want to go to, and that's when they open."

Savannah Mae sighed. "Oh, wow, that'll be cutting it short."

"I know," Hattie responded. "They're holding a dress for me, and I really want your opinion. Please?"

"Okay, as long as we're back by one o'clock, okay?" Savannah Mae was shaking her head, mentally kicking herself for agreeing to the shopping trip. It meant she would have to scramble the rest of the day and evening to make sure the house was in order for the party, something she had planned to do on Sunday morning.

"Great! See you at eleven," Hattie chirped and hung up. She whirled around to face her mother, sisters, Zach, and her dad.

"We're on. Mom, are you sure that the shop will hold the dress we picked out for Savannah Mae?"

Bonnie Ada nodded. "Of course, *cher*, they'll hold it."

"I hope this works," Hattie said. "I'm not sure how I'm going to convince her to get a dress for herself when we're supposedly going there to buy a dress for me. I guess I'll think of something."

Bonnie Ada smiled. "You don't have to. Everything is *c'est bon*. Remember, the dress is already paid for. You just need to get her to try it on. She's probably going to protest, and that's fine. Delilah the owner will hold it, and Zach will pick it up after you leave with Savannah Mae and bring it back to the house. *C'est tout!*" She turned to Honey and Dixie and Jack. "Everyone in and ready to decorate Savannah Mae's house while Hattie keeps her occupied?"

Everyone nodded. Honey pulled on her mother's sleeve. "Can we call ourselves Team Savannah Mae?"

Bonnie Ada looked down at Honey. "Of course, sha, I think that's a lovely idea. Now let's start pulling together all the beaucoup signs and decorations so we can be ready to leave right at eleven o'clock tomorrow."

"What about the cake?" Honey asked, a note of anxiety in her voice.

Dixie piped up. "It's ready to go, little sister. Don't worry, we won't forget it."

"You sure?" Honey asked, looking up at her sister, a look of worry in her eyes.

"Yep, absolutely. In fact, as the leader of Team Savannah Mae, why don't you be the one to make sure we get it out of the fridge?"

Honey's face lit up. "Okay!"

The next morning, all went as planned. Hattie got Savannah Mae out of the house and slowly drove her to the dress shop. Zach followed them in his car and parked half a block away so he could watch them leave the store—his signal to go in and get the dress. Moments after they left, the whole family entered Savannah Mae's house to prepare for the party.

Hattie and Savannah Mae walked into the small shop in downtown Waxahachie. Dresses of every fabric, style, and occasion hung on racks throughout the store. Hattie took her time looking at dresses on every rack. Delilah sidled up to Hattie and gave her a wink. After Hattie looked at every dress, she picked out a couple to try on. Delilah went in the back and brought out the dress that Bonnie Ada had bought for Savannah Mae.

"Hattie, why don't you try on this dress?" Delilah said, "It would go perfect with your blond hair and green eyes."

Hattie twisted her lips and cocked her head from side to side. "Hmm, I don't know."

Savannah Mae walked over and looked at the dress. She held out the skirt and ran her fingers over the silky, green fabric. Her mouth slightly dropped open. "Hattie, are you crazy? This is one of the most stunning dresses I've ever seen. What's not right about it?"

Hattie hunched her shoulders. "I don't know, it just doesn't seem like something that I would wear."

"Well, I would!" Savannah Mae responded.

"Then you try it on," Hattie proposed.

"Why should I try it on? I don't need a dress for a wedding."

"Oh, come on. Humor me. Maybe if I see how it looks on you, I'll like it so much that I'll want to try it on, too."

"Well, okay," she picked up the hanger and headed to the dressing room.

Delilah brought out another half-dozen dresses for Hattie to try on, to stretch out their time at the shop as long as possible. Savannah Mae stepped into a dressing room while Hattie took the one next door. Moments later, Hattie stepped out of her dressing room wearing one of the dresses and Savannah Mae came out right after.

Hattie caught her breath. The green silk dress hugged Savannah Mae's body in all the right places and made her eyes shine like emeralds. Her red hair shimmered as though she was standing in the sun. "Oh my!"

Savannah Mae turned to her. "What?"

"Sister, that is the most stunning dress I've ever seen."

"You like it? I'll take it off so you can try it on."

"No, no, I could never do the dress justice the way you do. It looks like it was custom-made for you."

"Well, it is beautiful," she said, fingering the fabric. Hattie watched her, noticing a look of wistful longing on her face. "However, I don't need a dress. You do."

Hattie hunched her shoulders. "Okay, well, I guess I'll keep trying on dresses."

For the next hour, Hattie took a long time trying on dress after dress. She turned down each one, finding something she didn't like about each of them.

"Come on, Hattie, you should get the yellow one, it's gorgeous," Savannah Mae implored.

"Naw, it just doesn't feel like me," she said as she stepped back into the dressing room. She walked out wearing a sapphire blue dress.

"Oh, Hattie, that dress is gorgeous. Seriously, it's the prettiest dress you've tried on today."

"You think so?"

"I know so! You should buy it. Look in the mirror. See how it makes your skin glow?"

"I appreciate your opinion, I do, but I really don't think I'm going to find a dress today," she moaned.

"Why not? You've tried on at least a dozen that were perfect for you."

Hattie hunched her shoulders. "I don't know. Guess I'm tired or not in the right frame of mind. Come on, let's go."

Savannah Mae rolled her eyes upward and shook her head. As they exited the dressing room Savannah Mae glanced back at the green silk dress, stopped, and gave it one last look. They stepped out of the shop and began walking down the street, in the opposite direction of the car. "There's a great little cafe just up the street that makes the best coffee."

Savannah Mae looked down at her watch. "Hattie, even though this has been fun, it's already past 12:30. I really should get home."

"Oh, come on, it won't take long. Besides, you said you wanted to be home by one o'clock. We still have time."

Savannah Mae sighed, realizing that her sister was not going to budge. When they reached the cafe, Hattie held open the door for Savannah Mae, giving Hattie just enough time to look down the street and observe her brother emerging from the dress shop carrying the green dress and giving her a thumbs up.

Hattie sipped her coffee as slowly as she could while Savannah Mae nearly gulped hers down. She was clearly getting impatient with Hattie, looking at her watch every five minutes. Finally, Hattie finished her coffee. "Okay, I'm ready to go," she said cheerfully, ignoring Savannah Mae's obvious anxiety. They got in the car and instead of heading to Savannah Mae's house, she drove to her own home.

"What are we doing here?" Savannah Mae asked, irritation threading her voice.

"Oh, just one more thing. It won't take but a second. Come on inside," Hattie grinned.

Savannah Mae reluctantly got out of the car and impatiently trudged up the walk to the front door. They stepped into the house and Hattie told her to follow her upstairs to her room. As soon as Hattie opened her bedroom door, Savannah Mae saw the green silk dress hanging on the closet door. In front of it on the floor was a pair of low heels, her own heels, from her own closet. Savannah Mae stood there, paralyzed. "What the. ..."

Hattie stepped over and gave her sister a hug. Savannah Mae stared at her. "This was all planned, wasn't it?" Hattie nodded, grinning.

"Are you even going to a wedding next month?"

Hattie shook her head. "Nope."

"I can't believe this."

"Believe it. Now go ahead and get dressed. I'll do your makeup for you when you're done." Hattie exited the room and closed the door behind her.

As soon as Savannah Mae was dressed and Hattie had applied her makeup, they got back in the car and drove over to Savannah Mae's house, arriving a little after two o'clock. Across the porch, a banner read "Congratulations, Savannah Mae!" They stepped inside the house, and everywhere they looked were decorations, most of them congratulating Savannah Mae, who felt her eyes filling with tears. She turned to Hattie and gave her a long hug.

"Thank you so much."

"You're not mad at me?"

"Well, I was a little. Now I see that you were given the toughest job of all, to keep me distracted and away from the house. I'm sorry if I acted annoyed."

Hattie grinned. Savannah Mae looked around the foyer and realized that everyone was there—Aunt Ruth and Lyle, Annabelle and Tim, Aunt Thelma, Uncle Keith, Gloria and Yolanda from the quilt guild, Travis and Howard Sheridan, Jack, Bonnie Ada, Hattie, Dixie, Honey, Zach, cousins Sue Ann and Charlene, plus a slew of cousins on her father's side whom she had yet to meet. She stood in awe as each person came up to give her their congratulations. She was about to turn away when she felt someone tap on her shoulder. She turned around to see Maggie grinning in front of her.

"Maggie, oh my God! You're here! How did you know?" Savannah Mae squealed, throwing her arms around her.

Maggie pulled back and turned Savannah Mae around. Travis was standing a couple of feet from her. "You can blame this guy," Maggie said. "He called and picked me up at the airport."

Travis stepped up and took Savannah Mae's hands.

"Darlin', you look like an angel that just swooped down from heaven," he said. He peered into her eyes, paralyzing her, rendering her unable to look away. Savannah Mae could feel her cheeks flushing and her knees weakening. "I mean it, Savannah Mae. You're breathtaking. And I couldn't be prouder of you."

Savannah Mae turned to Hattie, who stood within earshot. "Hattie, is this mascara waterproof?"

"No, why?" Hattie answered.

"'Cause it's about to spill down my face," she said.

Travis bent down and embraced her tightly, whispering in her ear, "If you'll let me, I'll give you the biggest kiss of your life later when your whole family isn't watching."

She looked up at him, her eyes sparkling. "Today's an exception. Deal, cowboy."

"Ok, y'all, it's time for gifts," Honey called out. "Let's go to the sitting room."

Everyone shuffled into the room. On an antique cherrywood table lay a pile of wrapped presents. In front of the table, was a wingback chair festooned with ribbons and a note pinned to the top with Savannah Mae's name. Honey escorted her to the chair and told her to sit down. Maggie nestled herself on the floor next to the chair. Savannah Mae opened gift after gift, oohing and aahing over each one, many of which were inscribed with her new name. She had to stop numerous times to dab her eyes to prevent tears from rolling down her cheeks and messing up the perfect job Hattie did on her makeup. When she finished, Travis stepped forward and handed her a small box wrapped in floral paper and tied with a chiffon ribbon. Slowly she unwrapped the gift to find a delicate gold chain. In the middle was her name, Savannah Mae, in script, dotted with tiny diamonds. Savannah Mae looked up at Travis in awe.

"You really shouldn't have," she started to say before he cut her off.

"Yes, I should've. You deserve it." He reached into the box, lifted out the necklace and clasped it around her neck.

"Thank you, Travis. I love it." She stared up at him until Zach broke the moment.

"Hey, I'm starving. Can we eat already?"

On cue, the whole family filed into the kitchen and brought out sliced brisket, pulled pork, a platter piled high with beef ribs, another with baby back pork ribs, Ruth's fried chicken and fried okra, Bonnie Ada's shrimp étouffée and jambalaya, beans, coleslaw, potato salad, homemade rolls, Annabelle's pecan pie, Keith's key lime pie, and Bonnie Ada's signature Doberge cake. Maggie and Hattie carried out a bucket of iced champagne and long-stemmed glasses. Howard Sheridan did the honor of opening the bottles, and Travis poured bubbly into the glasses, handing them to Hattie and Maggie to distribute around the room. He poured sparkling apple juice into a glass for Honey and the other younger cousins.

"Now, for the toast," Jack announced, raising his glass. "To our dearest Savannah Mae, who has come back to us. Congratulations, with all our love."

Savannah Mae had no sooner downed her champagne than Honey took her hand. "Come," she said, pulling her over to the food-laden table. "You have to take your plate of food first before we can."

"No, no, Honey, you go ahead. I'll wait just a bit."

Honey shook her head. "I can't. It's the rule." Worry crossed her face. She looked over at Bonnie Ada who nodded. "The guest of honor goes first."

Savannah Mae looked around at all the faces eagerly waiting to dive into the food. Zach's face paled, looking like he might faint. She chuckled. "Okay then," she said and started filling her plate. She had no sooner finished than Zach began heaping his plate with enough food to fill the stomach of the biggest football player on the hometown team.

When she finished eating, Aunt Ruth took Savannah Mae's hand and guided her into the sitting room, to the chair where Savannah Mae had laid the wedding dress quilt. A wistful look filled Ruth's eyes, as tears of a long-ago ache slipped down her cheeks.

"Is this made from the wedding dress that Emma sewed?" she asked, fingering the fabric.

Savannah Mae nodded. "I didn't want it to languish in that box in the attic. I decided to make it into a quilt as a way to both honor and remember her. Is that all right?" She searched Ruth's face for some kind of reaction.

Ruth patted Savannah Mae's arm. "My dear, it's more than all right. You have done both the dress and your mother a great honor. This way it will be seen and appreciated. After all, it is your heritage, too, not just your mother's."

One by one, all the guests entered the room to see where Savannah Mae had gone. Ruth told them the tale of the dress and how Savannah Mae found it in the attic and made it into the quilt. They all touched the quilt and looked at Savannah Mae in awe.

"This truly is the most spectacular quilt you've ever made," Maggie said, running her fingers over the tiny stitches. "What will you do with it?"

"I think I'll leave it right here so I can see it every day as a reminder of the love that brought me here."

"Oh, look!" Annabelle said, pointing to the family tree Savannah Mae had embroidered, framed, and hung on the wall. "That's the family tree I sent to Savannah Mae."

Everyone turned to look and walked up to it to find their own names.

"Savannah Mae, this is extraordinary," Aunt Ruth said. "Not only have you outdone yourself, but you've honored all of us."

Chapter Fifteen

Travis had been thinking a lot about what Savannah Mae had told him about Dennis and the accident on the way to her wedding with Scott. Something didn't sit right with him. As a lawyer and a former lawman, he had a lawman's sixth sense. Something was wrong, terribly wrong; he knew it lay deep in Dennis's character.

At the party, he pulled Maggie aside and asked her what she knew about the accident and the aftermath. She spilled every detail she knew and told him that she'd always suspected something had been covered up because the police began an investigation, and then suddenly, it was dropped with no public explanation. She shared with him that she watched how Dennis became increasingly obsessed with Savannah Mae and when Scott died, jumped at the opportunity to take over her life.

"Maggie, I've got a lot of contacts out there, people from my law school days. I'm going to look into the case."

Maggie pressed a hand against her heart. "Thank you, Travis. This has gone on too long and it really disturbs me that he's tracked her here. I'm afraid of what he might do. I told Lisbeth, I mean Savannah Mae, that there's something really off about him, but she won't listen. She wants to believe the good in people."

"I've picked up on that," Travis replied. "At this point though, she is taking him seriously. Did she tell you that she went for firearms training and bought a 9mm?"

Maggie nodded. "While I think that's a good idea, honestly, I doubt that if the situation arose where she had to use it against him or anyone that she could. We've known each other our whole lives. She doesn't have it in her."

"I have to agree with you, Maggie. Ya know, initially, I suggested she get a guard dog. She nixed the idea immediately. Said that Sophie wouldn't stand for it."

"She mentioned that," Maggie smiled. "She's crazy about that cat."

"By any chance do you have any details about the accident or any information that would help me look into this further?"

Maggie nodded. "Absolutely! I've got them on my laptop. It's upstairs."

Travis had no sooner given her his email address than Maggie scurried upstairs, fired up her laptop, and emailed him the files. She returned to the party and casually sidled up to Travis. "They're waiting for you in your inbox."

"Is your cell number on the email, in case I have questions?" She nodded. "It's possible that the guy is just your run-of-the-mill dirtbag," he said, "but I can't shake the feeling that there's something a lot more sinister going on."

"Listen to your gut," Maggie told him, "Because there is. And I've got an awful feeling that he will do anything to get her back. I'm truly afraid that he will harm her."

"Not on my watch," he said emphatically, his face clenched tight as an old-time sheriff ready to do battle with a ne'er-do-well.

On Monday morning, Travis opened Maggie's email, which provided a good start. He leaned back in his chair and let out a whistle. He needed to see the actual crash investigation file from law enforcement. He dug around online until he discovered that they were missing.

He picked up his phone and dialed an old friend from law school, Justin Schwartz, a prosecutor who worked for Los Angeles County, where the accident occurred.

"Hey, Travis," he answered.

"Justin, how are ya?"

"Not bad, and you? What's new in the Lone Star State?"

"Same old. Cattle keep calving, cicadas keep humming, and the fences keep needin' fixin'."

"What a life," Justin chuckled. "Are you practicing any law or just living the life of the gentleman rancher on that beautiful stretch of land?"

Travis laughed. "Yeah, I'm still practicing, which brings me to the reason for my call. I need your help on a case."

"What's up?"

Travis told Justin about Savannah Mae, her engagement, the car crash, his inability to read the law enforcement records, Dennis stalking her, everything.

"Okay, and may I ask about your interest in the case?"

"She's both a client and a friend. My dad handled her adoption, as well as the inheritance that brought her back to Texas. Justin, there's a lotta loose ends, things that don't add up. I understand that nothing ever came of it. Looks like it was never fully investigated nor was a case filed, which strikes me as odd considering there was a death in the accident. It's like a whole mess of cow pies. I need to see those law enforcement records because if there's anything not right here, and I suspect that there is, I've got to do something about it. This woman's life may be in danger."

"Is your interest in the case more than casual?"

"What difference does it make if it is?"

"None. You just sound pretty passionate about helping this woman."

"You're right. I fell for her the minute I laid eyes on her. As we like to say around here, she's pretty as a cherry pie, but it's more than that. She could be in real trouble."

"Okay, this sounds pretty interesting," Justin said. "I'll have to do some digging. I should be able to get the records to you in the next couple of days."

"Thanks, Justin. I owe you."

"Naw. Happy to help."

Chapter Sixteen

"Savannah Mae, do you ever miss living near the coast? Ocean breezes, walking on the beach?" Travis asked her one day over lunch.

Savannah Mae swallowed a bite of her Cajun chicken sandwich, sat back, and considered the question.

"Sometimes," she finally said. "Whenever it would get really hot at home, not hot like here, but what we considered hot, yeah, I'd go out to the beach. Usually, it was with Maggie. We spent a lot of time just hanging out there. She's a surfer."

"Maggie?" he arched a brow. "Didn't take her for a surfer."

"Oh, yeah. She's good. She's even won a few competitions. Here, I'll show you." She pulled up a video on her phone showing Maggie crushing a wave and coming out unscathed and still standing.

"I'm impressed," he said, replaying the video. "And do you surf, too?"

"Me? No. I love the water, but I'm not a board surfer, not like her. I've done some bodysurfing, which is fun, as long as the waves aren't too big. Maggie's fearless. She doesn't bother unless the waves are huge. Why do you ask?"

"Have you been to the Texas coast?"

185

She shook her head. "Maggie and I have talked about visiting some of the surfing beaches on one of her trips out here, but we've yet to do it. Why?"

"I thought that if you're missing water and beaches, I'd like to take you down to the Texas coast. Might be a nice distraction for a few days to go somewhere new, somewhere you don't have to think about a thing, other than where to eat supper. You can do some serious shell hunting, watch the seagulls catch fish, and swim in the gulf waters."

Savannah Mae's eyes widened, like a child who's learned she's going to Disneyland. The sides of her mouth curved into a little grin. "Where do you have in mind?"

"Now, that I can't tell you. Trust me to take you somewhere you'll love?"

Savannah Mae grinned. "Sure do, cowboy. When should I get ready?"

"How about we leave next Monday morning? Can you ask one of your sisters or cousins to take care of your house and Sophie? We'll be gone a few days."

"I'll see if someone can do it. Probably Annabelle and Tim— they adore Sophie. I'll make some calls when I get home. Oh, what town, and where will we be staying?"

"The family beach house, that's all I'm going to say." His eyes twinkled with amusement.

Monday morning, Annabelle and Tim moved into Savannah Mae's house, bidding her goodbye from the porch as Travis whisked her away in Old Nellie, his red pickup truck.

"How long is the drive?" she asked, trying to suppress her giddiness.

"Takes about four hours from here." He reached over and took her hand in his.

The trip passed quickly, and just after noon, they rolled into Galveston's historic district, home to countless Victorian homes. Savannah Mae was dumbfounded by the architecture, calling out for Travis to look at one house, then another, each more elegant than the last. He drove through the neighborhood, turned toward the other side of the island, and hung a right on Seawall Drive. Savannah Mae couldn't take her eyes off the beach; seeing the gulf waters for the first time brought back memories of growing up in a beach town. Her whole life she had drawn strength from the water that crashed on the shoreline. She would stand on the beach with water lapping at her ankles and often wondered whose ankles this very water had touched on a distant shore.

"Oh, Travis, please stop. I gotta get out. I just have to put my feet in the water. It's been so long."

"Hang tight, Savannah Mae. Where we're going, there will be plenty of sand and water, all you could want." He glanced at her and winked. "Remember I asked you to trust me?"

She nodded.

"Are you hungry? 'Cause we can stop if you want to eat."

"Okay, is there a place with a view of the water?"

"Yeah, we can do that," he said as he pulled into the parking lot of Gaido's Seafood Restaurant opposite the beach. Known for the gigantic blue crab resting on its roof, many considered it the best seafood place on the island.

"Welcome back, Mr. Sheridan. Nice to see you again," the hostess greeted them. She guided them toward a table with a window overlooking the water.

The waiter arrived and greeted Travis by name. "Your usual, Mr. Sheridan?" he asked.

Travis nodded and the waiter scurried off to get their drinks.

"Wow, you must spend a lot of time here. The staff knows you," Savannah Mae said as she sat down.

Travis winked at her.

When the waiter returned and set down two mojitos, a rum and mint cocktail, he asked if they were ready to order. Savannah Mae remarked that she hadn't had time to look at the menu.

"Do you mind if I order for us?" Travis proposed. "Everything on the menu is top-notch, you can close your eyes and point to anything, and you'll love it. However, I've got a few favorites that I think you'd like."

"Sure, I'm game."

"Nick, we'll start with jumbo lump crab served over sliced avocado with rémoulade sauce to share. The lady will have the pecan-crusted mahi-mahi, and I'll have the Parmesan-crusted red snapper." He looked up at the waiter "Thanks, Nick. I think that'll cover it."

He raised his glass, "A toast?" Savannah Mae nodded. "Here's to a relaxing few days on the island, free of stress and everyday cares."

"Works for me," Savannah Mae clinked her glass with Travis's and took a sip. "Oh my!" she purred.

"How could you know that I absolutely love mojitos?" She took another sip. "Is the place where we're staying near here?"

"Why?"

"'Cause I'm gonna have to come back here and have a few more of these. Maybe every day."

"Ha!" Travis laughed. "You just got here."

A glimmer filled her eyes, as a warm glow of the afternoon sun bathed her face through the window. "Yeah, but I really, really love mojitos. What a great surprise!"

Savannah Mae swooned over the crab and avocado appetizer and their fish entrées. They stole bites of each other's dishes. "Oh, my gosh," she said as she cleaned every morsel off her plate. "I didn't realize how much I missed fresh seafood."

"You don't eat seafood at home?"

"I do, but it's never this fresh. These taste like they caught them this morning."

"It's possible they did. At the latest, yesterday. They're well known for their seafood."

Nick returned to the table. Seeing the empty plates, he said, "I trust that everything was to your satisfaction?"

"Sure was, Nick," Travis remarked, patting his belly. "I'm feelin' as fine as the hair on a frog's head."

Savannah Mae snorted and quickly covered her mouth in embarrassment. Travis let out a roaring laugh.

"And you, madam? Did you enjoy your meal?" Nick asked. Savannah Mae didn't trust herself to speak and simply nodded.

When they got back into the truck, Savannah Mae apologized profusely. "I am so sorry. I hope I didn't embarrass you. I've never heard anyone say they felt as fine as the hair on a frog's head."

Travis grinned as wide as his mouth would go. "Well, sweetheart, you're in Texas, and here you never know what people are gonna say."

"Did you make that up, about the frog?"

"Oh, heck no. A lot of people say it. You've never heard it before?"

Savannah Mae shook her head. "Guess I still have a lot to learn."

"Yep," Travis agreed, thinking he would pull out a few more doozies in the coming days. It made him happy to see her laugh.

They traveled down the two-lane road, passing through Jamaica Beach. She took quick glances at him as he drove along the coastline. A good-natured smile was sculpted onto his face. A few miles later, they turned left down a small lane toward the gulf shore. They stopped at a large home painted Mediterranean blue overlooking the beach, and he pulled the truck into the covered parking area underneath the home. They got out, Travis grabbed their bags, and he led her up the internal stairs, unlocking the door at the top. They stepped inside and Savannah Mae stopped to look all around while he set their luggage down.

"Come," he took her hand. "You gotta see the view." He led her to the sliding glass doors, unlocked them, and pulled her onto the expansive balcony. The sea breeze blew her hair back. She stepped up to the railing, closed her eyes, and let the ocean air wash over her.

"I could stand here forever," she said with her eyes still closed. "This is about as close to heaven as it gets."

Travis stood behind her and wrapped his arms around her waist, laying his head on her shoulder. "Yep, it's about as fine as. ..."

"I know, I know, the hair on a frog's head," Savannah Mae said. "Ya know, I'm thinking it's even finer, maybe even as fine as the hair on a blue crab's head."

"That's really sayin' somethin'," Travis turned her around, took her face into his hands and kissed her passionately as the waves crashed on the shore. She didn't protest, melting into him.

He led her down to the bottom level, where they took off their shoes and headed out to a little wooden boardwalk that crossed from the property onto the beach. Soft, cerulean waves washed up on the shore. They strolled for what seemed like miles, collecting seashells, drawing their names in the sand with driftwood, and walking in and out of the warm, shallow water. They sat on the beach and watched dusk descend, hues of orange and magenta slowly sliding across the powder blue sky.

"Is this really your family home?" Savannah Mae asked.

"It's the family vacation home. We have an office in Houston, and whenever my dad or I have business in Houston, if we have a few extra days, we'll come down here to unwind. Doesn't take long for the place to work its magic."

"It sure worked on me," she whispered, her emerald eyes translucent, shining, and content.

"Don't get me wrong, I love my home, I love Waxahachie, but this," she said, reaching out her hand as though stroking the horizon, "this is truly paradise." She leaned against his shoulder, watching the waves crash on the shore.

When they got back to the house, Travis took her bag to one large bedroom and his own bag to another. She followed him into his room.

"I wondered how this was going to work," she said.

He turned to her, "How what was going to work? The sleeping arrangements?"

She nodded.

"Did you think I was going to push you into sleeping with me?"

"The thought crossed my mind."

Travis walked over to her, put his hands on her shoulders, and held her at arm's length, gazing straight into her eyes. "I hope that you know me well enough by now to realize that isn't my style. Yes, I am attracted to you. Intensely attracted. Yes, I think we've got something real special developing here. And yes, I hope it becomes something more. But I also know that you've been through a world of hurt, and you're still going through it with that Dennis fella. Whenever you're ready for something more, if you want something more, I'm here. I'm not going anywhere."

Savannah Mae broke his hold on her, and wrapped her arms around him, embracing him tightly. "Travis, you have no idea what that means to me." She rolled her lips inward to compose herself and looked up at him. "Some men would take advantage of a woman in a situation like this, figuring that she owed him something because he brought her to such an exquisite place. Travis, you are so different from any man I've ever met. You redefine the term *gentleman,* and I am so lucky to have you in my life."

"Savannah Mae, I am the lucky one. Now, let's stop getting all sentimental trying to prove who's luckier and see what's in the fridge."

"There's food here?"

"Oh, yeah, this is a first-class joint we run here," he mimicked in his best James Cagney voice.

They stepped into the kitchen, he opened the fridge, and they found a pitcher of mojitos and enough food to feed a family of eight for a week.

"Mojitos?" she gasped. "Who stocked the fridge? Who knew to have a pitcher of mojitos ready?"

Travis shrugged, poured them each a glass, and took out a variety of appetizers: Texas Twinkies with a note saying to heat them in the oven, black bean dip and chips, deviled eggs topped with sweet jalapeño relish, Frito pie, and a few peanut butter cookies topped with Hershey's kisses.

"Oh, my goodness," Savannah Mae barely got the words out looking at all the food.

"I thought that we'd eat a bit, then drive into town. There's an Artwalk in the Historic District tonight where the artists serve champagne in their studios. There're some real talented artists in Galveston. Sound okay?"

"Oh, more than okay. What a treat. You know you're spoiling me, right?"

"Absolutely. That was the whole point of bringing you here. Eat and drink up, darlin'."

After dining, Savannah Mae walked down the hall and stepped into her room to freshen up. She didn't see her suitcase and realized she was in the wrong room. She turned to leave when she saw a framed photo of a young boy on the wall. Savannah Mae stepped up to it to get a closer look. He was clearly a happy child, a grin spreading across his face as he looked into the camera lens, smiling with pure innocence. She ran her forefinger over the photo, musing about who the child was and why his photo was hanging on this wall. It mesmerized her so much that she didn't hear Travis enter the room.

"Are you lost?" he asked, an annoyance in his voice.

She heard his sharp tone, spun around quickly, and shook her head. "No, no. I thought this was my room. When I realized it wasn't I started to leave and saw the photo of this beautiful boy. I couldn't take my eyes off of him. I'm sorry, I didn't mean to be nosy."

Travis stared hard at her, his arms crossed over his chest.

"May I ask who he is?" she asked timidly, noticing a perturbed side of him she'd never seen before.

"He's my son," he answered curtly.

Savannah Mae felt her heart skip a beat. Her jaw dropped open slightly. "Your son? Where is he?"

Travis swallowed hard, clearly trying to settle his emotions and not doing a particularly good job of it. His face flushed. He balled his hands into fists that pushed against his sides.

"He died in a swimming pool at a neighborhood party. My wife was supposed to be watching him. She turned away, and in moments he drowned. I was out of town at the time."

A deafening, choking silence filled the room. The anger and sadness in his eyes made her feel numb and mute, and unable to express any words of comfort without sounding trivial. They continued to stare at one another.

"My God, Travis," she finally said. "I can't say how sorry I am." She ran her hands up to the sides of her face, holding it, afraid if she let go, she would break. Mustering the courage to say something, anything, to relieve his sorrow she softly murmured, "Parents aren't supposed to bury their children."

Travis jabbed his hands into his pockets and stared at the floor. He heaved in a big breath of air, and after a few moments, he looked up, the angry flush fading from his face, his voice calmer. "Thank you, you're right. Parents aren't supposed to bury their kids, it's supposed to be the other way around."

Savannah Mae moved to leave the room; Travis caught her arm. "You're probably wondering if I'm still married. I'm not."

"Travis, you don't have to talk about this."

"Yeah, I do," he pressed the conversation. "I've been wanting to tell you because this is a big part of me. It was my worst nightmare, one I couldn't foresee, and now one I can't forget." He looked away for a few moments and back at her. "I know it was an accident, and we were equally grief-stricken. I wanted to move on, I tried to move past it, but I couldn't because I could not stop thinking about how her negligence led to his death. I knew that I'd never be able to forgive her for that. In the end, it destroyed our marriage."

Savannah Mae stepped closer to him and gingerly wrapped her arms around him, holding him for several moments until he backed away. He reached down, clasped her hand, and silently led her out of the room.

"Come on, let's go into town. I don't want this to spoil our evening," he said looking down at her, holding her gaze. Savannah Mae watched his eyes soften, the harshness of a few minutes before gone.

The next morning, golden light bathed the room as Savannah Mae awoke to a knock on her door. She looked at her watch. It was already 9:30.

"Come in."

Travis walked in carrying a tray with coffee cups. Savannah Mae began to get out of bed.

"No, no, stay right there," he said.

"Breakfast in bed?" Savannah Mae asked.

"Nope. Just coffee," he smiled. "Sit up."

She placed a pillow behind her back. He handed her a cup of coffee, and as she sipped it, she glanced up and saw a painting leaning against a mirror above a chest of drawers. It was of an older woman, her silver hair spilling down her back. She was sitting on a chair in front of a tall window, soft beams of daylight flooding the room, cascading over her like delicate lace. Savannah Mae felt a strange, familiar sensation come over her.

"I know it must have seemed rather spontaneous of me to buy that painting, and it was. Even so, I'm glad I bought it. I can't explain why I was so drawn to it. I just knew that I had to buy it because it was supposed to be mine."

Travis looked over at the painting and then back at Savannah Mae. "It's more than a little ironic that the woman in the painting has that mysterious look in her eyes that you sometimes get. It's almost as if the artist painted it of you, of an older you. Remember she remarked about that when she was wrapping it up?"

Savannah Mae nodded. "Yeah, she also said decades of painting have taught her that while faces change over a lifetime, the eyes don't," Savannah Mae recalled. "I think I bought it because she also said that someday my grandchildren will look at the painting and ask who painted it of me. I loved that."

She sat holding her coffee, mesmerized by the painting and feeling its magnetic hold on her. Travis coughed into his fist to get her attention. She looked up at him and then back at the painting.

"Okay, lazy bones, time to get up. I've got something planned for us today."

She tilted her head to the side. "Planned? What?"

"Just get dressed in something comfortable. Loose clothing. Sneakers. And put on some sunscreen, we'll be outside for a while."

She nodded.

"Okay. Meet you downstairs in 30 minutes. We have a reservation in town."

Half an hour later, Travis and Savannah Mae got in the truck, and he handed her a granola bar. She looked at him and raised her eyebrows.

"Breakfast," he stated.

"Aren't you going to eat something?"

"I already ate while you were sleeping."

A short while later, they pulled up in front of a shop with a sign that read "Segway Tours."

Savannah Mae looked at the sign and back at Travis. "We're taking a Segway tour? That's cool, but I don't know how to ride a Segway."

"Nobody does until the first time. It's fun, and it's a great way to see the town."

"Okey dokey," she said, getting out of the truck. "I'm gonna take your word for it."

They walked into the shop, met the manager, watched a safety video, picked out helmets, and began practicing on the Segways. The guide instructed them and their fellow Segway riders to follow him outside and around the block. By the time they came back to their starting point, Savannah Mae was zooming around like she had been riding a Segway her whole life. She looked over at Travis, a big grin plastered on her face.

"You're right! This is bowls of fun!"

The guide explained that they would be seeing some of the tree sculptures of Galveston, carved from century-old oaks that had fallen during Hurricane Ike in 2008. Local artists used chainsaws to carve them into whimsical sculptures. A few minutes later, they pulled up in front of a larger-than-life-size Dalmatian, carved from a tree that stood on the grounds of City Hall near a fire station. Painted white with big black dots, he looked like he was about to jump on a fire truck any minute. The guide took them down Post Office Street and stopped near the backyard of a three-story, stately Victorian home.

"Oh, Travis, look at that!" Savannah Mae pointed to a tall, slender angel cradling a small bunny in her arms. "Who would have thought to carve a tree like that?"

"Actually, it was the owner's idea," the guide interjected. Everyone looked at him. "The homeowner once worked for *Playboy*."

A buzz flew through the group of tourists. One man called out, "You mean she's a *Playboy* bunny?"

The guide answered, "Well, that was years ago. She also runs a rescue bunny sanctuary. And now, y'all know a little town secret. Let's move on. ..."

They dashed around town seeing a carved pod of dolphins cresting a wave, several mermaids, the Tin Man and Toto from the Wizard of Oz, a geisha, a giant outstretched hand reaching for the sky, a guitar, and a grandmother reading a book to her grandchildren.

As they pulled back up to the tour office, Travis asked, "Have a favorite?"

Savannah Mae pursed her lips, thinking. "I don't know if I could choose just one. There were several. Maybe the two herons? Or the lion nodding off to sleep? No, no, it was definitely the angel cradling the bunny."

"Did the guide's story about the homeowner influence you?"

Savannah Mae scoffed. "Absolutely not. I thought it was very clever."

They returned their Segways, walked outside, and collapsed in the truck.

"You know, riding a Segway is kinda exhausting. I can feel my backside and legs aching a little," Savannah Mae remarked.

"Like the way you feel after riding a horse?"

"Yes, as a matter of fact, that's exactly how it feels," Savannah Mae replied. "Oh, Travis, that was amazing. Really, really amazing. Whew!" she blew out a puff of air. "Thank you so much."

"You ready for some mimosas on the beach?" he grinned at her.

"Hello! Take me to your castle, dear man. I'm more than ready."

They spent the rest of the day on the beach, sharing a picnic lunch, collecting more shells, walking for miles, and basking in the serene gulf waters. Savannah Mae couldn't remember the last time she felt so tired, yet so exhilarated that she doubted she would be able to sleep that night. Every nerve in her body felt alive, as though an electric euphoria was coursing through her veins. Even so, her mind was at ease, a tranquility filled her and eased the anxiety Dennis was trying to force into her life. Dusk began to fall as the sun pitched into the horizon. The moon rose over the water, and speckles of stars peaked out of a dark blue silken sky. Travis gathered some nearby wood and built a fire on the beach in front of the house.

"Hey, tend the fire for a few minutes, will ya?" he asked as he turned and ran up the stairs into the house. He brought down toasting forks, marshmallows, a chocolate bar, and graham crackers.

She sighed, a little smile crossing her lips. "What will you think of next?"

He shrugged. "I'm sure I'll come up with something."

They dined on s'mores, and cuddled in front of the crackling fire, watching the undulating flames moving like a hypnotic dancer enticing her lover. He stared at her hands and ran his fingers over her fingers, as though by touching them he would learn everything about her, all that she kept inside, the deepest secrets of her subconscious. Although she smiled, he knew that her fears were never far away. He could feel it and see a tinge of worry in her eyes.

She turned and looked up at him. His eyes seemed more silver than gray, more brilliant than usual. She reached up and outlined his face with her forefinger.

"You all right?" he asked.

"I have not been this at peace or felt this safe in a long time. You did that by bringing me here. By all that you've done for me. Your kindness is overwhelming me, in a good way."

He kissed the top of her head and smiled. They sat for several minutes watching the fire and breathing in the sea air, letting it fill their senses.

"Remember I told you that I haven't always been a lawyer?" he said, breaking the silence.

She looked up at him. "Yeah. Didn't you join your dad's law firm after law school?"

"I think I also told you that I worked in law enforcement for several years before that."

"You did. Were you a police officer?"

"Close. I was a deputy in the Tarrant County Sheriff's Department."

"Why did you leave?"

"Don't get me wrong, I loved the work. I did a lot of community outreach, really got to know people, and helped them. I was in the process of applying to be a Texas Ranger. I'd gotten great feedback on my interviews and was told I was the leading candidate for their open position."

"So, what happened?"

He looked away, then back at Savannah Mae. "My son's death turned my world upside down. I couldn't focus, couldn't prioritize. I was falling apart, which was unlike me. I told the Rangers I was withdrawing my name and took a leave from Tarrant County. I wanted to go back to work, but my heart wasn't in it, and when you're working in law enforcement, your heart has to be in it or you jeopardize the lives of those you work with and the public's safety. My dad suggested I go to law school and come to work for him. I clerked for him while I was in law school. Then when I graduated and passed the bar, I joined the firm. I bought the ranch not long after as a place I could retreat to, a place where nature and the horses helped me heal."

She turned to look him in the eye. "This explains a lot. You know, there's something to be said for destiny."

"How so?"

"For some time, I've thought that my destiny has never been my own. It was decided long ago, by my birth parents and by my grandmother before I was born. And by the wonderful people who adopted me. And yet, that same destiny brought me back here. And your destiny took you from law enforcement to practicing law to the ranch that you love. In my case, all along, my history has been about my people, my family, and all they've given me and given up for me. It took me coming to Texas to understand what was missing in my life. It's always been about the love that has surrounded me. Even if I didn't know it. And now, just when I least expected it, I'm finding a different kind of love."

The night air stilled around them as they stared at one another, eyes locked, until Travis took her hand.

"Travis, do you understand what I'm saying?"

"Perfectly," he raised her hand to his mouth, gently brushing it with his lips.

Chapter Seventeen

ust after noon the next day, as Travis pulled up in front of Savannah Mae's house, Annabelle and Tim came out to greet them.

"Hey, cousins," Savannah Mae called to them, stepping out of the truck. "Did Sophie let you get any sleep at all?"

"Barely," Annabelle answered. "She sure is an affectionate cat. We loved taking care of her."

"I can't thank you enough," Savannah Mae smiled at Annabelle.

"It was our pleasure. Hey, let me help you with your things." She picked up the wrapped painting. "What's in this thing? It feels like a picture."

"It is! Come inside, and I'll show it to you."

Travis started to follow when Tim asked him to show him something in his truck's engine.

"Sure. It's running a little hot right now," he said, opening the hood.

As soon as Annabelle and Savannah Mae were out of earshot, Tim turned to Travis.

"Look, I needed an excuse to talk to you."

Travis furrowed his brow. "What's up?"

"The second night y'all were gone, a strange guy came to the door asking for Savannah Mae. We wouldn't tell him if she was there, and he began demanding to see her. Said he was her fiancé. Annabelle and I had just come back from practicing at the range, and the guy saw our holstered guns. He got really upset. Guess he doesn't like guns. Anyway, we told him to leave or we'd call the police."

"Let me guess. A blond guy in designer clothing, lots of swagger, acts like he owns the place."

"You know this guy?"

"Sort of. He's been stalking Savannah Mae, and there's a restraining order against him. He's not supposed to come within 500 feet of her house."

"Is he her fiancé?"

Travis shook his head. Travis rolled his lips inward, bit down, and made a conscious effort not to say much. "Thanks for letting me know. The guy is a real piece of work. Annabelle isn't telling Savannah Mae, is she?"

"No, no, we decided that I'd let you know, and you could tell her. We didn't want to upset her."

"Wise move. Thanks."

"Savannah Mae isn't in danger, is she?"

"Not on my watch, she isn't. Thanks again, Tim."

Travis and Savannah Mae helped Annabelle and Tim take their belongings to their car, while both of them scratched Sophie behind the ears, and bid the cousins goodbye. They stood on the porch waving as Annabelle and Tim drove away.

"I have to take care of a few things at the office and should get back to the ranch," Travis said, cradling Savannah Mae's face in his hands. She nodded, and he bent down and lightly brushed her lips with his. "By the way, would it be okay if I pulled up the security footage on the house?"

Savannah Mae pulled back. "Why? Is something wrong?" A note of alarm infused her voice.

"Not sure. I just want to check the footage. Tim said he saw shadows outside, and someone came to the front door demanding to see you. From Tim's description of the guy it sounds like it was Dennis. I want to see what the cameras caught."

Savannah Mae pinched her brows together.

"Listen, don't worry. I'm gonna check it out. I'll call you after I review it, okay?"

Savannah Mae nodded. "Okay. Oh, Travis?"

"Yeah?"

"Thanks for taking me to Galveston, and for everything. And thank you for talking me into having those cameras installed."

He nodded, bent down, kissed her lightly on the cheek, and left the house. He turned back just as she was about to close the door. "One more thing. ..."

"I know," she cut him off. "I'll make sure all the doors and windows are locked."

He tipped his cowboy hat to her and walked down the steps to his truck.

Chapter Eighteen

ravis drove straight to the law offices in downtown Dallas and pulled up the security camera footage of Savannah Mae's house. Just as Tim described, he saw Dennis confronting Tim and Annabelle at the front door. He scrolled slowly through the next several days and saw him walking about the property in the evenings, looking in windows, as well as parking across the street and watching the house with outrageously oversized binoculars, which in spite of the seriousness, made Travis chuckle.

"You're a piece of work," he said to the image of Dennis in his car with the binoculars. "Jerk."

He continued scanning the video up through the present day to see if he had been in the area when Travis dropped Savannah Mae off at home earlier in the day. He was not but figured it wouldn't be long before he resurfaced. He picked up his phone and dialed the cell phone of the Ellis County sheriff.

"Hey, Travis," the sheriff answered. "What can I do ya?"

"Remember the restraining order that was issued on behalf of Savannah Mae McDonald—she used to be called Lisbeth James—in Waxahachie?"

"Yeah, I do. You and I went to the house, confronted the guy, and I told him that if he got within 500 feet of the house, I'd cuff him. How's that workin'?"

Travis provided details of the video and expressed concern that the guy was going to keep coming back. "Savannah Mae is strong. She wants nothing to do with him. You and I have seen plenty of sleazy characters like him. He's such a loose cannon that I'm worried he may harm her."

"I see your point," the sheriff said. "In normal circumstances, the restraining order should have contained him. Obviously, this guy thinks that the law doesn't apply to him."

"Exactly. Could you assign one of your deputies to do hourly drive-by surveillance?"

"If things aren't busy, I can do that, but if this guy is as shrewd as he seems to be, he may duck if he sees one of our cars. For maximum protection, I suggest she hire an off-duty officer to keep watch overnight."

"Duly noted, thanks for your help."

Next, Travis pulled up the law enforcement records that Justin sent him. He leaned back in his chair and let out a long, slow whistle reading through them, backing up the document several times to reread portions to verify details. The report stated that Scott's car was tampered with, as well as the driver's side seat belt. When the steering and brakes ceased working, the car veered off the road, and when the car headed full bore into a large tree, the driver's seat belt failed, causing the driver to go through the windshield, an impact that killed Scott immediately. When the passenger, Dennis, was interviewed by the police, it was observed that not only did he not suffer any major injuries, but he was also extremely nervous, was sweating, and refused to answer questions. The final record stated that Dennis was the likely suspect, and he would be charged with first-degree murder. After that, there were no further notes. It appears that nothing ever happened, that Dennis was not charged, and the case was dropped.

"What?" Travis shouted at the screen. He picked up the phone and called Justin. "Hey, sorry to be abrupt, buddy, but I just read the accident report you sent me. Did you know that Dennis Dragna was never charged and the case was dropped?"

"Yeah, I did. I wanted you to see the details for yourself. There was some really bad stuff going on surrounding this incident. It involves people with a higher pay grade than me."

"So, that's it? The case got dropped, no follow-up?" Travis asked.

"As far as the police and the court are concerned, it was. There's someone else you should talk to who can give you more background than I can."

"Who's that?"

"An investigative reporter who got to the bottom of the incident. He's pretty skittish to talk about it. Tell him you're a friend and that I recommended he speak with you. I'll warn you, he'll be reticent and will likely speak with you only if you agree not to reveal your sources."

"Done. Text me his name and number. Thanks."

Travis reached out to the reporter who, as Justin warned him, was guarded. He told Travis to call him in the evening at his home where he would be able to speak more freely.

When Travis called that evening, the reporter first asked for his promise that he would not divulge where he learned the information that he was about to share with him.

"You got it," Travis said. "Sounds like this is a bigger story than I expected."

"You have no idea," the reporter remarked. "First off, I discovered that Dennis Dragna comes from a very wealthy Los Angeles family with underworld connections that have been operating in L.A. since before Prohibition."

"Okay, how does that factor into the accident?"

"I was just getting to that. Dennis's wealthy family paid off the DA and a judge not to indict Dennis for murder."

"What?!"

"Yeah, furthermore I discovered a litany of charges filed against Dennis for various misdemeanors, all dismissed by the same judge."

"Unbelievable," Travis remarked, running his hand over the top of his head. "Why didn't anything come of your discoveries? Why didn't any articles appear?"

"That's where this story gets ugly. I talked ad nauseam with my editor about my findings. He was totally behind me. The first article, the bombshell article, was written and ready to go to press. Then, before that happened, I began receiving anonymous threats against my life and against those of my wife and kids."

"What?"

"Yeah. I'm pretty sure that the threats were the work of Dragna's family."

The reporter told Travis that he couldn't risk the lives of his family and told his editor he had to walk away from it. His editor wasn't happy about it but understood, saying he would find another reporter to take over the story. When the editor explained the situation to other staff reporters, no one wanted any part of it. Understandably, none of them was willing to risk their lives for the story.

Travis thanked the reporter and dialed Justin. "Hey, just talked to your reporter. This is a bona fide colossal cow patty."

"That's why I wanted you to talk to him. Not sure what can be done at this point."

"Justin, you're getting soft in your old age. Of course, there's somethin' that can be done."

"Yeah? Like what?"

"Like moving the case to another county and reopening the investigation there," Travis responded. "That a-hole got away with murder. If it can be proven that he did it, and he gets put away, Savannah Mae will be able to live her life without fear. And I'm gonna make sure she gets that."

Travis hung up the phone and sat back on his couch, stretching out his long legs on the rustic wooden chest he used as a coffee table and punching one of his fists into the palm of his other hand.

Chapter Nineteen

inally, several months after Savannah Mae first met with her, the private investigator called to say she had found Emma, who now went by the name Emma Lisa Jenkins. She had married 25 years before, never had a family, and was now living in an assisted living home in the Savannah, Georgia, area.

"Assisted living? Are you sure?" Savannah Mae asked. "Why would she be there? She can't be more than 48 years old."

"Due to federal HIPAA privacy laws, I was not able to find out anything about her medical condition. I was, however, able to confirm that she is definitely a resident in the home. All I can offer you is the name, location, and phone number of the place. Do you want it?" the investigator pressed.

"Of course." Savannah Mae took down all the info, hung up, and sat dazed, staring at the piece of paper. She pulled out her laptop and looked up the home. Then she called Aunt Ruth, who was relieved to hear about Emma but heartbroken that she suffered some medical condition that warranted her living in an assisted living facility.

"I'm going to fly out there and see her. Will you come with me, Aunt Ruth?" Savannah Mae asked, a pleading tone in her voice. "I just knew she was still alive. Though I must admit I never dreamed she would be in an assisted living home."

"Of course, dear. I can't imagine what happened for her to end up there. I wouldn't miss this trip for anything."

Three weeks later, they landed at the Savannah/Hilton Head International Airport on a warm day, skies a light blue with scattered puffy clouds dotted above. They rented a car and, before they departed the lot, Savannah Mae put the home's address into her phone. A half-hour later, they pulled up in front of the facility. "This is it, Aunt Ruth. Are you prepared for this?"

"Yes, I think so, dear. It's been a long time coming. Are you?" she reached over and squeezed her niece's hand. Savannah Mae nodded. She got out of the car, opened the trunk, and reached into her travel case. She took out the wedding dress quilt.

"Oh, my, what did you bring that for?" Aunt Ruth asked, her eyes wide with surprise.

"You know, I'm not sure," Savannah Mae answered. "I hadn't planned on bringing it, but when I was walking through the living room on my way out, I saw it. Something told me that I should bring it along. I packed it at the last minute."

Aunt Ruth wrapped her arm around Savannah Mae's shoulders, giving her a gentle squeeze. They walked to the door. Before they entered, Savannah Mae stopped and looked at her aunt.

"Ready?" she asked the older woman.

"Yes," Ruth nodded. "If you are."

They entered the building and stopped at the desk to ask where to find Emma Jenkins. The fuzzy-haired receptionist pointed down a long hallway. A sign indicated that the hallway led to the independent living unit.

"Excuse me, but we thought she lives in the assisted living section," Savannah Mae said.

"No. She's definitely in the independent living section," the woman responded. "Once you enter independent living, go to the end of the hallway. She's in the last room on your right."

They thanked the receptionist and walked down the hall, where they found the room with Emma's name on the door. Ruth and Savannah Mae looked at one another and knocked on the door. They heard footsteps, followed by the door opening. A tall woman with shoulder-length striking red hair, dressed in a colorful blouse and pants, wearing pumps, jewelry, and makeup opened the door.

"Yes?" she started to say, looking at Ruth and Savannah Mae. Then her face froze.

"Emma?" Ruth asked.

"Is that you, Ruthie?" Emma asked.

Ruth nodded just as Emma stepped out and threw her arms around Ruth, hugging her so tightly that Ruth had to peel her off so she could see her face to face.

"What are you doing here?" Emma asked, wiping at the tears falling down her face.

"I should be asking you the same thing," Ruth responded.

"How did you find me?"

Ruth put her arm around Savannah Mae's waist. "Your daughter, Savannah Mae, found you."

Emma's jaw fell open as she looked at Savannah Mae. "You're my daughter? Really? This isn't some kind of joke?"

Savannah Mae said, "No, I really am your daughter. My name is Savannah Mae McDonald."

Emma reached over and touched Savannah Mae's curls and ran her fingers across her cheek. "You must be. You have our red hair and Jack's eyes. Come in, both of you, we have a lot to talk about."

When Savannah Mae sat down, Emma noticed that she had something in her lap.

"What is that?" she asked Savannah Mae.

"It's your dress," Ruth answered, "your wedding dress made into a quilt." Savannah Mae got up and placed it in Emma's lap.

Emma's eyes widened, and her mouth slowly dropped open as she began to unfold the quilt. "Yes, yes, I recognize the fabrics. I'd forgotten all about it. Figured that Mother threw it out when I left home."

"No, she didn't throw it out," Ruth told her. "She never forgave herself for making you give up Savannah Mae and not allowing you to stay with Jack. She hid the dress in the attic, and Savannah Mae found it when she inherited the house. She made it into the quilt."

Emma pulled up the quilt and buried her face in it. "So many memories," she said, hugging it in her lap.

Over the course of several hours, Emma learned that Fannie Lee had died and left the house and an inheritance to Savannah Mae, which brought her to Texas where she worked with an investigator to find Emma. In turn, Ruth and Savannah Mae learned that Emma was in perfect health and had been living in the independent living unit since her husband died. She no longer wanted to keep up a house and knew that the independent living unit at the facility offered resort-like living, meals made by a chef, and the option of moving into assisted living or the nursing home should her health decline.

"I really have the best of all worlds here," she said as she waved her hand around.

"Why didn't you ever come home or at least call and let us know what happened to you?" Ruth asked. "We've worried over you for 30 years."

"Oh, Ruthie, I was so young and stupid. When Mother wouldn't let me stay married to Jack or keep my baby girl," she smiled affectionately at Savannah Mae, " I blamed all of you and decided that I would punish everyone. In the end, I was the one who suffered because not only did I lose my baby and Jack, but I also lost all of you. I suppose you could say that I lost myself."

"Mama—oh, may I call you Mama?"

"Of course," Emma responded, taking Savannah Mae's hand into her own.

"Mama, are you happy here?"

"Well, I suppose I am. I have a few friends here and in town. I don't have to lift a finger, the facility does everything for me."

"I understand, Mama, but are you happy?"

Emma looked away, seeming to compose her thoughts, then back at Savannah Mae. "Happiness is a decision. It's not external, it's internal. When I lost Larry, I was devastated and I couldn't pull myself together. I realized that I couldn't stand to be in the home I'd shared with him because everything I looked at reminded me of him. I was depressed, to say the least. So, I decided to sell the house and most of our belongings and move in here. It's okay."

"Emma, you shouldn't settle for 'okay.' Life is richer than that," Ruth said.

"Yes, well that's the hand I was dealt, or rather the hand I dealt myself."

"It doesn't have to be that way," Savannah Mae interjected.

"Sometimes it does," Emma responded sadly.

"Have you ever thought about coming home?" Ruth asked.

"Actually, I have, numerous times. But I figured that after I deserted everyone and vanished, no one would want to see my face again."

"I can tell you right now that you are wrong!" Ruth stated emphatically.

Emma let out a long sigh. "Even if I wanted to, moving halfway across the country isn't in my budget. I managed to get a special reduced rate when I moved in here. I live on a fixed income from Larry's life insurance that covers my rent here and my car payment. There's not a lot left over. My savings are pretty meager."

Ruth and Savannah Mae exchanged glances and smiled.

"Emma, you have more money coming to you than you could ever spend."

Emma sat back in her chair. "What money? What are you talking about?"

Ruth opened her eyes wide. "We told you that Mother died. She left you a substantial inheritance in her will. She left an inheritance for all of us."

Emma blinked trying to make sense of it. "Mother did that? After what I did, she included me in her will?"

"Of course, she did, Emma. She never stopped loving you."

"And even though she didn't want me, Grandma included me in her will, too," Savannah Mae added.

Emma sat there in stunned silence. Finally, she asked, "Is there enough for me to buy a home in Waxahachie? This place is nice, and it's been a great place to live but, to be honest, I'd really like to live in a real home again."

"Mama, there's more than enough, but you don't have to do that. Come live with me! You know how big the house is. "

"She's absolutely right, Emma. The house is so big, you can have your own floor, if you want it," Ruth reassured her.

"Well, I wouldn't want to impose. After all, Savannah Mae, it's your house now."

"It wouldn't be an imposition, Mama. I mean it, come home. Live with me."

Emma looked back and forth repeatedly from Savannah Mae to Ruth. "Well, if you two are serious...."

"We are!" Ruth and Savannah Mae said together.

"Then let's stop babbling and organize this move."

Over the next couple of days, Savannah Mae and Ruth helped Emma pack all her possessions and arranged to have a company move everything to Texas. Savannah bought seats for them on a flight going into DFW, where Lyle would pick them up. The night before their flight, Savannah and Ruth treated Emma to supper at Vic's on the River, a Southern-style restaurant overlooking the Savannah River. They shared several low-country dishes: classic crab cakes, succotash, fried green tomatoes, and shrimp and grits, accompanied by a bottle of white wine and a dessert made of a praline pecan shell over fresh peaches and ice cream.

"The food at the home was wonderful, but nothing like this!" Emma declared. "I haven't eaten like this since before my sweet Larry got sick."

"Do you remember cousin Charlene's cooking?" Ruth asked.

Emma closed her eyes and placed her hands over her heart. She opened them, "I sure do. She was such a good cook. That woman could make me eat anything, even foods I normally wouldn't touch. I've thought of her so many times. How is she?" she asked.

Savannah Mae looked at Ruth and grinned. "She's fine, more than fine, and she's going to stop by the house when we get home," Ruth said.

"I can't believe it." Emma said, a bit of excitement infusing her voice. Emma looked at the two of them. "It's more than I could have hoped for, to return home with the two of you. And now, to see Charlene again, well, that is like a spoonful of freshly whipped cream on a coconut custard pie."

Ruth laughed. "As I recall, Charlene used to make that pie."

"She sure did, and chess pie, and buttermilk pie, and sorghum pie, and cherry pie, and—"

"Stop, Emma, you're making me hungry, and I'm too full to even think about food," Ruth cajoled. "Let's get out of here and go to the hotel."

Emma nodded. She reached out and took both Savannah Mae and Ruth's hands into her own. "Thank you both for taking me home. I was wondering, could we leave a little early and make a couple of stops on the way to the airport?"

Savannah Mae and Ruth nodded.

"I have two very dear friends that I want to stop and say goodbye to. They've been so good to me. Ever since I moved into that independent living place, one or both of them visited me every week, sometimes twice a week. We'd play cards, or go to the movies, or go out to supper, or play miniature golf. I wouldn't have gotten through living there without them, especially after Larry died."

"Consider it done, Mama," Savannah Mae said.

Chapter Twenty

After a family reunion at DFW airport, Emma, Ruth, and Savannah Mae climbed into Lyle's mega SUV.

Upon arriving at the house, the family carried the luggage into the house and was met by Thelma and Keith, who embraced Emma so hard she thought she might break. After they let go, a very tall, elegant woman, Stella, stepped up and stood in front of Emma, tracing her face with her eyes and grasping her hands.

"Emma, never did I think I'd see you again. I've missed you so much."

Emma smiled fondly at her childhood friend, then looked over at Savannah and Ruth. "You can thank these two, they're responsible."

The four women stood in silence staring at one another, a look of soundless, private joy washing over their faces.

"Stella, you have hardly aged a day since I last saw you," Emma remarked. "You still have that perfectly smooth ebony skin, glowing from the inside out," she said, reaching over and caressing her cheek. "What is your secret?"

Stella chuckled. "Oh, Emma, you know the secret. It was your Mama who taught me to quilt. Remember the quilts we made for my cousins when their house burned down?"

Emma nodded. "I haven't thought about that in years. Yes, I remember. We worked on those quilts for months."

"Well, all those quilts got me going and have kept me busy since we were children. And if I'm busy, as my Mama used to say, it keeps me out of trouble."

Emma grinned. "You and my daughter, Savannah Mae, need to get acquainted. She's a quilter, too."

Stella looked over at Savannah Mae with a wide-eyed look of surprise. "Is that so?"

Savannah Mae shrugged. "Guess it runs in the family."

"Well, I can't wait to see your handiwork," Stella declared.

Keith coughed into his hand. "Savannah Mae, where do you want Emma's luggage to go?" he asked.

"Hmm, I'm not sure." She turned to Emma. "Which bedroom do you want?"

"Is my old bedroom being used?" she asked gingerly.

"It's all yours and waiting for you, if you want it."

Emma and Savannah Mae marched upstairs, with Ruth, Thelma, and Keith close behind. Emma walked down the hall and into her old room; her mouth fell open.

"Is it okay, Mama? You seem surprised."

"I-I-I-I am. This room hasn't changed since I left home. Look," she pointed to several stuffed animals and a doll with a porcelain face on the bed. "Those were my favorite toys when I was little. I can't believe they're still here."

"That's because Mama didn't want to change a thing," Ruth told her.

"She was waiting for you to come home," Thelma added. "We all were."

Emma stared at the toys, the walls, everything, her eyes wide with disbelief. She placed the case holding the wedding dress quilt on a stool at the base of the bed. "I've thought about this room so many times. All my childhood memories live here."

She walked around touching the colorful cotton quilt on the bed that Fannie Lee had made, the toys, and the pictures on the walls. She opened drawers to find little treasures she'd left behind years before, trinkets and little rings and miniature doll quilts and little silver scissors that used to fit her child-size hands and glass animals and smooth stones she collected. Finally, Emma plopped down in a chair in front of the vanity, placed her elbows on the top of it, and rested her face in her hands, her head pitched downward.

"Mama? Are you okay?" Savannah Mae leaned over her.

"Yes," she said, without looking up. "This is all very emotional for me. I was so stupid to walk away. Please give me a few minutes to gather myself."

Savannah Mae, Thelma, and Ruth looked at each other and left the room. They stepped into the hallway and walked to the stairway. Before heading down, Ruth told Savannah and Thelma, "Let's leave Emma be for a while. Last night I called Cousin Charlene and told her that we would be bringing Emma home today. Charlene said she would make her a special meal. Lyle told me he talked to her before the plane landed and she would be bringing the food right about now. When Emma comes down and eats somethin' she'll cheer up a bit."

"Do you really think so?" Savannah Mae asked, worried that the return home was too much for her mother.

"I do, sweetheart. Your mother is resilient, and it's not like we talked her into returning home. She wanted this, and she wants a life with you."

"Okay," Savannah Mae nodded. "I sure hope you're right."

Savannah Mae, Thelma, and Ruth went into the kitchen, where they found Lyle, Annabelle, Tim, Keith, and Charlene. They explained what had happened and that Emma needed some time. As Ruth predicted, Emma came downstairs a while later, looking much improved. Everyone turned to look at her, trying to gauge her mood. She didn't disappoint them.

"My, I can't believe how this house has hardly changed since I left," she stated cheerfully. "It's like it's frozen in time. Savannah Mae, I'm surprised you haven't changed it at all."

Savannah Mae smiled and held her head slightly to the left. "That's because I wanted it to be exactly as you remembered it when you came home. Grandma must have felt the same way. She was the one who left it like this."

"How did you know I would? Come home, that is."

"Because I believed it. In my heart, I knew you were still alive. I just needed to find you."

"Oh, baby girl, you're everything I wished you'd turn out to be," she said, embracing her so long that Savannah Mae wasn't sure she would ever let her go.

Charlene coughed into her hand to get their attention. Emma let go of Savannah Mae and looked at Charlene, who stepped over and embraced Emma, then stepped back.

"Cousin, you haven't changed at all," Emma's eyes scanned Charlene's face.

"You're sweet, Emma, even if it's not true. Now, if y'all don't mind, I made a real nice lunch and it's gettin' cold."

Everyone retreated to the dining room where Annabelle and Tim had set a pretty table with a vase filled with roses picked from the garden. Charlene insisted everyone sit and no sooner had they done so than she began bringing in platters of food: King Ranch chicken casserole, greens cooked with bacon, buttermilk biscuits, squash casserole, and peach cobbler.

"Oh, sweet Charlene!" Emma declared, "You remembered my favorite dishes."

"Of course, I did. It wouldn't be your homecoming if I'd prepared spaghetti or somethin'." Charlene sat down, and the hungry group dove into the food.

Later that evening, after everyone had gone home, Savannah Mae and Emma retreated to the living room, where Savannah Mae showed her mother the framed family tree on the wall.

"You're on there, too," Emma said, pointing to Savannah Mae's name. Savannah Mae simply smiled. "You made this, didn't you?" Emma asked.

Savannah Mae nodded, adding that Annabelle had created the tree and sent it to her, and she had it printed on muslin and embroidered it.

"It's quite remarkable," Emma said as she traced her fingers over the family tree.

They sat down on the big wingback chairs. "Are you tired, Mama? Do you want to go to bed?"

"I'm tired, baby girl, but in a good way. No, I don't want to go to bed. Tell me about you, your life, I want to hear everything. And don't you leave out a single detail, young lady."

Savannah Mae told her everything about herself, her adoptive parents, her life in California, Scott, the letter from Howard Sheridan, meeting Thelma, Keith, Ruth and her family on the front porch when she moved into the house, calling Jack and meeting his whole family and how wonderful it had been having sisters and a brother, something her adoptive parents couldn't give her.

"Have you got yourself someone special?" Emma quizzed her, figuring as her mother, she had a right to know.

"Yes, sort of," she answered, and told her about meeting Travis. "Honestly, we're just friends. It's nothing serious."

"If that's the case, why do your eyes light up talkin' about this Travis fella?"

Savannah Mae blushed and changed the subject.

The next morning, the doorbell rang. Being closest to the foyer, Emma answered the door.

"Hello, ma'am, I'm Travis Sheridan. You must be Savannah Mae's mother, " he said, his lips forming a wide smile as he removed his Stetson and handed her a bouquet of wildflowers. "Welcome home."

"Please come in," Emma looked up at him, opened the door wide, and took the flowers. "I've heard all about you."

"Oh, that could be bad or good. Sure do hope it's the latter," he grinned, his silvery eyes gleaming.

"It is," Emma responded just as Savannah Mae came around the corner.

"I see you two have met," Savannah beamed at Emma and Travis.

"Yes, we have," Travis said. "Mind if I take you two fine ladies to lunch?"

"I'll get my purse!" Emma answered quickly, turned, and ran up the staircase.

"You're slick," Savannah Mae cracked a smile.

Travis put both hands on his chest. "Who, me?" he protested, like a schoolboy caught with his hand in the cookie jar.

"You're trying to charm and impress my mama. I see what you're doing."

Travis bowed his head. "Oh no, I would never do such a thing," he teased, glancing up to see Emma coming down the stairs.

After a long lunch at Travis's favorite barbecue restaurant where Emma met Gracie and couldn't stop talking about how she missed good ol' Texas barbecue, he dropped them off at home and went on his way.

Before they had even made it up the front stairs, Emma stated emphatically, "You aren't just friends."

"Whaddaya mean?" Savannah Mae turned around to look at her.

"I know I haven't been in your life very long, but I can tell when a man is infatuated with a woman, and that Travis is spellbound by you." Emma gave her a knowing small smile.

"Mama, I don't know what you mean. Seriously, we're just friends, good friends."

Emma cast her a circumspect glance. "Savannah Mae, a man does not look at a woman like that when they're just friends, even good ones. You can tell me all you like about how you're friends. I saw something much bigger when I caught him looking at you when you were facing away. That man is in love with you."

Savannah Mae blushed a deep shade of red, turned, and ran up the porch stairs to give her face time to calm down. As soon as they entered the house, Savannah Mae hurried up the staircase, yelling behind her that she was going to freshen up and be down shortly.

She stepped into her room, closed the door, and stared at her bright red face in the mirror.

Late that afternoon, the doorbell rang and, once again, being closest to the door, Emma opened it. Her jaw dropped when she saw Jack McDonald standing there alone. They stared at one another. Savannah Mae walked in from the sitting room and saw her father. She stepped up to him and planted a light kiss on his cheek.

"Mama," she turned to Emma, "aren't you going to invite Dad in?"

Emma quickly composed herself. "Of course, sweetheart. Hello, Jack. It's good to see you." She stepped back to allow him through the entrance.

"It's good to see you too, Emma," he responded, not taking his eyes off her.

Sensing they needed some alone time, Savannah Mae ushered them into the parlor, "I'll make some coffee," she said to a mute audience that continued to stare at one another.

Savannah Mae took as long as possible to make the coffee. She put the cups, sugar, and creamer on a tray and walked back into the parlor. She set it down on a coffee table, handed each of them a cup, picked up her own, and said she had some emails to respond to and if they needed her, she would be upstairs. Neither one responded; she wasn't sure they even knew she was there.

When she was out of earshot Jack said, "Emma, you look good."

"As do you, Jack," Emma responded. "You're as handsome now as the day we ran away to get married."

They watched each other for several more minutes until Emma broke the silence.

"Jack, I'm so sorry," she began, slightly shaking her head. "I've regretted my actions every single day. Losing you and Savannah Mae has been an unbearable heartache."

"Don't dwell on that, Emma. It's the past. What's done is done."

"Yes, but it didn't have to be that way. If I'd only had the strength to stand up to Mother, we could have stayed together and raised Savannah Mae ourselves." A few moments of silence passed. "I understand you have a lovely wife and a nice family now."

"That's true," he said tenderly. "For a long time, I waited for you to come back. I prayed that you would return. But you didn't answer any of my letters, and when Ruth told me one day that no one in the family had heard from you, I figured I was part of the collateral damage." He reached up and ran a hand over his face. "I didn't know if you were alive or dead. I grieved for you, for us, as though you had passed away."

"Oh, Jack," Emma began to weep quietly, resting her face in her hands. "I should never have let Mother drive us apart."

"Emma, it would have taken a presidential order and half of the U.S. Army to stop your mother. She was determined not to let us stay together or keep our daughter. I would have done anything to keep the three of us together, but your mother had other plans, and when you succumbed to her wishes, I had no choice but to accept it."

Emma continued to weep, reaching up and wiping away the tears as they fell. "You have the life and the family that was supposed to be ours," she mumbled.

"No, that's not true. I have the family that was supposed to be mine," he responded, trying not to sound as harsh as he felt. "I would like you to meet them sometime. They adore Savannah Mae and are curious about what her mother is like. Will you come by for supper sometime?"

Emma looked up at him. "That's very nice, but don't you think it would be a bit awkward?"

"Not for us, it wouldn't. The family wants to meet you. Perhaps when you're more settled in, you and Savannah Mae could come by for something informal. Maybe a barbecue in the backyard."

Emma nodded her head, wiping her eyes. "Yes, that would be nice. But it'll probably be a while."

"'Til then," he said, standing up. Jack bent down and kissed Emma lightly on the cheek. She watched him walk out the front door. As soon as the door closed behind him, 30 years of grief and tears poured out, spilling onto her dress, soaking her like a summer rainstorm.

Chapter Twenty-One

It had been a year since Savannah Mae had moved to Texas, and she could not have been happier. She'd found her mother and father, both of whom had become a big part of her life. She counted more family than she could fathom on both sides. Plus, she and Travis seemed to be moving toward something, albeit at her own very slow pace. Her quilting was thriving, and she was getting a reputation around the gun range as a sharpshooter. The instructor, Julie, suggested she start entering competitions because she was getting that good. When Savannah Mae called and told Maggie what Julie said, Maggie let out a howl.

"You sure have come a long way, girlfriend. I'm proud of you."

A few weeks later, as the days grew shorter and the temperatures finally began to abate, she came home one day to find her front door unlocked and slightly ajar. She took out her phone, dialed Travis, and told him what she found.

"Call 911, and most important, don't go into the house. It's too dangerous," Travis cautioned.

"Travis, I have to. Mama is in there. If someone broke into the house, I have to protect her. It might be Dennis."

"Stay out of the house, please. He isn't going to bother with your mother, but he sure will bother with you. Stay put. I'll be there in twenty minutes."

After calling 911 and hearing the police operator also tell her to stay out of the house, she hung up, removed her Smith & Wesson 9mm from her purse, took off the safety, and holding it behind her back, cautiously went inside.

She stepped into the dining room and found Dennis sitting at the table examining the framed name change document that had been hanging on the wall. He looked up when she entered the room.

"What is this?" he yelled at her, waving the frame above his head. "Why did you change your name? Why didn't you wait to change it to my name when we get married?" His face was clenched, stiff and rigid, like a wolf about to lunge at its prey.

Savannah Mae tightened her grip on the gun, running a finger over the safety to make sure it was off. It was.

"Dennis, the last time you were here, I told you in no uncertain terms to leave and never come back. I also told you that we were not engaged, nor would we ever get married. Or have you forgotten that little episode?"

"I have a right to be here!" he yelled at her, the veins in his neck jutting out.

"Like a coyote in a hen house? No, you don't. I've had it with you, Dennis." Her voice gradually grew louder. "Not only have you illegally broken in, but you have no right to be in my house. Furthermore, there's a restraining order against you, which you are aware of, to stay at least 500 feet away from me and my house."

Dennis burst out laughing. "You think that meaningless piece of paper is going to keep me away? You're dumber than I thought."

Savannah Mae ignored his comment and suddenly noticed flares and a can of gasoline on the table. Her eyes narrowed as she turned to focus on him. "What are those doing on the table?"

"Whaddaya think?" he taunted her.

"I don't know. What are they doing there?" she pressed, trying to control the panic she felt rising in her chest.

"Since you aren't too bright, I'll tell you," he mocked her. "Obviously, you need an incentive to leave this old clunker, so I'm just going to make it easy for you."

Savannah Mae shook her head. "What are you planning to do Dennis?"

His upper lip rose as he lifted one of the flares. "Haven't you ever seen one of these?"

She stared at him, not giving him the satisfaction of an answer.

"These things can start fires, Lisbeth. All I gotta do is dump some gasoline on this rug, break open a flare, and throw it down on the rug, and poof! Instant fire. One should do it. This whole room with all your rugs, curtains, furniture, and pretty knick-knacks will go up in flames in less than a minute. Won't take long for the whole house to burn down."

"Why on earth would you do that?" she asked, barely above a whisper.

He belly laughed as though he'd heard a ridiculously funny joke. "Are you serious? You really don't get it? Okay, fine, I'll play along. Lisbeth, since you obviously have some weird attachment to this house that is preventing you from returning home and marrying me, I'll just get rid of the obstacle. Problem solved."

Savannah Mae's eyes widened in astonishment. "You would burn down my house to get me to marry you?"

"Now you're getting the picture," he responded, a smug smile sweeping across his face. "You know, I tried a few more subtle gestures that you ignored. It didn't have to come down to this."

"Like what?"

"I had your water turned off, set fire to your shed, and tampered with your fake cowboy's truck, figuring you would get tired of living here in this godforsaken place and return home. But, no, you were too stupid to see all the signs I left for you."

"That was you?" her eyes widened.

He smiled with a deranged look of satisfaction. That was it, Savannah Mae had reached her limit of insults and threats that she'd tolerated in the hope that he would leave. It was now obvious that he was truly crazy and wasn't going to leave, and that he had every intention of burning down the family home. Her home.

"Dennis, have you lost your mind? You won't get away with burning down my house."

"Yeah, I will. Here's the deal, Lisbeth, and I'm only going to make this offer once, because if you don't take it, there won't be any second chances."

"Deal? What deal?"

"You leave right now with me, return to California, and marry me, or I burn down the house with you in it."

Savannah Mae's jaw dropped. "You would murder me?"

"Sure thing, sweetheart. If I can't have you, no one can."

She held up her hand. "Wait a minute. I was going to marry Scott. You were his best man. You were fine with my marrying someone else. Why the change?"

Dennis broke out in a sick laugh. "Oh, that. There was no way I was going to let Scott marry you."

Savannah Mae momentarily lost her voice as she watched a diabolical look creep over his face. "You murdered Scott to get to me?"

"Okay, so now you get it. Lisbeth, you need to understand that I'm capable of anything, and I will do whatever is necessary to get what I want."

"And what you want is me?"

"Your brain cells are kicking in. Good girl! Now come along nicely," he said, standing up from the table, and I won't burn down this old house."

Later she could barely recall that she swung her hand around and pointed her gun at him. "I'm only going to tell you once, Dennis. Get out of my house. Now!"

"Oh, that's rich," he snickered. "Like you know how to use that thing. Even if you do, you won't shoot me. You haven't got the guts."

"Don't test me, Dennis. I'm serious."

Still laughing, he walked toward her. Though her insides were roiling, she didn't back down. She had trained for this at the gun range and knew she could protect herself. A voice in her head kept repeating that she was worth it. When he got within two feet of her, the police barged in through the open door. The noise momentarily distracted Savannah Mae; she turned her head toward the noise. Dennis grabbed the gun, and with the other hand, put a choke hold around Savannah Mae's neck. He pointed the gun at her head and looked straight at the police.

"Leave right now, or I swear I'll shoot her."

Savannah could feel him start to tremble. For all his big talk, she could tell he was scared and was fairly sure he'd never used a gun before. She regretted taking off the safety, knowing that he might accidentally shoot her. The officers pointed their guns at Dennis, their red lasers beaded on his head.

He yelled at them, "I come from a very powerful family who will make sure all of you lose your jobs if you don't leave."

"Well, is that so?" the flak-jacketed lead officer said. "Well, Mr. Dragna, in case you hadn't noticed, you're in the great state of Texas, and we do things a little differently around here. First of all, you don't call the shots, we do. Men like you who try to harm someone do not dictate how this is gonna go. I suggest you surrender peacefully."

"Ha! What a joke! Think again. This is going my way, or it's not going any way at all. Understood?" he bellowed back using his most commanding voice.

"Quite," the officer answered. In his peripheral vision, he noticed movement on the stairwell but kept his eyes focused on Dennis.

Outside, both SWAT and Travis arrived at the same time. An officer in the garden wearing a listening device advised the team and Travis what was going on inside. Travis started to move around the house, heading for the back door. The officer in charge told Travis he could not enter the house. He stopped and turned around. He knew better than to test the officer.

Dennis continued to hold Savannah Mae in a choke hold while the police and now SWAT stood in the front foyer, officers still drawing a bead on him. His face was distorted with madness. A sour, contorted grin spread across his lips. And his eyes bled a wildness, like a savage animal penned in with no escape. Savannah Mae could feel him sweating through her clothing. Suddenly, his whole body went stiff. Dennis felt a gun to the back of his head.

"Listen, boy, you let go of my daughter, or I swear, I'll blow your head off. And I don't mean next week, I mean now!" said a voice more thunderous and frightening than a tornado whipping across the prairie.

Dennis released his choke hold. Savannah Mae twisted around and grabbed her gun from him, and pointed it at Dennis, while

Emma kept her gun pressed against the back of his head. The police moved in, handcuffed Dennis, and escorted him out of the house into a waiting police car. As soon as he was away from her, Savannah Mae set the safety back on her gun and threw her arms around Emma, holding her tight.

"Where'd you get that gun?" she asked, pulling back and looking down at her hand.

"Right where I left it 31 years ago," Emma responded.

"Where'd you leave it, Mama?"

"Under a floorboard in the corner of my closet. Your grandpa gave me the gun a long time ago to go shooting out in the back-country. He told me to hide it in a place no one could find it except me."

Savannah Mae took the gun and opened the chamber. "Did you have fresh ammo that you used to load it? There's only one bullet in the chamber."

"No, didn't have any. That bullet's been in there at least 30 years, maybe longer."

"Mama, that bullet probably wouldn't have worked. It's too old."

Emma winked at her. "True, but he didn't know that."

As soon as Travis saw the police taking Dennis out of the house, he bounded up the stairs, two at a time, and seeing Savannah Mae and Emma, he ran to them and enveloped Savannah Mae in a tight hug nearly forcing all the air out of her lungs. She pulled back.

"Travis, hey, I'm okay. You know, today could have ended quite differently had you not convinced me to learn how to protect myself. Even though I knew that I was worth protecting, and Mama, too, in the end, it was Mama who saved me." She looked at Emma who smiled endearingly at her daughter. "She is one brave mama bear."

Savannah Mae watched Travis's eyes. He bent back down again and held her tight. She ran her arms tightly around him and didn't let go until a police officer interrupted them to interview Savannah Mae and Emma about the sequence of events. Along with every detail, Savannah Mae told the officer that Dennis admitted to killing Scott in order to get to her.

Chapter Twenty-Two

The police interviewed Travis the next day. He told them everything he had learned about Dennis and the accident that killed Scott. He turned over all his notes to the district attorney, who, after reviewing all the material plus Dennis's actions at Savannah Mae's house, determined that they had more than enough to put him away for a very long time. A few days later, Travis stopped in at Savannah Mae's and suggested they go out to eat, somewhere without a lot of noise. He drove her to Farm Luck Soda Fountain & Dry Goods in the historic downtown district of Waxahachie.

Savannah Mae's eyes grew wide when they walked into the brightly lit, old-timey, sweet parlor. It looked and felt like a 1950s soda shop.

"Haven't you been here before?" Travis asked.

"No, how could I have missed this place?" she said, looking all around. "I thought we were going out to supper."

"We are. They serve sandwiches, wraps, soups, and salads if you want that kind of thing, but since we're here to celebrate something major, I thought we could have something more decadent."

"Such as?"

"Check out the soda fountain menu."

Savannah Mae read through the menu, a big grin spreading across her face, as her eyes danced with childhood whimsy. A waitress dressed like someone out of the 1950s asked if they were ready to order. Savannah Mae looked at Travis.

"Ya wanna split a banana split with me?"

"Sure."

"What would you like to drink?" the waitress asked.

"A chocolate malt," Savannah Mae replied quickly.

Travis's eyebrows shot up in surprise. "Really?"

"Yeah, you said we're celebrating something, so I'm going all out."

"That's true." He looked up at the waitress. "I'll have a phosphate with raspberry syrup."

After the waitress left, Savannah Mae asked, "What's a phosphate?"

"Hmm, kinda hard to explain. They're kinda sour and tangy, and they're flavored with sweet syrups to compensate for the sourness. "

"Well, aren't you just a wealth of knowledge!" she laughed. "You know I'm going to have to take a sip of yours, don't you?"

"Okay, but only if I get to slurp your malt."

Savannah Mae stared at him bug-eyed. "No slurping allowed."

"Then no phosphate for you!"

"Hey, do you know the history of this place?" Savannah Mae asked, looking around.

"It was originally the Waxahachie Bank & Trust, built in the late 1800s. See that big vault door down the hallway?" he pointed to the back of the restaurant. Savannah Mae turned around and looked. "That door is supposed to weigh as much as my truck."

"Is that why it's still here? Because it's too heavy to move?"

"Probably. Maybe they keep it as a point of interest. They use the inside as their kitchen."

"No way!"

"Go check it out for yourself," he said, pointing to the back.

Savannah Mae started to get up when the waitress brought their banana split, Savannah Mae's malt, and Travis's phosphate soda. No sooner had she set them down than Savannah Mae grabbed the phosphate soda and took a sip. Travis simultaneously snatched her malt and took a big slurp, making Savannah Mae laugh and nearly snort up the phosphate. She slapped her hand over her nose to prevent it from going everywhere.

"Are you about to snort up my phosphate?" he asked, trying to be serious.

She nodded, about to break out in giggles, knowing she was going to really embarrass herself if she spewed it everywhere. She shut her eyes tight and looked away until she could completely swallow the soda. Then she looked back at him, grinning.

"Can I have my malt back?"

"Only if you give me back my phosphate," he said grinning.

Slowly they traded, each one cautious that the other one wouldn't keep up their end of the trade. They did, though, and settled into sipping their drinks and sharing the banana split.

"So, what are we celebrating?" Savannah Mae asked.

"Your freedom."

"Huh?"

"Dennis will never bother you again. He's being charged with aggravated kidnapping, which is a first-degree felony in Texas. He's going to prison, Savannah Mae. It's just a question of whether he gets the minimum of five years or the maximum of 99 years. Or he could get life in prison, plus a hefty fine. If he does serve a shorter sentence, afterwards California would probably extradite him to face first-degree murder charges in Scott's death. Either way, he won't be going anywhere for a very long time. He's probably going to end up in one of the worst prisons where he may not survive."

"I don't understand," Savannah commented. "Why wouldn't he survive prison? He's not that old."

"Because inmates have a code; they don't like criminals who've harmed women or children. And they're not fond of arrogant SOBs like Dennis. With his good looks and highfalutin ways, he probably wouldn't make it to the end of his sentence...."

Savannah Mae felt the last bit of residual tension from her ordeal finally melt away. "Travis, I could not have gotten through this nightmare without you."

"It's over, and now you can live your life without fear. I'm just glad I was around to help."

Life soon returned to normal, and Savannah Mae and Travis spent more and more time together. Yet, Savannah Mae still held back emotionally, as though they were just casual friends. Once a week, they rode horses on the ranch, and when the weather got a little warmer, they returned to Galveston for several days.

Travis surprised her by secretly inviting Maggie to join them. She was waiting for them at Gaido's restaurant when Travis and Savannah Mae drove into town and stopped for lunch. Maggie told them that she didn't intend to spend all her time with them; she planned to surf some of the area beaches, and then drive her rental car to Corpus Christi and South Padre Island to check out the waves. When Savannah Mae asked her if she was thinking of moving to Texas, Maggie said she might if she found a few breakwaters to her liking. She referred to her visit as a "scouting trip."

Savannah Mae bought another painting, and they took another Segway tour, exploring a different part of the historic city. Mostly though, they spent time on the beach collecting seashells and watching waves crash on the shore. She was finally fully at peace, knowing that her life was no longer in danger. In the evenings, they watched the sun descend on the distant horizon and cuddled by a stone ring, tending a fire that danced to its own rhythm. Travis never tired of gazing into her eyes to get a glimpse of the spirit that burned within.

Even though they became nearly inseparable, Savannah Mae still couldn't give the relationship her all. She held back in subtle ways, and Travis knew it. He patiently waited for her to mend her wounded heart and recover from the trauma with Dennis.

⚘

One day, Savannah Mae told Emma that the previous spring she had submitted the wedding dress quilt online to the International Quilt Festival in Houston.

"That's wonderful. What is this festival?"

"Mama, it's one of the most prestigious quilt shows and competitions in the world. And I just received notice that it's been accepted into the competition."

"Oh, my! This sounds like a big deal."

"It is."

"You didn't have to do that. I love it just the way it is."

"Mama, I'm doing it for me. I used to enter a lot of competitions when I lived in California."

"Really? You're so talented. You must have won quite a few."

"I did, but I never had the courage to enter the Houston show. People compete from all over the world. The wedding dress quilt is the first one I've ever felt was worthy of the competition and might have a chance of winning a ribbon."

"Now, Savannah Mae, I'll admit that I don't know too much about the quilting world these days, but even so, I'll bet your quilt wins. I've never seen anything like it," she looked adoringly at her daughter.

"Thank you for your faith in me, Mama. Honestly, I don't think it's going to win. The competition is very stiff. It's just something I want to do."

"Then you have my blessing with one condition."

"Anything."

"You're going to Houston to see it on display, I assume?"

"Yes, of course."

"I want to go with you. Who knows, maybe Ruth or Bonnie Ada or Thelma or some of the girls will want to go, too."

"Really?"

"Really. Now go pack up that quilt and ship it to Houston. We've gotta pull together a girls' trip."

A few weeks later, on the day before they were to leave for Houston, Travis stopped in unannounced to see Savannah Mae. She grinned as soon as she opened the door, her eyes twinkled at the sight of him.

"This is a nice surprise! I didn't think I'd see you before we left town."

He stepped inside, removed his hat, and stared straight at her. "I came to ask you what you're afraid of."

She slightly shook her head. "Excuse me? What are you talking about?" She searched his face for a clue.

"I think you know," he bore his silvery eyes into hers, holding them like a magnet.

Savannah Mae looked away and swallowed hard because she did know and expected that this conversation would come up eventually. Still, she wasn't ready for it. She felt her eyes start to sting. She turned back. In a fragile voice, she murmured softly in a hushed tone.

"Losing you," she rolled her lips inward before continuing. "Scott left such a hole in my heart that I'm afraid to love again. I fear that if I love you with everything I've got, something's going to happen to you. And I couldn't take that. It would destroy me."

Travis placed his hands on her shoulders. "Savannah Mae, I get it, but you must know, especially by now, that I'm not going anywhere. Nothing's going to happen to me. I will be here, always. Loving you."

She looked away. "You're not the problem, Travis. I am. I think I'm damaged."

"No, you're not," he said emphatically, tenderly turning her face back toward him. "I don't accept that. Now I know you're getting ready to go on your girls' trip to Houston, so I want you to think about something while you're away."

She sucked in a big breath of air. "Okay," she said. "What?"

"Marry me."

Two simple words. They hung in the air, paralyzing her for several moments. Finally, she broke free.

"Oh, oh, wait a minute," she protested putting her hands up in front of her face and taking a step backward. "That's a big deal. I didn't expect this," she gasped, turning away.

"Why not?" he asked, stepping up to her, placing his hands on her shoulders again and stopping her from walking away. "We've been seeing each other for quite a while. You know I love you, and I'm pretty sure that you love me, even though you won't say it. I would do anything for you, you know that. We spend nearly every day together. What's the difference between what we're doing and tying the knot so we live together and don't spend hours every day driving back and forth to each other's houses?"

"I-I-I don't know Travis, I need time to think," she said, her voice fragile, on the edge of cracking.

He let out a long sigh. "Take all the time you need, darlin'," he said reluctantly. He turned toward the door and put on his hat. Just before he opened the door, he swiveled back. "You know where to find me when you've made your decision."

Travis left the house, and after she closed the door behind him, Savannah Mae leaned her back against the door and slid to the floor. She broke down, whimpering at first, followed by heaving sobs. Emma was in the kitchen, and when she heard her crying, she walked into the foyer.

"What's wrong, honey?"

Savannah Mae sobbed with despair barely getting out the words. "He ... asked ... me ... to ... marry ... him."

Emma kneeled in front of her and put her arm around Savannah Mae's shoulders. "Good Lord, baby. Why are you cryin' about it?"

"I'm scared, Mama. I love what we have, but he wants more, and I don't think I can give it to him. I don't think I can return the kind of love he has for me."

"Come here," she said, lifting Savannah Mae up, taking her hand, and guiding her to a chair at the breakfast table in the kitchen. Gently, she pushed down on her shoulders and made her sit.

"Don't make the same mistake that I did."

Savannah Mae looked up at her, tears still streaming down her face.

"Baby girl, I should have fought for Jack and for you. Because I didn't have a backbone and couldn't stand up to my mother, I lost both of you. I've regretted it every day of my life. Now I'm tellin' you, if you don't grow yourself a backbone real quick, you're going to lose that good man and you'll regret it all your days."

Savannah Mae nodded that she understood, yet the tears kept coming.

⚜

The next morning, Emma, Savannah Mae, Ruth, Annabelle, Thelma, Bonnie Ada, Dixie, and Hattie piled into Bonnie Ada's big SUV. They checked into their hotel as soon as they got into Houston, and the next morning the family headed to the George R. Brown Convention Center for the opening of the show. Everyone noticed that Savannah Mae was not her usual cheerful self. They tried making jokes, asking quilting questions, even tickling her to no avail.

"Sister, aren't you excited?" Dixie finally asked.

"Yeah, don't you want to see if you won?" Annabelle pumped her.

"Of course," Savannah Mae said, trying, though failing, to sound upbeat. Though she knew she was putting a damper on their girls' trip, she couldn't help herself. All she could do was think about Travis and how if she told him no, she would be driving a knife into his heart, and into her own as well. Yet, the idea of agreeing to marry him terrified her. She was sure she carried some kind of bad luck mojo that might kill Travis. She knew she wouldn't be able to live with that either. She wished that she and Travis could return to those lighthearted days before those two simple words, *marry me,* changed everything.

They walked to the area cordoned off for the top prize-winning quilts. They meandered around the exhibit area looking for hers. Dixie moved ahead, turned, and called back to the group, "It's over here, at the front of the row." The group walked down the row and stopped when they found Savannah Mae's quilt pinned with the "Best of Show" blue ribbon rosette and displayed on a large divider wall, cordoned off by a rope four feet from the quilt. A dozen or more people were leaning over the rope trying to get a closer look at it. To the side stood a woman wearing white cotton gloves and an official show badge. She repeatedly told the onlookers to stay back and not touch the quilt.

"Well, that's strange, why can't we touch the quilt?" Emma remarked to the family. "It's been touched by so many of us, what's a few more fingers?"

The white-gloved woman turned to Emma, alarm in her voice. "What do you mean? When did you touch it?"

"When my daughter gave it to me, and every day since," she said, pointing to Savannah Mae.

The white-gloved woman looked straight at Savannah Mae and asked, "Are you Savannah Mae McDonald?"

Savannah Mae nodded.

"We've been trying to contact you to let you know that you won. Would you please step over the rope and tell our audience how you made this stunning quilt?"

Savannah Mae broke into a small smile, did as requested, and told the audience the story of the quilt. She pointed to her mother, telling them it was she who had made the original wedding dress.

"How did you come up with using this classic design for all those fabrics?" one woman asked.

"Usually, quilters use cotton, how did you know that all those non-cotton fabrics would work?" another implored.

"What techniques did you use to quilt those delicate fabrics? That must have been very difficult," a third woman remarked.

As the onlookers moved on and new people crowded around to marvel over the quilt, she repeated the story, and again after that for the next two hours. Finally, the white-gloved woman told her to go enjoy the show and to come back after lunch the next day to talk to the audience again. Savannah Mae felt a bit better having been distracted for a while, but fell into another slump as the day wore on. Even though the next day she was in no better spirits, she returned to her quilt to talk about the story behind it and the process.

Toward midafternoon, Travis showed up and stood in the back of the audience listening to Savannah Mae talk. She didn't see him, though the family did. Hattie saw him first and whispered to Dixie, who told Annabelle, who whispered to Ruth, who told Thelma, who told Bonnie Ada, who pointed him out to Emma. They all watched as Travis slowly moved to the front, stepped over the rope, and walked up to Savannah Mae, who was standing at the side of her quilt. The white-gloved woman stopped him.

"Sir, please return to the area behind the rope. You can't be back here."

He smiled at the woman, removed his cowboy hat, got down on one knee in front of Savannah Mae, and pulled a small velvet box out of his suede jacket pocket. Savannah Mae stood there in shock, staring at him, one hand covering her mouth. The crowd began applauding, and her eyes began to dampen, glimmering like sunshine when it hits water, stinging the backs of her eyes. Travis opened the box and gazed up at her.

"Savannah Mae McDonald, will you do me the honor of marrying me and being my wife 'til death do us part?"

She stared numbly at what lay inside the box, and up at him, then finally nodded, trying to blink away her tears. Slowly, she held out her left hand. Travis took her hand into his and gently slid the vintage diamond ring onto her finger. They were oblivious to the dozens of people crowded around who had erupted into loud cheers. He stood up, took her into his arms, and kissed her gently. Travis stood back and Savannah Mae pulled him toward her and kissed him long and hard. Claps, whoops, and hoots exploded from at least a hundred onlookers, including those of the family. They heard none of the noise and saw only each other.

Her throat tight, she leaned in and whispered into his ear, "I love you more than you can ever know and will to my dying day, Travis."

He smiled, put his hat back on, reached down, and picked her up in his arms, as a groom carries a bride over a threshold, stepped over the rope, and said, "Ladies, if you'll excuse us, we have a wedding to plan." He headed toward the exit through a crowd that parted like the Red Sea, followed by Emma, Ruth, Thelma, Bonnie Ada, Annabelle, Dixie, and Hattie, each of them wiping their eyes.

The End

Reader's Guide

The Wedding Dress Quilt

BY JEFFREE WYN ITRICH

1. The main character of the story is Savannah Mae. Throughout the book, her life changes quite a bit. Do you feel she also changed or only her circumstances? In what ways did she grow, and in what ways did she stay the same?

2. Did the main character's quilting and creativity help her along her journey?

3. How did you feel about the ending?

4. Family plays a large role in this story. Do any of Savannah Mae's relatives remind you of anyone in your family? If so, in what way?

5. Which character do you most relate to and why? Who was your favorite character?

6. Which location in the book would you like to visit and why? Would the story have played out differently in a setting other than Texas?

7. Which moment or scene prompted the strongest emotional reaction for you?

8. Was there a time that you disagreed with a character's action or choice? If so, what was it? Would you have written it differently?

9. If this book were made into a movie, who would you cast in the leading roles? Are there any actors that would be perfect for any of the supporting characters?

10. If you could ask the author one burning question, what would it be?

11. What was the most surprising, challenging, or intriguing aspect of the story?

12. What do you think is next for the cast of characters?

About the Author

Jeffree Wyn Itrich was born and raised in San Diego, California. She began writing as a child when she discovered a book filled with her mother's personal writings. The book inspired Jeffree to write. And write she did, filling countless journals with stories and essays.

In school, an English teacher recognized her ability and urged her to follow her literary dreams. She attended the graduate school of journalism at the University of California, Berkeley.

Her first book, *The Art of Accompaniment* was published by North Point Press in 1987, where it was named a Book of the Month Club and a Better Homes and Garden Book Club selection.

She used her journalism education to work in medical communications where she wrote hundreds of articles about medical therapies over a twenty year period. Even with a busy life, she never lost her passion for writing fiction. To date, she has had two novels, one cookbook, and a children's book published. In addition, *Chicken Soup for the Soul* has published thirteen of her stories.

Following her family's roots, she moved to the small town of West, Texas, in 2018. *The Wedding Dress Quilt* marries her love of quilting and Texas where her family settled more than 150 years ago.

Visit Jeffree online and follow her on social media!

Website: jeffreewyn.writerfolio.com/writing

Goodreads: goodreads.com/goodreadscomjeffreewyn

Pinterest: jeffreei

Facebook: JeffreeWyn/

Blog: jeffreewynawriterslife.blogspot.com

YOUR NEXT FAVORITE

quilting cozy or crafty mystery series is on this page.

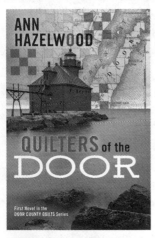

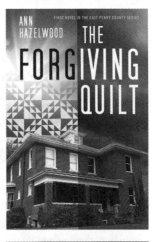

Want more? Visit us online at ctpub.com